She touched, seared and finally ignited a flame that he claimed as his own.

He burned. His body ached to make her his.

How and why were meaningless—reason ceased to exist. All he could do was react.

Groaning, he thrust his hands back through her hair. He urged her head up and brought his mouth down, possessively, hungrily, as though his life were dependent on drinking in her sweetness. And in that second, in the coldly remote hollows of his heart, the imperishable flame sparked a small, steady ember.

"My lord . . . Brice," Elora choked out, not certain how she had come to be in such a position.

His lips sought the silken column of her throat while his hand eased her nightgown from her shoulder.

"No," she exclaimed, trying to pull her nightgown back into place. "No, you mustn't."

Yes, Brice thought, *I must. My life is here, in this woman.*

Books by Elizabeth Ann Michaels

Destiny's Will
A Jewel So Rare
From a Silver Heart

Published by POCKET BOOKS

Elizabeth Ann Michaels

POCKET BOOKS

New York   London   Toronto   Sydney   Tokyo   Singapore

An *Original* Publication of POCKET BOOKS

POCKET BOOKS, a division of Simon & Schuster Inc.
1230 Avenue of the Americas, New York, NY 10020

ISBN: 1-4165-0705-1

This Pocket Books paperback printing September 2004

10 9 8 7 6 5 4 3 2 1

POCKET and colophon are registered trademarks of Simon & Schuster Inc.

Cover art by Jim Griffin

Printed in the U.S.A.

For Ann,
My sister and best friend

Acknowledgments

To Mary Beth, Chris, Phyllis, Kim, Becky, Ann, Linda, Peggy and Christi, for standing by their local author.

To the Brunetti family, for their loving support. (Aunt Do, this one might make you blush.)

To Caroline, for pushing, prodding, editing and never losing faith.

And to "Dude and Dad," for always, *always* being there.

My heartfelt thanks to you all.

Prologue

Hampshire, England, 1815

In the shadows of his family's ancient stone chapel, Brice Warfield stood as though carved from granite. Oblivious to the cold or the wind, he stared at the familiar tall spire, his face scourged by a sorrow that threatened to destroy him.

His anguish was absolute; of the heart as well as the mind and body. Anger, frustration, resentment, disbelief; all warred with his sanity and thrust him into the blackest realms of despair. Pain ravaged his being, bitterness withered his soul.

"Brice?"

The softly spoken whisper came from behind, but he remained unmoving.

"Brice, please come back to the house with me. Standing here will not . . . will not bring them back."

It was as honest a statement as any Brice had ever heard. But he didn't want the truth. It only served to remind him of all that had happened in the four days since they had received word. It felt like four lifetimes.

He spun around and fixed his sister with a damning stare. "You have it only partly right, Vianne. Yes, standing here is completely useless. But then, all my efforts to save Mother and Father and Robbie were completely useless. All the arrangements I made to free them from prison, all my influence with the British government, all the money at my disposal were completely useless."

"Brice," she pleaded in a voice strangled with tears. "You did everything you could."

"It wasn't enough."

"Then nothing would have ever been enough. There was no escape for them. You have to accept that."

"No."

"Yes!" she cried desperately. "I know you loved them, Brice. I know they meant the world to you. But you cannot blame yourself for . . . for . . . their deaths."

Brice watched grief consume his sister and he pulled her close. As he had done countless times since their childhood, he held her as she cried out her misery. But unlike all those times in their past when he had offered words of comfort to a distraught little sister, only silence existed between them now.

There was nothing he could say to ease her suffering, for his own was too great to overcome. All too clearly, he pictured the faces of their parents and elder brother as he had last seen them, before they had made the mistake of traveling to Paris. They had been happy, carefree, looking forward to visiting the city that had been denied to most of the world for years. They had had no way of knowing that they would die there, their lives snuffed out by Napoleon's command.

The silence lingered until Vianne's tears dwindled. Only then did Brice drop his arms.

"Will you come back with me?" Vianne asked gently. "The vicar is here to make arrangements for a service."

Brice stiffened. Bitterness drew his features into a terrible mask, the green of his eyes chilling with an iciness that rivaled winter at its very worst. "The vicar can go to hell."

Vianne gasped. "You can't mean that?"

"I mean exactly that."

Precisely that and a great deal more. As far as he was concerned, the vicar could take his church, his benedictions and his God and go to the devil. They were all worthless, just as his money and power, his hopes, prayers and dreams were all completely and utterly worthless.

2

Chapter

1

London, 1818

BY THE FEEBLE LIGHT OF THE MOON, BRICE BARELY SAW THE woman emerge from the swirling mist hugging the street. Her cloaked figure was barely an arm's length away, but it wasn't until she gave a shrieked cry of warning that he became fully aware of her presence.

He turned, and in the next fraction of a second, his senses took in every detail of his surroundings. His mind registered the scene as though simultaneously viewing a series of paintings done by some master's hand.

The coachman appeared frozen in place, his face registering a numb shock at the woman's strident voice. The footman securing the horses posed in a crouched position, his startled eyes directed toward the back of the vehicle. From behind one rear wheel, a quick spark and a flash illuminated a puff of smoke and the nebulous form of one who raised and fired a pistol.

The danger of the moment crashed into Brice's brain. Instinct urged him to elude the flintlock's deadly missile, yet there had been no time to react and motion seemed suspended, slowed to a frustratingly sluggish crawl. In an eon-long second, images of his entire life coalesced in his mind, evoking the beloved faces of his parents and brother.

Regrets ravaged his heart, twisted at his gut with thoughts of all that could have been.

He could picture the lead ball tearing into him and his body slumping to the ground in agony or death. Every muscle, every nerve and fiber of his being tensed for the blow, the searing pain.

Instead, there was only the woman suddenly stepping between him and the raised gun. For an instant, he had a glimpse of her pale face, her eyes widened in shock and her lips parted on a pained gasp. She seemed to hover on the brink of taking another step, but her shoulders arched and her hands rose to clutch helplessly at the air.

She collapsed in his arms. The impact of her soft body brought reality flooding back, and he gathered her close, holding her limp body protectively.

"My lord!" the coachman exclaimed, jumping down from his high seat and rushing to Brice's side. "Are you hurt, my lord?"

Brice swung the unconscious woman up into his arms, but his piercing green gaze was riveted to the shadowed area behind his coach. Whoever had fired the pistol had fled.

"I'm fine, Holloway." But that was stretching it a bit. Someone had just tried to kill him and most likely would have succeeded if not for this woman's actions.

Cursing, he climbed the front stairs of his town house just as the heavily carved door opened and a tall, flustered-looking butler rushed onto the landing.

"My lord, I heard the shot. Is all well?"

Brice had neither the patience nor the inclination to bandy words, especially when it was perfectly obvious that the situation was far from normal. "No, Cobb, all is not well. Send for the surgeon, damn it." His fierce tone sent Ambrose Cobb off to do as he was told.

Not bothering to speak another word to anyone, Brice stalked into the marble-tiled foyer, past the small cluster of servants who had gathered to whisper and stare in wonder. He didn't spare them a glance as he made for the curving stairway, carrying the woman's slight weight with ease.

He took the stairs two at a time and made his way to the second floor and the suite of rooms that connected with his own. His face drawn rigid with concentration, he gently laid the woman on the high four-poster bed, easing her to the pillows with infinite care.

Straightening, he studied her cloaked form carefully. She seemed a fragile young thing, lying so still. Despite the pallor of her skin, she was exceedingly lovely. The contours of her face were molded into a delicate oval, her high cheekbones giving way to the clean line of her jaw. Her nose was straight and pert above generously curved lips, and blond brows arched over eyes, the color of which he could only guess.

Strands of blond hair had escaped their simple twist and framed her face, making her appear precariously frail. In the soft light filling the room, her pale features appeared to be fashioned of delicate porcelain. He knew that she was no china doll, though, for she possessed whatever inner strength it took to save his life.

Brice shook his head in total, unrelenting disbelief. *Why?* Why had she, a complete stranger, put herself in such danger for him? It was as much a mystery as why anyone would want to see him dead.

The swish of stiffly starched black skirts sounded from behind him and he turned to see his housekeeper bustle into the room, a basin of water and a stack of towels clasped in her plump hands.

"I thought there might be a need for these, my lord," Mary Cobb offered on her way to the bed. "Until the doctor arrives."

Brice sent her a wry look. "I see the details have spread throughout the staff."

"Yes, my lord," she replied sympathetically. The lace ruffle of her mobcap fluttered with the dismayed shake of her head. "We are all terribly shocked to think that such a thing could have actually happened. I trust you are unharmed, my lord."

Brice ignored the question and the genuine concern that

had prompted it. "Spare me, madam." His voice was as bleak as winter's raw wind.

"As you wish, my lord, but we are most grateful to this young woman for saving your life." She placed the towels on the bed beside the woman and fussed worriedly. "The poor thing. Do we have any idea who she is?"

Brice snorted in disgust. "More than likely someone bent on self-sacrifice." But even as he spoke, the notion struck him as curiously rare. As far as he knew, noble, well-intentioned people did not exist. Not without a price, at any rate. On an indifferent note, he wondered what the charge was for saving a life these days.

The corner of his mouth quirked down at the thought. As much as he would like to get past the situation, he could not ignore the fact that this young woman had prevented his own death. That was a weighty truth with which to deal and whether he wished it or not, he felt a disturbingly uncomfortable responsibility toward her.

Grumbling low in his throat, he stared down at her. He had no idea how seriously she had been injured, but she was unconscious and that was not a good sign.

"Mrs. Cobb, help me get her out of her clothes." He unbuttoned the cloak's simple fastening and only then realized his housekeeper remained unmoving.

"Do you have a problem, Mrs. Cobb?"

"No, my lord. I mean . . . Oh, dear."

Even in the subdued light, Brice could see a healthy flush stain Mrs. Cobb's rounded cheeks. "Put aside your embarrassment, Mrs. Cobb."

"I will try, my lord," she managed in a miserable voice. "But if you will pardon me for saying so, this is a task best suited to another woman."

He ignored her chagrin as so much nonsense. "I believe the situation demands that you set aside your delicate sensibilities for the time being."

"Of course, my lord. I meant no offense. I only meant that you are, after all, the Most Noble Marquess of Warrington."

"What in blue blazes does that have to do with anything?"

6

he snapped, rapidly losing his temper. "Now, either do as you are told or get out."

He was glad to see her shake off her amazement and rid the unconscious woman of her shoes.

Easing the woolen cloak away from the woman's shoulders, his gaze dropped immediately to the wide stain of blood that soaked the fabric of her blue dress from midriff to hip.

"Damn," he muttered, his green eyes glittering from beneath his lowered brow. Up until now, he had only assumed that she had taken the shot. The blood was a grisly confirmation that he had been horribly accurate.

His curse drew Mrs. Cobb's attention. At the sight of so much blood, she gasped, clasping her hands to her mouth.

"Dear Lord in Heaven," she whispered, her face growing sickly pale.

Brice could not contain his jeering smile. "Don't waste your breath seeking assistance from that quarter, madam. This woman's fate lies solely in mortal hands." With jerking motions, he yanked off his black evening jacket and rolled back the cuffs of his shirt. "Now, if you will lend your assistance, please."

Together they removed the woman's clothes. Each piece, from the simple blue muslin dress to the light corset and thin chemise, bore the small round hole caused by the pistol's ball.

As soon as the last of the garments were removed, it was obvious where the ball itself was lodged. Blood flowed freely from a ragged puncture in the woman's side, just below her left breast. Beneath the smear of blood, the skin around the wound was swollen and had taken on a bluish tint.

Brice scowled fiercely. This was no mere scratch, but a serious wound that could possibly see this woman dead. The cold reality of that made his muscles clench tightly, but he brutally forced the effect away, greatly resenting his ungovernable response.

Irritated with his own reaction, he reached for a towel. "Bloody hell. What business do you have running about saving people's lives, imposing your benevolence on the unsuspecting?" Despite the roughness of his voice, he pressed the cloth to the wound with exceptional care.

"Mrs. Cobb." He drilled his gaze into hers. "I want the surgeon here in the next five minutes."

"Yes, my lord," she murmured, her eyes rounding. Swiftly, she gathered up the bloody garments and fled.

In the wake of Mary Cobb's exit, silence filled the room. Only the ticking of the gold filigree clock on the mantel could be heard, but Brice was oblivious to its sound as he concentrated on doing what he could to save this unknown woman. He sat beside her, keeping a firm hand on the towel pressed to her side. Blood had already soaked into the fabric, but the heavy bleeding had abated somewhat.

His gaze lowered along the slim column of her throat to her shoulders and the abundant slope of her breasts, and he couldn't contain his look of annoyance mixed with puzzlement. Who was this woman? She had come out of nowhere to save his life. Yet what had she been doing walking the streets of Mayfair at night and alone at that?

The obvious answer lay in that age-old profession. He had to admit that he did not want to think of her as a whore. And logically he knew that prostitutes who plied their wares on the streets rarely wandered into this part of the city.

She could be a servant, out on some errand for her employer, or out meeting some admirer. She was beautiful enough to attract any man's attention. Still, none of that rang true. The clothes she had worn were of fair quality. Nothing as grand as the gentry would wear, but well made and certainly more costly than what a mere parlor maid or a scullery wench could afford.

A low moan escaped the woman's lips, drawing his gaze to her face. Her smooth brow puckered and her eyelids fluttered briefly. She turned her head to one side and shifted her shoulders, but her movement, slight though it was, brought a grimace to her face and another groan to her lips.

Brice laid his hand on her shoulder, holding her in place

against any further activity. "Don't move," he whispered, watching as she slowly regained consciousness.

Through her parted lips, she drew an unsteady breath then swallowed hard. Again, her head turned away, as though in the remnants of her shock she was trying to escape the pain that she was only now beginning to feel.

Slowly her eyes opened and pure, undiluted blue stabbed straight into him with stunning force. Brice felt the breath knocked from his body. He felt incapable of looking away. All the muscles in his chest constricted, gripping him in one huge excruciating knot.

He fought for breath as reality vanished. The boundaries of his existence now went no further than her eyes and for endless seconds, he felt fused with this woman, an extension of her, while her very essence ripped him open and coursed to the core of him.

Hope, trust, faith . . . *love.* Each invaded him, twining in on themselves, spiraling outward in all directions, reaching for a part of him long dead. He didn't know how or why, but he felt them capture his mind and body, and he struggled to escape their hold.

Then with literally a blink of an eye, reason returned. She clenched her eyes against the pain and Brice was freed from whatever force had held him. Like an arrow that was suddenly released from the straining tension of a bow, he jerked back and dragged in one aching breath after another, his heart pounding furiously as though he had run an arduous course.

Shaken, he squared his shoulders and glared down at her. *What in the devil had happened?* Looking into her eyes, he had been pulled into some trance, some illusion where only she existed. Traces of that overwhelming sensation still lingered in the periphery of his awareness, warming the ends of his nerves.

Determinedly, he clamped down on the crazed, jarring feeling. It was madness, utter madness most likely brought on as an effect of nearly being murdered. He shoved the weakness away and focused his attention on the situation at hand.

"Try to lie still," he ordered.

Drawing as deep a breath as she could, the woman opened her eyes, grimacing at the effort that small act took.

"Where am I?" she asked, her voice low and laced with pain.

"I've brought you into my house."

She seemed to digest that for a moment, remaining silent until she could gather the strength to say more. "Who are you?"

"Brice Warfield." He watched her strive for another breath. "But more importantly, who are you?"

She swallowed before answering. "I'm Elora Simmons."

"Throwing yourself in the path of the shot was a foolhardy thing for you to do, Elora Simmons. You put yourself in grave peril for my sake."

Elora gave the tiniest nod of her head. When she spoke her words were oddly calm. "Is my own life forfeit then?"

Brice knew it was a valid question, but, for some reason that was beyond comprehension, his mind thoroughly refused to entertain it. Instead, he searched her face, and knew, absolutely *knew* with every ounce of his being that he could not let this woman die.

"No." The word was a declaration that defied all and any argument.

Elora drew another shaky breath, but before she could say anything, she gritted her teeth and arched back against the bed, digging her heels into the mattress.

Brice's hands shot out of their own accord. Instincts he had thought long-dead, innate impulses he had assumed had been destroyed years ago swamped him, demanding he lend her whatever strength he could to ease her pain. Driven by some inner force he could not seem to control, he curved his fingers around the soft contours of her shoulders and gathered her to him.

"You just saved my life," he snarled. "I'm not about to let you die. Breathe, damn it, hold on to me and breathe."

Against his arms and chest, he could feel her body

trembling, could feel the warmth of her tears hot against his neck. His arms tightened, but he was helpless to do more than that. Frustrated, he was forced to wait out the moments until at last her body went limp in his arms and he heard the gentle rush of her exhaled breath.

Tensing, he leaned away and scanned her face, expecting to see the slumberous mask of death. Instead, he saw her looking up at him, her beautiful eyes tired and glazed over, but very much alive.

Those eyes. Looking into the indigo depths was like looking into pure and raw emotion.

Too many emotions.

As though burned, he pushed from the bed and stared down at her, suspicious, resentful. She was making a mockery of his self-control, forcing him into a role of compassionate champion, a task he could not fulfill.

Hands clenched into tight fists at his sides, he silently decreed that the doctor had better arrive immediately.

No sooner had he finished the thought than Mary Cobb entered the room, escorting a harried-looking Dr. Bingham.

"My lord," she whispered, her voice lowered, no doubt in deference to the ailing young woman. "Dr. Bingham is here."

A host of disparaging remarks balanced on the tip of Brice's tongue. Fortunately for the doctor's sake, he swallowed all but the most imperative statement.

"Tend to her, doctor. *Now.*"

Through the haze of her agony Elora heard the command and struggled to understand. She concentrated on drawing in air, but her side felt on fire, her leg and chest blazing. It seemed as though every muscle in her body was twisted tight against the assault and all she could do was surrender to a low cry.

Helpless tears slid down her cheeks as she fought back the nausea and dread. Brice Warfield had told her she was not going to die, but she sensed that he had stretched the truth for her sake.

She didn't want to die. She was only twenty-one and there

was so much in life she had yet to experience. Love . . . and marriage and children. She wanted all those, had hoped that they would be hers someday. If she died now, she would never have a chance for her dreams to come true.

Her mind fled from the thought of death and sought sanctuary in the sight of Brice Warfield standing at the foot of the bed. His arms about her had been a soothing balm and she wished he would hold her close again, surrounding her with his strength. Instead, a wiry man approached her.

In vain, she tried to focus on him, but the room seemed to bend and grow dim. A buzzing sounded in her head and try as she might, she could not hear anything other than the insistent whir in her ears.

Her strength rapidly waning and her grasp on reality slipping, she struggled to put one coherent thought after another. Notions flitted through her mind and ran together in a jumbled collection. She didn't know this small, somber man, but she couldn't think clearly enough to question or understand his presence. She vaguely realized that she was lying naked for all to see, but she could not summon the strength to rise and cover herself. The pain in her side was about to swallow her whole, and all she could do was stare in mindless amazement.

She looked to Brice once more for help and found him silently regarding her. Amidst the swirling grays that threatened to engulf her vision she saw the green of his eyes, the black of his hair, his tall powerful figure. Some intuition compelled her to trust and rely on him and mentally she reached out for him.

"Brice." It was an agonized, beseeching whisper, barely audible and torn from her lips, but Brice heard it.

Carefully, he returned to sit at her side and took one of her icy hands between his own.

Elora curled her fingers into his palms and savored the warm reassurance his touch brought. "Please don't leave me."

"I won't, sweet."

The endearment brought a weak smile to her lips. It

seemed to melt away when she noticed the bloody stain on his clothing. "I didn't realize dying was such a messy affair."

Brice's brows lowered fiercely. "You are *not* dying," he told her in no uncertain terms. Turning his head sharply, he skewered Ridgely Bingham with a challenging look.

Clearly reading the silent message Brice was sending, the doctor nodded in jerking motions. "I will do my best, my lord. But the shot must come out as quickly as possible." He gestured uneasily to Elora's torn and bloodied flesh. "She has lost a great deal of blood, and will lose more." He paused, obviously choosing his next words with great care. "There is no guarantee that she has the strength for the ordeal. Strong men have . . . that is, I can make no promises that she . . ."

The stare of glinting green eyes brought him to a stuttering halt. His gaze shifted to Mrs. Cobb before returning to Brice and finally settling on Elora. "I will do my best."

Elora was barely conscious of the preparations going on around her. She never felt Mary Cobb grasp her ankles in a secure grip. The figure of the doctor as he moved back and forth beside the bed was a distant shadow.

Only the firm pressure of Brice's hands on her shoulders penetrated her abused senses. Only his unwavering gaze pierced the icy numbness that encompassed her. What little reasoning she retained at that moment was centered completely and totally on Brice. Her entire universe began and ended with him.

The first touch of the surgeon's hands on her side shattered the bounds of her sanity. Pain tore at every fiber of her body, convulsed her muscles and ripped her nerves with unrelenting force. Waves of agony ground their way from her stomach to her lungs and up to her throat in a scream of torturous suffering.

The last thing she saw before darkness claimed her was the shattered look on Brice Warfield's face.

Chapter

2

Shadows and silence enveloped Brice like a weighty mantle. Their combined effects created a bleak atmosphere in which his mind insisted on dwelling. The events of the night still ran through his veins like some strange energy, robbing him of the serenity he desperately wanted.

Sitting beside the four-poster in which Elora lay, he shut his eyes briefly and gave in to a coughing laugh that had nothing to do with humor. His grin was as cynical as his mood, and his thoughts were deeply rooted in self-mockery.

After all these years he was still susceptible to his emotions. He had thought himself beyond such a weakness, but it would seem that there was still a chink or two in his hide that was not impervious.

It was annoying to admit that fear had somehow penetrated his armor. And of course a certain amount of concern for Elora Simmons had penetrated also. But he'd be damned if he was going to take either seriously. He had simply gotten caught up in the histrionics of nearly losing his life. It would have been enough to rattle anyone, but it was over and done with and he was in full control again.

In full control.

Lacing his hands together over his chest, he slouched more deeply into the cushions of the chair and reluctantly

14

gazed at Elora. She lay unconscious, the blanket and sheet pulled to her shoulders. From all appearances, she looked to be sleeping peacefully. But beneath the covers, her body was wrapped tightly in layers of bandages, her skin overly warm to the touch.

He stared intently at the serene contours of her profile illuminated by the fire's glow. Only an hour past, those very same features had been contorted with unspeakable pain. In his mind he could still see her eyes locked to his as though he were the very source of her strength.

Shaking his head, he considered just how much strength Elora Simmons would need. The surgeon had estimated her chances of survival as poor. She was young, but she had lost too much blood. The shot had been lodged against a rib, missing any organs within, but the shock to her system had been severe. She was healthy, but there was always the chance that the wound could become putrid.

Another scoffing laugh shook his shoulders, but this time it was underscored with blatant defiance. In one smooth movement, he rose and stepped to the bed. Boldly, he gave her an assessing look, unconsciously willing her to open her eyes.

"I am not your strength, Elora. Do you hear me? I am *not* your strength."

The sound of his own voice drew him up short.

"Bloody hell." Disgusted and uncomfortable with his own behavior, he stalked away, sneering at the absurdity of it all. Three hours ago, he had never even set eyes upon this woman. Now, he was keeping a bedside vigil like some impulsive idiot.

He needed to put his life back on its normal course, exactly where he had left off three hours ago. Toward that end, he strode to the door that led to his bedroom and entered the spacious chamber, continuing on into his dressing room. Despite the lateness of the hour, he rang the corded bellpull before crossing to a chimera-legged tripod table. There, he lit a thin cigar and drew heavily on the gray smoke.

He took his time to savor the fumes. They were familiar, routine, and they went far in reestablishing his personal sense of equilibrium.

The cigar clamped between even white teeth, he stripped off his bloodied cravat and tossed it onto a nearby chair. His fingers were making steady progress on the buttons of his shirt when he noticed his valet in the doorway.

"Come," he ordered, squinting through the cigar's silver haze.

Fently entered the dressing room, his rigid stance the quintessence of studied decorum.

"My lord?"

Brice glanced over his shoulder as he poured water from a porcelain pitcher into its matching bowl. "Send word to my secretary that I want him back from York as quickly as possible."

Not a flicker of emotion crossed Fently's face, nor did it ever. The deep lines remained set, the gray brows immobile.

"Very good, my lord. Do you wish for me to lay out your clothes?"

"No," Brice replied, too restless to tolerate Fently's methodical ministrations.

"As you wish. Will there be anything else, my lord?"

"No."

"Very good." Fently nodded. He had his instructions, but he hesitated in taking his leave. Brice knew there was something else on his man's mind. He raised his brows in inquiry.

"What is it, Fently?"

"I beg your pardon, my lord," he began slowly. "But I wish to express how glad I am that you have escaped this situation unscathed."

Brice hung the towel about his neck and raked the damp strands of black hair off his forehead. Openly, he studied his staid valet and the corner of his mouth twitched slightly.

"Going maudlin on me, Fently?" he drawled. Something that by a stretch of the imagination could be called derisive humor touched the green of his eyes.

16

"Nothing quite so inspiring, my lord."

Brice laid the towel aside and stepped to the Chinese lacquered armoire. "Yes, well, you won't have to worry about seeking employment elsewhere quite so soon. I am still very much alive and capable of ensuring your salary."

Fently's face retained all of its solemnity, but Brice noticed his valet's neck took on a reddish hue. "My concern was solely for your welfare, my lord."

Brice threw him a pointed look. "That's quite noble of you, Fently." Withdrawing a fresh shirt, he slipped it on.

The discussion obviously at an end, the valet exited. Behind him, Brice finished with his shirt, oblivious to Fently's unusually taut bearing.

His mind set on the evening's events, Brice made his way into his bedroom in search of a brandy, but his steps were halted by a crashing sound coming from the bedroom in which he had left Elora.

"What the devil?" In seconds, he was through the connecting door. His gaze darted to the bed. The shadowed area revealed only thrown back covers and rumpled pillows.

In one all-encompassing glance, he scanned the entire room, coming forward as he did so. He spotted Elora standing before the fireplace, a small side table tipped over by her feet. Amazed, his pace slowed. She was precariously near to death, so how she had managed to leave the bed was beyond him. But there she was, seemingly mesmerized by the flickering reds and golds of the flames.

He closed the distance between them, stopping only when he was within arm's reach of her. Still, she continued to stare at the fire, unconcerned by her condition, oblivious to his presence and heedless of her near-naked state.

The latter did not, however, go unnoticed by Brice. He had been fully aware of her beauty as he had removed her clothing, but time and the urgency of the moment had prevented him from fully appreciating her splendor.

Now, with the fire's glowing hues dancing over her gentle curves, he was keenly aware of just how beautiful she was. His reluctance to be near her evaporated. He didn't stop to rationalize whether his observation was timely or not. He simply gave in to a reflexive impulse and drank in the sight of her.

The long length of her fair hair shimmered with light, the waves creating mysterious swirls that beckoned. Her face showed no signs of pain, but rather reflected an inner serenity that only enhanced her loveliness. The slope of her shoulders and the contours of her legs were trim while the fullness of her breasts positively invited a man's caress.

Beneath his snug fitting pants, he rose up fast and hard. He ground his teeth at the unexpectedness of his reaction. Unbelievably his body was making demands, demands that were impossible for too many reasons. The thick bandage wrapped about her ribs was a grotesque reminder of reason number one.

Lifting a hand, he curved his fingers over her shoulder.

"Elora, what are you doing?"

She turned her head slowly, her eyes feverish and squinting ever so slightly. As though in a dreamlike state, she scrutinized every line and curve of his face, then lifted a hand in mute examination.

Brice's brows lowered as she traced a finger over his high cheek to the edge of his jaw. Her gaze followed her finger's searching path as it skimmed close to his chin and sought his mouth. There, both finger and stare lingered.

A tingling tremor began in Brice's lips, coursing down his neck to his chest. Caught off guard, he stood motionless as the trembling warmed every nerve along the way. A gentle heat collected in the region of his heart, quickening his pulse.

Stunned, he drew a sharp breath. He was beginning to react to her touch in the same way he had reacted when he had first looked into her eyes. He could feel the twinges of that compelling sensation where she became part of his being. The feeling was sheer lunacy . . . and too dangerous for his peace of mind.

"Elora," he whispered harshly, but she silenced him, lifting her hand to his forehead. Suspiciously he stood immobile while she traced the lines of his scowl with a butterfly's caress. She took her time until the gentleness of her touch smoothed his frown away.

Seemingly satisfied with her accomplishment, she lowered her hand and looked away briefly. But her gaze quickly returned to Brice once more.

"Sir, I'm so cold." Uncontrollably, her bottom lip quivered. "Could I have something to keep me warm?"

The simplicity of her plea was as unexpected as her touch had been. Automatically, Brice retreated from both . . . and from the woman responsible. He took refuge in total exasperation and the scowl returned to his face.

Shaking his head, he declared, "You have no business being out of bed."

Nonetheless, he removed his shirt and draped it over her shoulders. Careful not to strain her injury, he guided her arms through the sleeves. That done, he fastened the buttons down the full length.

"You are most kind, sir," Elora murmured weakly.

Brice's only reply was to carefully pick her up and carry her back to the bed. He settled her beneath the covers, then stepped away, stern words of warning just waiting to be uttered. The rebuke died on his lips when he saw that Elora was already asleep. He jammed his fists on his lean waist.

"The last bloody thing I need is to play nursemaid."

Minutes later, he was fully clothed, standing at one of his bedroom windows, issuing orders to Fently once more.

"Have Mrs. Cobb sit with Miss Simmons through the night."

"Very good, my lord."

"I do not want her left alone. Do you understand?"

"Yes, my lord."

Everyone had better understand because, Brice swore to himself, he would be damned if he was going to return to Elora's side now or any time in the near future. She had the most abominable effect on him.

That settled in his own mind, he turned his attention to the view from the window. With a pensive eye, he watched the fog roll and curl. As thick now as it had been hours earlier, the layer of misty white captured his attention and goaded him into thinking about the attempt on his life.

He had never given much thought to his own death. Since it was inevitable, it was worthy of little contemplation. But he had always assumed the time would be somewhere in the future, certainly not that night and not prompted by a murderer's hand. Laughing caustically, he decided he was going to have to give the matter of his death serious thought, since someone else was obviously doing that very same thing.

His lips thinned as he considered who might be responsible. As far as he knew, he had no real enemies, so it was a distasteful and extremely disagreeable prospect to have to consider one's acquaintances capable of murder. However, as much as he wanted to discredit the notion, he found himself giving it closer scrutiny.

He made a mental list of those who held a grudge against him, and why. Ruefully, he had to admit that there were several possibilities.

To start with, there was little love lost between himself and the Earl of Stanley. The earl had a penchant for the gaming tables, and a streak of incredibly poor luck whenever Brice decided to pick up the cards. Just last night, Brice had lightened the earl's pockets by twenty-five thousand pounds. Stanley had stormed from their club, white-faced and furious, muttering oaths of retribution.

It was entirely possible that Stanley had acted on his threats. But it was just as likely that the Duke of Westford had finally given vent to the animosity he had harbored for years.

The grudge was long-standing, and Brice knew, founded for the most part on the duke's jealousy. The man made no secret that he coveted Brice's collection of ancient artifacts, one rare and treasured Egyptian papyrus in particular. On more than one occasion, Westford had threatened to go to any extreme to best Brice in the game of collecting Eastern antiquities.

Add to that the fact that years ago, Brice had entertained a brief but intense affair with Westford's wife. It made little difference to the duke that the dalliance had been conducted according to all the peculiar precepts the *ton* followed in such matters. And that Westford himself was a philanderer of the worst sort. He had never forgiven Brice and over the course of time had nurtured his hostility into a full-fledged hatred.

Swearing, Brice scrubbed a hand across his forehead in irritation. It was all absurd; someone trying to kill him and him trying to determine who. He could think the thing to death and still not have the answers.

He shoved away from the window and stretched full-length on his bed. Against his will, he found himself staring at the door to Elora's room. When he realized what he was doing, he yanked his gaze to the ceiling. Unfortunately, that did not prevent his mind from picturing her on the other side of the door.

"Bloody hell. First a nursemaid and now a simpleton." He could not seem to control his thoughts about her, and the more he thought, the more he realized some startling qualities about the woman.

Elora Simmons had made the ultimate sacrifice for him. He couldn't think of anyone who would do such a thing, especially for a total stranger. In return she had asked for nothing more than a shirt to keep her warm. Even hours ago, when she had been completely lucid, she hadn't even asked that a doctor be summoned.

There was an elemental generosity in such a manner, an artlessness that struck a chord deep within him. That in itself was extremely unsettling. He wasn't accustomed to such selflessness nor did he know how to react to it. Most people viewed him in terms of his wealth and station in life, and tried to use both to their own advantage.

Elora had done the exact opposite. She had offered herself up for his benefit and in return wanted nothing more than to be kept warm.

The image of her face flooded his mind. As clearly as if

21

she were lying atop him, he could see her delicate features surrounded by golden waves of hair and beseeching eyes filled with pain. He could feel the touch of her hand on his face, infusing him with warmth and . . . and what? Somehow, she permeated his being and made his reality vanish.

No! He shook his head to clear his vision, and pulled himself back to the present. He stared hard about his room. *This* was reality. This solitary life he had created for himself.

Reality had nothing to do with some tender, self-sacrificing woman who prompted emotions he would not tolerate. And it was *not* pain-filled blue eyes that ripped into him until he felt he had a soul.

Chapter

3

THE SOUND OF GENTLE SNORING DREW ELORA'S EYES OPEN. STILL caught up in the remnants of sleep, she slowly turned her head toward the source of the thick breathing and found a plump woman slouched in a nearby chair. Distantly surprised, Elora discovered that she herself was in bed, and briefly she wondered where she was.

She recalled the evening's events immediately. She had been making her way along Berkley Square in search of Lord Ashton's residence, where she would assume her new position as governess. Intent on finding the correct address, she had been hurrying along through the dense fog when she had spotted a coach in waiting. It had taken her several seconds to realize that the indistinct shape behind the vehicle was that of a man with a raised pistol.

At that same instant, she had nearly stumbled upon a tall, dark-haired gentleman who had loomed up out of the fog, oblivious to the danger he was in. Fear for his safety had chilled her blood and she had tried to warn him, to cry out.

The next thing she knew, she had awakened in this bed. The man had been by her side, sitting close and telling her she wasn't going to die. After that, her memories were fragmented.

She lifted the covers and peered at her clothed form. Her side still ached dreadfully, but the agony that had previously consumed her was gone. Beneath the voluminous shirt she was wearing she could feel the bandage wrapped around her with all the pressure of a corset. She was more than a little uncomfortable, but it was a small price to pay to still be alive.

Experimentally, she tried to lever herself upward against the pillows. Her entire body protested vehemently. Holding her breath, she shut her eyes and laid back once more. She would not be leaving this bed any time soon. She faced that fact as she opened her eyes and looked about. But she also conceded that her stay was dependent solely upon the gentleman's discretion.

Her smooth brow furrowed as she tried to recall his name. But it remained elusive, overshadowed by other impressions of him that were much stronger.

His eyes were green, a deep verdant hue that had been fiercely intense, filled with powerful but unnamed emotions that even now caused a ripple to race up her spine. His voice was deep, the sound mellow and somehow comforting. And he was strong. She could still feel his arms holding her through the hideous pain.

Brice Warfield.

His name was Brice Warfield. Just knowing that brought a smile to her lips.

The plump woman in the chair stirred slightly, her snoring sputtering off into a choking cough. The sound captured Elora's attention and silently she watched the woman awaken.

The woman blinked back the effects of her nap then yawned deeply, resettling her mobcap. She turned to look at Elora and her hands froze in midair. Evidently amazed that her charge was finally awake, she came to her feet.

"Oh, I declare, but it is good to see you with us." A jubilant smile lined her round face. "I am Mary Cobb, miss, the housekeeper, and I've been watching over you. How are you feeling? Are you in much pain?"

Elora returned the smile, grateful for the woman's concern. "Only a little."

Mary nodded with apparent motherly wisdom. "That will pass in time, now that you're on the mend. We were all quite frantic about your condition."

"Thank you."

Looking somewhat surprised, Mary Cobb laid her hand over her ample bosom and exclaimed, "Oh no, miss, you have nothing to thank me for. It is I who should be thanking you. You were simply wonderful saving the marquess the way you did."

Elora was suddenly at a loss. "The marquess?"

"Yes, the Marquess of Warrington." Mary's head tilted to one side as if in confusion. "Don't you remember?"

"I remember a gentleman by the name of Brice Warfield."

"That's right. Brice Warfield is the Marquess of Warrington, but I suppose there wasn't time for polite introductions the other night."

Elora blinked, her amazement escalating by the second. "The other night?"

Mary shook her head sympathetically. "Yes, miss, you've been here for two days now."

"Two days?" Elora could hardly believe it.

"You really have been outside of things, haven't you, miss?"

Somewhat dazed, Elora agreed weakly, "Yes, I am afraid so."

"Well, don't you fret about anything. We'll have you right in no time." She smoothed the silk coverlet, her hand lingering lightly on Elora's arm. "You just rest and I'll run down and get you some broth. Cook has had a pot simmering just for you."

As if the mention of soup could induce hunger, Elora felt a distinct emptiness in her stomach. She was definitely hungry.

"Thank you, Mrs. Cobb."

"Oh, my pleasure, miss. Now, is there anything else you'd be needing?"

Elora shook her head, but changed her mind when a sudden thought struck. "Mrs. Cobb, there is something; my clothes case and reticule. I believe I dropped them when I called out to the marquess." She glanced away with a slight frown as she tried to remember exactly what she had done with her possessions. "I'm not certain where they are."

Obviously seeing her puzzlement, the housekeeper allayed her worries. "We have your things, miss. The coachman found them right out in front where you left them." She reached into the bedside table and withdrew the black reticule from the drawer. "I've kept this close by for you, and I took the liberty of unpacking your clothes."

She handed the drawstring purse to Elora, then made her way across the room. There she paused and gave Elora a huge beaming smile filled with gratitude before quietly exiting.

Reticule in hand, Elora squinted slightly as she watched Mary take her leave, and marveled at the housekeeper's elation. It was obvious that the woman was delighted for the marquess's safety. Apparently, the Marquess of Warrington was greatly revered by his servants.

Her thoughts turned to the marquess. He was a wealthy man, if the room was anything by which to judge. She opened her reticule and removed a pair of wire-rimmed spectacles and slipped them on. The splendid room was suddenly brought into sharp focus.

Midmorning sun shone brightly through two sets of windows dressed in heavy, pale blue brocade. The fabric complemented the cerulean coverlet on the bed and the plush rose-patterned carpet covering the floor. The highly polished furniture was ornately elegant, boasting intricately carved Egyptian figures and gold inlaid Turkish engravings.

Lord Warrington had exotic tastes, it would seem. In all her life, Elora knew she had never seen the likes of such furnishings. Living in the solitude of the country, she hadn't had the opportunity to do more than read about such treasures. Now, she was surrounded by the very articles themselves and counted herself quite lucky. She decided that London was certainly filled with surprises.

Dangers, too, her mind added. The idea that the marquess had nearly been shot to death was appalling, and impossible for her to reconcile in her own mind. She would never understand how or why one person would wish to harm another. Violence had never made any sense to her.

Tormenting remembrances of her past clutched at her heart. Her stepfather's cruelty had been incomprehensible and frightening as over the years he drank and gambled away the trappings and privileges of an affluent merchant. She and her mother had lived under his tyrannical domination, terrified of provoking his temper that could erupt for no discernible reason. What pleased him one day could very well incite him to raise his fist the very next.

And he had raised his fist. Often and with punishing force. She could still feel the fear that would consume her at his bellowing rages and brutalizing attacks. Just the thought made her want to pull the covers about her protectively.

It had been so different with her father.

Her sorrow fell away like a lacy mantle in the breeze to lay bare the cherished memories of her childhood. Her father had been a teacher in Yorkshire, and they had lived a simple life. That had not stopped her parents, however, from sharing a rare and abiding love. It had only been natural for that love to permeate her world. Her mother's tender embrace, her father's compassionate laughter; she had held those close to her heart like a sacred talisman through all the dark years with Harmen Gillet.

To this day, her stepfather's name made her nerves quiver. But she had the satisfaction of knowing that he had never been able to brutalize her soul. *That* was still graced by love.

Distracted by her thoughts, her unfocused gaze was on the reticule she still held. But an unnerving sensation assailed her and she looked up, trying to determine the cause of the feeling. She found it at once and blinked in surprise.

The marquess had entered the room and was lounging in

the doorway with negligent, long-limbed grace. His arms crossed over his chest, his head cocked to one side, he openly watched her. A disarmingly real aura of masculine authority encompassed him and reached out to Elora clear across the room.

Unaware that she did so, she silently returned his perusal. The first time she had seen him, she had been wracked by pain. Agony and the darkness of the night had made it impossible for her to garner a clear picture of him. Now in the light of day, her discomfort at a tolerable level and her glasses perched on her nose, she had a perfectly clear view of the man.

He was unlike any man she had ever, *ever* seen before. His face was ruggedly sculpted with high cheekbones and a jaw that was unyielding. The green eyes she remembered so well were accented by straight black brows, while his lips were chiseled into firm lines that gave no hint of humor. His hair was unrelieved black, the soft strands catching the sunlight and glinting blue.

It was an extraordinarily handsome face, possessing the same kind of strength that was evidenced in the broad width of his shoulders covered by the dark blue jacket, and the long line of his legs sheathed in gray trousers. But underlying all that strength, there was a strange emptiness, a coldness that made her want to wrap her arms about herself. She imagined his age to be near thirty-five, but he seemed older somehow.

This wasn't how she remembered him. Amidst the incomplete images of that night, she had formed an impression of someone teeming with emotion, not this man who seemed so remote. Isolated. Detached. But unnervingly compelling.

"Hello," she managed. A little breathlessly, she watched him push away from the door and saunter toward her.

"I see you've decided to open your eyes." Coming to stand at the foot of the bed, he stared at her with a suspicious intensity that made her uncomfortable.

"Yes, I'm finally awake." She regarded him closely. "Is . . . is something wrong?"

"Why do you ask?"

"Because of the way you're looking at me." Unconsciously, she settled her glasses more firmly on her nose.

He smiled thinly and his skepticism seemed to vanish. "I don't recall ever seeing a woman wearing spectacles."

"Yes, well." She sighed in relief, for she had gotten the impression that he had been looking at her as though she were somehow a source of trouble. Thankfully, he had managed to smile and allay her fears. She did not want to do anything to provoke the man. Or any man for that matter. "We are not all blessed with perfect eyes."

"Then it appears that vanity does not run in your veins, Miss Simmons. Courage is more your style." He paused, looking thoughtful. "You've made Mrs. Cobb a happy woman."

"Have I?"

He leaned a shoulder against the bedpost. "Definitely. Our paths crossed on the stairway and she was all aflutter with your awakening."

Warmed by the housekeeper's concern, Elora could not contain her smile. "That's very sweet of her. She seems a nice person."

Brice's gaze lowered to her delicately molded lips. "Well, be prepared to become the chick to her mother hen. She's got a captive patient since you'll be confined to that bed for a while."

He had inadvertently raised the very matter that had worried Elora earlier. "I didn't mean to inconvenience you in this way."

"I'd hardly say that saving my life qualifies as an inconvenience."

"No, of course not. But I am, as you say, confined to this bed, for a while at least. I do not wish my presence to be a burden to you or your staff." Behind her glasses, her crystalline blue eyes darkened on an afterthought. "Or your wife."

A hint of a scoffing laugh worked its way from Brice's throat, joined by a dismissing shake of his head. "I have no

29

wife, Miss Simmons. And as far as my staff is concerned, they do as they're told." His voice took on a sardonic edge. "Besides, they've been waiting breathlessly for two days for the chance to serve you. I believe they see you as a combination of their knight in shining armor and a fair damsel in distress. Trust me, you will not be a burden to them."

His words should have belied her worries, and for the most part they did. But while he had assured her of the servants' reaction to her presence, he had made no mention of how he personally felt about having her in his home.

She searched his face, but his set features gave her no clues. "Thank you," she said somewhat lamely. "It was never my intent to put anyone to such bother. I had only just arrived in London and I was simply trying to locate the residence of Lord and Lady Ashton."

"James Ashton?"

"Yes, Lord James Ashton. I have been hired as governess to his children."

In what appeared to her as a curiously discerning look, Brice narrowed his eyes. "The Ashtons reside several houses that way," he informed her, indicating the direction with a nod of his head. "The cabman should have known that when he dropped you off the other night."

"Oh, I didn't arrive by coach, my lord."

"I beg your pardon?"

"I was making my way on foot."

Silence. For a space of three heartbeats, not a sound, until Brice slowly crossed his arms over his chest, his studied movement causing his jacket to rustle subtly. Then a dangerously low, *"What?"*

Elora's heart thumped. Every tautened line of his body exuded an unmistakable air of disapproval. She had only to look into his bleak eyes for confirmation.

This was the very thing she had wished to avoid. Under his heavy, yet unspoken censure she felt compelled to hastily explain. "I know walking through London was dangerous, but I didn't have a choice. I had enough money to obtain passage on the coach from my home in Yately to the Peacock Inn here in London." Her face fell slightly. "I hadn't counted on prices here being quite so exorbitant."

She fingered her reticule, thinking how dismayed she had been when she had discovered she hadn't had enough money to afford a cab. The driver had been as patient as he could manage, but he had taken little pity on her. The best he had been able to do was give her directions to Berkley Square.

"Ashton made no provisions for your travel, I take it," Brice commented critically.

"No," Elora replied. She waited nervously for his reaction to that. When all he did was mutter something beneath his breath, she glanced away, suddenly feeling very foolish and very tired.

She knew it wasn't her fault that Lord Ashton had left her to her own devices, and she certainly was not to blame for her deplorable lack of funds. But circumstances since her arrival in the city had been less than wonderful, and she was beginning to see just how naive she had been.

She sighed again. The position as governess had been the answer to her prayers. It represented the source of income she desperately needed to start paying off her stepfather's debts. Suddenly she wondered if she hadn't been pinning her hopes to a false sleeve in thinking everything would be all right once she took up her post in the Ashton household.

The door to the hall opened and Mary Cobb entered with a tray, grinning hugely. It was a warming sight, and Elora clung to it with high hopes. Things would work out, she told herself. She would just have to keep faith.

"Here we are, miss." Mary nodded to Brice as she crossed to the bed. "A nice bowl of chicken broth. And a pot of tea."

Touched by the housekeeper's concern, Elora smiled. Behind her spectacles, her eyes glowed with a startling intensity.

Abruptly, Brice shoved away from the bedpost and headed for the door. "I'll have my secretary send a note around to Ashton," he commented curtly over his shoulder.

At the door he paused and glanced back, his face as rigid as his stance. Then, he left the room as quietly as he had entered.

Taken aback by his brusque departure, Elora stared at the closed door for a moment before looking worriedly at Mary. "Mrs. Cobb, did I say anything to offend his lordship?"

The housekeeper's lips pursed as she poured tea into a china cup. "No, miss, you didn't. The marquess is . . . he is a difficult man to understand at times. Don't let that put you off."

Elora peered at the door again. Brice Warfield was indeed a complex man. He had come through what for most people would have been a harrowing experience, but he displayed no outward signs that he was glad to be alive. That very private element of gratitude that one wallowed in when one managed to survive was missing from his manner. Even his humor, what little there had been of it, had been horribly hollow. It was the same kind of emptiness she saw in his eyes, a coolness that was mocking and bleak.

He was not a happy man. If she hadn't seen it on his face then she knew it in her heart. However, his presence had filled the room. Now, with him gone, she felt inexplicably bereft of his company.

"This should perk you up a bit, miss," Mary said, spooning the chicken soup from a small tureen into a bowl.

Elora reluctantly put away her thoughts about Brice Warfield and concentrated on eating. With Mary's assistance in sitting up, the broth was soon gone and she was leisurely sipping her tea.

"Thank you, Mrs. Cobb," she said on a contented sigh. "I feel better already."

"Your color has improved, miss. That's a good sign."

"I'm sure it's because of the wonderful soup. Please tell cook it was delicious, even better than my mother's."

"Your mother is a good cook, then?"

"She was." Lowering her cup to its saucer, Elora's expression became wistful. "She died several years ago."

"I'm sorry, miss. It's a hard thing to lose your mum. But do you have any other family?" Her voice rose expectantly. "Someone who might be worried about you?"

"No, my father died when I was a child and my stepfather . . ." Her voice skidded to a halt.

How could she even consider Harmen Gillet? Because of his selfish, mean-spirited ways, she was left to face the host of creditors to whom he owed an enormous amount of money. And he? She had no idea where he had run off to. No, she would not care to contact him even if she did know where he was.

"No. There is no one else."

"Well, while you are here, miss, you won't be alone. Mr. Cobb and I will make certain of that." She took the empty cup from Elora and set it on the tray. "You are truly wonderful, miss, and I just shudder to think what might have happened if you hadn't come along."

"The woman has no business wandering about loose," Brice announced to himself as he descended the stairs. She had done no more than smile at his housekeeper and he had felt a warm, disturbing shiver shoot up his back. He had quit the room at once.

She was a menace, he decided, not only to his peace of mind, but to herself. In the short time he had talked with her, he had seen her emotions play all over her face. She had been as transparent as all hell, her distress and hopes flashing about unchecked, making her seem more vulnerable than she already was. Ingenuousness of that kind could get her into serious trouble, especially in Ashton's house.

"Bloody hell." He was mildly familiar with the Ashtons, as they lived only four houses up. But he was very aware of their reputations. James Ashton was a lecherous despot, his wife, Judith, nothing less than a querulous shrew. He wouldn't wish the pair of them on anyone.

Gravely, he considered Elora's impartial manner to the entire matter. Either she wasn't aware of the type of person

33

for whom she would be working, or else she was a glutton for punishment. Mockingly, he decided that she was both. That could be dangerous. *She* was dangerous.

"She's a walking menace," he repeated, entering his study.

"My lord?"

Brice glanced up to find his secretary standing at the French doors. "Marcus, you made good time," he snapped, not bothering to explain his comment about Elora Simmons.

"I came as soon as word reached me," Marcus Quinn explained.

Brice gave his stout, sandy-haired secretary a brief look as he took a seat behind his mahogany desk. "I didn't expect you until tonight."

"I thought it imperative that I arrive with all haste." He came forward with his words. "You are unharmed, my lord?"

Spreading his hands wide, Brice ignored Marcus's obvious concern. "I believe we can be fairly certain of that since I am not bleeding all over my desk."

The droll tone made Marcus wince. "Please bear with me, my lord. I simply needed to be reassured. This has all come as a shock."

"You needn't remind me." Brice shifted one stack of papers onto another. "The entire affair is damned ridiculous."

"Did you happen to see who fired the pistol?" Marcus asked with extreme caution.

"No."

"And the woman?"

Brice's head came up. "What about her?"

"Was she able to tell you anything?"

"As in who would want to kill me?" Brice gave a caustic laugh. "No, she had little to say as she was otherwise preoccupied with trying to stay alive." And with wreaking havoc on his insides. Only moments ago, he had gotten caught by her sapphire eyes. No matter how cautious he had been in approaching her, that same overwhelming sensation he had experienced two nights ago had assailed him once again.

Silently, he cursed a blue streak. What was it about her that rendered his control over his body useless? He responded to her in a way in which he had never before responded to any other woman.

Coming to his feet, he strode to a side table for a thin cigar. His movements precise, he lit the tobacco, pushed Elora from his mind and focused on the matter at hand.

"I want you to contact the Bow Street Runners," he told Marcus, exhaling a fine stream of smoke.

"A wise decision, my lord. I will see to that immediately."

"You will keep this quiet. The last thing I want is to have this bandied about as drawing room prattle."

Marcus didn't reply quite so readily. When he did, Brice heard the man's skepticism. "No one will learn of this from me, my lord, but you must realize how quickly news travels."

Brice clamped down hard on the thin roll of tobacco. Marcus was right. The *ton* thrived on gossip. The smallest bit of hearsay swept from one parlor to the next like a wave of the Black Plague, with results that could be just as devastating.

It was an inescapable fact, and as Brice stood there, he was forced to face another truth. *Miss* Elora Simmons was at this very moment residing in a bachelor's household. If, and more likely when, the particulars of this entire situation got out, her reputation wouldn't be worth a whore's curse. No one would give a damn that she had saved his life, or that he regarded most women with a fair amount of respect. It would be assumed that he would give his masculine appetite free rein, and her name would be trampled under the dictates of polite society.

Shoving aside his jacket, he thrust one hand into his pant's pocket. "Of all the bloody predicaments."

"My lord?"

"I suddenly have need of a chaperone."

Marcus stuttered for a moment. "Y-yes, you are quite right, my lord. I hadn't thought of that, but I can see the necessity. Is there anyone that you would prefer?"

Brice would prefer not to have anyone at all. He was extremely guarded about his personal life and the presence of a chaperone in the house would mean an encroachment on his privacy. But there was no alternative that he could see.

"Send a note to Viscountess Redsdale."

Marcus's eyes rounded enormously. "Your sister, my lord?"

Taking a deep draw on the cigar, Brice paused and gave his secretary a meaningful look. "Put your eyes back in your head, Marcus."

"Yes, my lord," Marcus said, visibly trying to school his features into a placid countenance.

Brice thought the man failed miserably, and it was little wonder. It had been years since he had wished to have his sister in the house. Ever since the death of their parents and brother, he had estranged himself from Vianne. Oh, he was civil to her whenever they happened to meet, but he made damn certain those times were very infrequent.

"I will take care of the matter at once, my lord."

Brice knew he had shocked Marcus. Still, he offered no explanations and quickly concluded their meeting. He had had enough of the matter for one day. He was done thinking about attempted murders, nefarious plots . . . and Elora Simmons.

An afternoon spent inspecting some prime horseflesh and an evening engaged in cards at his club kept his thoughts occupied and otherwise removed from the state of his affairs. It wasn't until he climbed the stairs to his room that night and dismissed Fently that he was forced to think about the situation at all.

As he shrugged out of his evening jacket and stripped off his white cravat, he counted himself lucky that no one at Watier's had approached him with comments about the incident. That was not a guarantee that the rumors would not spread, only that apparently no one at the club had heard yet.

Working the buttons of his shirt, he looked distractedly to the door connecting to Elora's room and his fingers stopped. For the first time since he had entered his room, he noticed a light coming from beneath her door.

A quick glance to the clock on the mantel confirmed that it was well after two in the morning. He couldn't imagine why she would have a candle burning at this hour.

Opening the adjoining door, he found Elora in bed asleep, and quite unexpectedly, he was lured forward by the exquisitely appealing sight she presented.

The brace of candles glowing from the bedside table illuminated the slight flush on her cheeks. The waves of her hair spilled over the pillows in a luxurious disarray of flowing gold. Resting on the bridge of her nose were her spectacles while beneath one delicate hand lay an opened book.

With infinite care, he removed the thin wire frames and set them aside, then found his gaze arrested by the creamy perfection of her skin. She was lovely. Even with the effects of her condition taking their toll, she possessed an elegant beauty that was most rare . . . and so damned tempting that blood rushed through his body with alarming speed.

He jerked back, holding his breath against the sudden heat that curled into the pit of his belly. Stunned at the unexpectedness of his reaction, he started to rein in on the desire infusing him, but instead he absorbed it for a few agonizing seconds.

How long? How long had it been since he had responded to a woman so unconsciously? Years. Yet twice in the span of only a few days, desire for Elora had surged up in him, hot and demanding, ignoring all and any reasoning. The sensation brought back memories of his youth, of unbridled passions.

His thoughts soured. The past, all of it, belonged in the past. There was no separating the good from the bad. It was all dead and buried.

Breathing deeply, he regained control. Unclenching his fists, he studied the book across Elora's lap. She had managed to raid his library, no doubt with Mrs. Cobb's help. He couldn't begrudge her that. It had to be damned annoying to lie immobile all day, bandaged up the way she was. He wasn't certain he could tolerate such a hindrance.

Carefully he lifted her hand and pulled aside the thick volume of art history. His touch was as light as possible, but still, the slight shift in her arm caused Elora to stir.

As though it were the most natural thing for her to wake up and find him standing over her, she smiled a dreamy smile, full of delight.

"I fell asleep," she murmured. "I was reading that wonderful book on ancient Roman sculpture, but I could not stay awake."

Her face was as expressive as ever. Happiness mixed with expectancy in an enchanting combination that Brice could not ignore.

"You shouldn't be tiring yourself out," he commented in a taut voice. "Now, go back to sleep."

Elora's smile vanished abruptly as he reached to extinguish the candles. "Must you go, my lord? I thought it would be nice to . . . to talk."

Brice turned his head sharply to look at her, her obvious dejection impossible to miss. Mentally, he squirmed. She wanted nothing more than polite conversation. If she were any other woman, that would be an easy task for him. But she wasn't any other woman, for no other woman would have risked her life for him. No other woman affected him as she did.

On an inward sigh, he relented. He knew it wasn't the wisest thing for him to do, but he sat beside her.

Elora's smile slowly blossomed once more. "I was so hoping you would stay," she said without the slightest bit of coyness.

Her candor surprised him and he regarded her dubiously. "Are you always this brutally honest?"

"Yes, I suppose I am."

"Didn't anyone ever tell you that such lack of prudence can get you into trouble?"

Her mouth turned down at the corners as she plucked at the coverlet. "There have been others . . . my stepfather, who have found fault with my manner."

Brice's brows flicked upward. "Do not misconstrue my words, Miss Simmons. I find nothing wrong with your manner."

"Oh?" If he had said she was the most beautiful woman on earth, Elora couldn't have looked more pleased. "Thank you. I like you, too."

He scoffed. "You barely know me."

"True, but I still like you."

"More of your honesty?"

Elora had to laugh. "Yes."

"You are an amazing woman, Miss Simmons. I can well imagine a great many people who, in your place, would be moaning in abject misery at this very second, while you have the forbearance to actually laugh." He shook his head in disbelief, then surprised himself by asking, "How are you feeling?"

Elora's eyes sparkled with mischief. "In all honesty?" She lifted her slender hands in a shrug. "I hurt."

"Damn it," he admonished. "Why didn't you say something?"

"Because complaining serves no purpose, especially in this instance. Little can be done to alleviate the pain, so it is useless to mention it."

Brice choked back a curse. "If you aren't the damnedest woman. Where do you get these notions of yours?"

"What notions?" she queried in genuine confusion.

"Notions like lying in pain without uttering a word. Notions like speaking whatever is on your mind." A sudden strain chilling his face, he drilled his gaze into hers. "Notions like throwing yourself in front of a fired pistol in order to save a complete stranger." He hadn't meant to state it so bluntly, but for days he had wondered what her motives had been.

39

"My lord," she implored, her expression reflecting amazement and worry. "I am by nature a forthright person. These notions you mention are not idle whims or careless impulsiveness."

Unaware that she did so, she laid her hand on his forearm. "I did not want you to get killed. How could I have lived with myself if I had done nothing to try and help you?"

Brice's eyes locked with hers, his vision filling with clear, pure blue . . . and he was caught. The voice of his inner self compelled him to move, to leave now before it was too late. But a wraithlike version of her coalesced into a blinding white light and speared through him, this time seeking out his heart and prompting a flood of ungovernable emotions he hadn't experienced in three years.

Genuine hope, unfettered by his habitual disdain, rose up inside him, holding him immobile. A true sense of compassion replaced his customary derision, and for the first time since the death of his family, he experienced that awful sense of vulnerability attack him. Intuitively, he felt the protective barriers he had erected crumbling before the radiance that seemed to emanate from Elora.

The combination of feelings was overwhelming and he jerked back, fighting for mastery of his senses, battling against the force that threatened his sanity. He shoved to his feet in one powerful move.

"My lord?" Elora stared up at him in dismay, her voice echoing her trepidation.

His body held rigidly, his face contorted with rage, he spat, "Damn you." He ignored her startled gasp as well as her look of hurt. "Damn you for ever coming into my life."

Chapter
4

HORRIFIED, ELORA STARED AT THE DOOR BRICE HAD JUST slammed behind him, his bitter curses still echoing through her mind. His anger had come out of nowhere, and had been directed solely at her. But why? She could find nothing in their conversation that would warrant his reaction.

Releasing a tightly held breath, she looked distractedly about the room. From amidst the varied blue hues and stark, gilded hush, the most awful dismay descended upon her. The weight of it brought her close to tears.

Her presence was obviously unwanted . . . worse, resented. Despite his assurances to the contrary, Brice Warfield wished her out of his life. It was a horrible realization, cruel . . . but oh, so familiar.

Tormenting memories rushed unbidden to mind, and try as she may, she could not evade them. How could she ignore ten years of her life, years during which her stepfather had considered her a burden? He had treated her like some unwanted pest, an annoyance to be barely tolerated. Her mother had protected her from the worst of his animosity, but after her death, his resentment had taken full flight.

Blindly, she reached to the bed stand for her spectacles and put them on. The resulting clarity seemed to give focus to her agitated thoughts.

"There's nothing else to do," she whispered raggedly.

She drew back the covers, then slowly turned onto her side, slipping her legs over the edge of the bed. But as careful as she was, pain burst through her, radiating out to the farthest tips of her limbs.

Moaning, she curled into a tight ball, trying to roll into herself in silent defense. Her attempt was futile and she crumpled to the floor, eyes clenched shut, gasping for breath.

Nausea swamped her, a nasty companion to the cold dots of moisture that beaded her brow. For eternally long seconds, she could do nothing more than clutch the bedding in tight fists and will the pain away.

One minute became another, and another. The agony decreased by small degrees, finally lessening enough to allow her an even breath. Opening her eyes, she swallowed hard, then took hold of her resolve.

Exercising every bit of caution she possessed, she levered herself upward, bracing her weight against the bed. Little by little she came to her feet on shaking legs.

The walk to the armoire was considerably easier. The worst of the strain was past and she made good use of her upright stance.

Her choice of dress was a simple matter. Several of her gowns buttoned down the front. She chose one. Brice's shirt fell to the floor, and with scrupulously modulated movements, she eased the dress into place. The immodesty of forsaking undergarments was completely ignored. Given her disability and her haste to be gone, she thought herself justified.

She slipped her feet into low shoes and donned her cloak, newly laundered and mended. Disregarding the throbbing in her side, she collected her reticule, then made her way from the room.

The long, dimly lit hall was unfamiliar to her. She had no idea in which direction the stairs lay, but she chose to go left. With slow steps, a poker-straight back and a rigid jaw, she made her way through the house. The stairs proved to be especially frustrating, limiting her progress to a limping, one-step-at-a-time descent. When she finally reached the first floor, her energy was severely drained, forcing her to rest against the balustrade in sheer exhaustion.

Her muscles quaked; the simple act of breathing became arduous. The front door appeared discouragingly far away. Briefly, she considered if her course of action was at all wise, for crossing the marble floor suddenly took on all the proportions of crossing the English Channel. The prospect seemed daunting, as daunting as Brice Warfield's stormy face and angry curses.

Pride came to her rescue. She would be a burden to no one.

It was tenacity alone that urged her to the door. But once there, it was a set of locked knees and a shoulder propped against the panel that kept her upright.

"What the devil do you think you are doing?"

Her eyes flew wide and every nerve in her body twitched reflexively at the sound of Brice's scorching voice. How many times had she heard that same kind of anger from her stepfather? The furious tones filled her with dread.

Her every move a study in precision, she turned until her back was against the wall. In something close to fear, she found Brice advancing upon her with the long strides of a predator, and a formidable scowl that bore into her until it seemed to fill her vision.

If she hadn't already been pressed to the wall, she would have stepped back. Everything about him, from his fists jammed on his waist to his booted feet planted firmly apart, was overwhelmingly intimidating.

Alarm snaked its way through her, and it took all of her self-control to swallow the plea that formed on her lips. Experience with Harmen Gillet had taught her that no amount of imploring would spare her if an angry man chose to physically vent that anger. All she could do now was wait and hope that Brice Warfield was not such a man.

Bravely, she peered up through her glasses at him and said, "If you would be so kind as to have my belongings sent on to Lord Ashton's, I would appreciate it." She held her breath, anticipating his reaction.

Brice stared hard at the defiant face raised to his. "Do you have a death wish, you little fool?"

She didn't pretend to misunderstand his growled words. She was growing increasingly weak with each passing minute and she could well imagine that he saw as much. "What I have, my lord, is a great desire to be gone."

"Just like that?" he sneered, snapping his fingers. "In the middle of the night."

"Yes, now," she retorted with supreme dignity. Dimly, she thought to snap her own fingers, but she could not muster the energy. And even if she could, the act might prove to be too provoking. "I wouldn't dream of inconveniencing you a moment longer."

Brice dismissed her raised chin and cool voice, for the vulnerable, wounded-pride look on her face made a mockery of her *sangfroid*.

Bending low, he scooped her up into his arms. "Don't ever play faro, Miss Simmons. You don't have the face for it."

Elora's breath caught in her throat, along with her fear and indignation. It wasn't until Brice was halfway up the stairs that she found her voice. Unfortunately, it emerged as nothing more than a low, fatigued murmur.

"My lord, put me down."

"And have you bleeding all over my carpets? I think not, madam."

He didn't say anything more, and for that, Elora was extremely grateful. She was also extremely relieved. He had not lifted a hand to hurt her and that went far in draining the tension from her limbs. She was wearied to the very core of her being and quite against her will, her body melted against the powerful strength of his arms.

Brice carried her back to her room, and set her on the bed.

There he thrust a tanned finger beneath her nose and snarled, "Don't move." Turning away, he strode to the bellpull and gave it a decisive yank.

Elora sat immobile, not because of his curt command, or because of the horrible weakness pervading her body. She sat still because total confusion held her captive. In all her life she had never met such an astonishing man. His behavior was beyond her comprehension. One minute he damned her for being there and in the next, he refused to let her leave.

Slowly, she removed her glasses and pressed cool fingers to her aching forehead. The strength that had sustained her up until now was nearly gone. It was a bleak realization given the fact that she still had to contend with Brice Warfield. The thought was not encouraging.

Squinting slightly, she watched him approach. His chiseled face was wiped clean of expression, his green gaze a chilling void.

"Please do not make this difficult, my lord. I do not intend to stay and I am too tired to argue the matter with you."

"The matter is already decided. Mrs. Cobb will be here shortly to help you with your clothes."

"You have no right to keep me here. Why, a half hour ago you didn't even want me here."

"The hell I didn't."

"How can you say that?" she cried indignantly. "You stood right there and damned me for ever coming into your life."

"That doesn't mean I am going to let you walk out of here and kill yourself."

"You are exaggerating."

"Madam, you can hardly stand. If I had not stopped you, you would have collapsed out there in the street. What would you have done then? Crawl to Ashton's house?"

His sneer brought blue fire to her eyes. "I would rather crawl my way through all of London than remain where I am not wanted."

Abruptly, Brice turned away, cursing beneath his breath. But just as quickly he swung back, bending low until his face was level with hers. "I will say this only once, Miss Simmons, so you had best listen well. You are not leaving this house until I say you are fully recuperated."

Elora didn't need her glasses to discern his implacable air of command. He meant exactly what he said. He would keep her here until he felt she was well enough to leave, despite the fact that he had no authority to do so. The gall of that sparked her ire and prompted her to be less cautious than she normally would have been.

"You can't stop me from leaving," she railed.

"I just did."

"With no regard to what I might think?"

His jaw clenched and when he spoke, his voice was as empty as his eyes. "Miss Simmons, I don't give a bloody good damn what *anyone* might think." He matched actions to words and reached for the fastening of her cloak.

Suddenly, it was all too much for Elora. His callous, overbearing manner stripped her defenses down to nothing. He had made his contemptuous feelings perfectly clear. To be confronted with his disdain now was only demeaning, leaving her feeling useless and humiliated.

"Don't," she got out in a broken voice, grasping his hands with her own. Weak tears filled her eyes. Embarrassed, she tucked her chin, turning her head away. "Please . . . don't."

Brice's hands stilled. He looked down at her lowered head, and whether it was the touch of her cold, shaking fingers or the miserable, choked sound of her voice that caught him, he couldn't tell. Regardless, he stepped back, and scrutinized her forlorn figure.

What he saw displeased him greatly.

How that affected him displeased him even more.

Swearing, he stormed into his room, not sparing her so much as another glance.

"Damn it all to hell!" he snarled to the four walls. "She's making a shambles of my existence."

He did not want to feel anything for her, but the tears in her eyes had been like a jab to his stomach. And the misery implicit in the sloping curve of her shoulders had him feeling like a heel.

Bloody hell, he was not a cad. If he hadn't stopped her, she could have hurt herself further. To his way of thinking, that made him a gallant savior. Then why did he feel as though he had just crushed a rare and delicate flower?

He stalked the length of the room and back. Every step of the way, her image accompanied him. He could still see her standing against the front door, proudly clinging to a strength she didn't have. Her face had been drained of color, her eyes glazed with pain . . . and something else.

Fear. He came to a sudden halt to consider that. As helplessly as she displayed her emotions, her fright had been blatantly apparent. But what in the devil did she have to fear from him?

"Nothing."

He resumed his trek across the room, all the while trying to purge himself of unwanted emotions. Emotions Elora Simmons had somehow called forth from a part of him dead for three years.

Damn her! He did not want to feel sympathy or regret. He did not want to feel *anything*.

Throwing himself into a chair, he braced his elbows on his knees and lowered his head into his hands. Emotions choked his mind like vile, contemptible debris. Ruthlessly, he shoved them away, refusing to surrender. He couldn't. Not ever again.

His fingers clasped tightly, forming a taut fist he scrubbed over his lips. By whatever means, he had to gain control, to nullify these sensations attacking his body, devouring his mind. He could not leave himself unprotected against Elora Simmons and all she inspired.

He had no choice. Hope was as dead as his brother. Love was a callous nonentity that slept with his parents.

* * *

Green eyes resolutely empty, Brice entered the British Museum at precisely ten the next morning. Striding into the museum's main hall, he readied himself to deal with the host of museum officials waiting expectantly for him.

He turned the corner into a short hall and literally bumped into the Duke of Westford. "Your grace," he intoned politely.

The duke nodded in reply. "Warrington."

"This is an unexpected pleasure." It was the most tactful thing Brice could say. Given the attempt on his life, he couldn't help but view the man in a different light. "With the whole of London at our disposal, it's rather amusing that we should both be in the very same spot at the very same time."

As though he detected an offensive odor, the duke's face furrowed into a grimace. "What brings you here this hour of the morning?"

"I could ask the same of you." Brice eyed the thin peer with interest. "But that would be a waste of time and energy. We both know we have penchants for antiquities." What Brice didn't know was if the duke also had a predilection for murder. His eyes narrowed slightly. "I understand, Westford, that your latest expedition to the East has produced some remarkable artifacts."

The duke's spare chest expanded. "And did you also hear that we may have found one of the most rare bronzes to date?"

Brice knew it to be common knowledge, as the papers had been full of the story the week before. But how like this pompous oaf to make an issue of it. "If it's true, you're to be congratulated."

"What do you mean, 'if it's true'?" Westford demanded.

"Only that." Spreading his hands wide in a gesture of supreme nonchalance, Brice shrugged. "Nothing conclusive has been decided about the piece. It may very well be as old as believed, and then again, it might not."

The duke drew himself up into what Brice found to be a

poor parody of an aggressive stance. "You'd like that, wouldn't you, Warrington?"

"On the contrary, I'd very much like the piece to be the genuine thing."

"I can just imagine why," Westford retorted in roiling sarcasm. "You'll never add the piece to your collection. Not as long as I have anything to say about it."

It was all Brice could do to keep from laughing out loud. The Duke of Westford was a pitiful braggart, spurred on by an even more pitiful envy. It was damned annoying to have to stand there and tolerate the man, but the single matter of a pistol fired in the dark forced him to endure.

Letting some of his irritation show, Brice goaded, "There is nothing you have that I want, Westford. What a shame the same cannot be said of you." With great satisfaction, he watched his comment hit its mark. The duke's face turned red with a rage he did nothing to conceal.

"You bastard," Westford hissed.

"Tell me something I don't already know."

"I'll tell you that you will rue the day you ever decided to play this game, Warrington."

"What game is that?"

"Trying to best me in collecting the world's priceless treasures."

"Just how do you intend to win, Westford? I already own the Sennedjem Papyrus, the one piece you consider to be point, game and match."

Westford's neck strained against his cravat. "I'll go as far as needs be, mark my words."

"Oh, I intend to," Brice commented levelly. But as he watched the duke march off, he wondered to what lengths the man would go in his jealous quest.

All the way to murder?

The question lingered in his mind through the rest of the morning. As he inspected the latest shipment of artifacts from the expedition he had financed to Egypt, he considered the Duke of Westford from all angles. Was the man capable of murder? The only answer Brice arrived at was that anything was possible.

By early afternoon, he emerged from the museum and headed for his club, more than ready to leave the unresolved question of the duke with kohl vases and canopic jars. All three had an air of fable about them and he felt sorely in need of reality.

Still, the dose of truth that hit him broadside when he stepped down from his phaeton and threw the reins to his waiting tiger was far too sobering. He barely had time to hand his gloves and hat to one of the footmen before he was accosted by two of Watier's members.

"Warrington, by God, I wouldn't have believed it if I hadn't heard about the thing this very minute. Damned if a man can't walk out of his own home without being reduced to carrion."

One of Brice's black brows slowly rose. "Heard what?" But damn, he already knew. News of the incident the other night was finally making the rounds.

The rotund baron sputtered, yanking his chin to his neck. "Why this matter of that pack of scoundrels attacking you. Nasty state of affairs. There ought to be a law."

"There was only one scoundrel," Brice corrected blandly.

"Only one you say?"

"Still, damned cowardly," the baron's companion added. "But you look to be in good shape, Warrington. I didn't expect to see you up and about so soon."

The baron thrust out his massive chest and corrected his friend. "You've got it all wrong, all wrong. The marquess here didn't take the shot. To hear Ashton tell of it, some chit of a girl, his governess in fact, was the very one to save Warrington's hide."

"Ashton?" Brice queried.

"None other," the baron affirmed. "Was in the card room earlier, filling everyone's ears. Says you sent some note around, excusing his governess from her duties while she's on the mend."

Brice mentally throttled James Ashton. He had also made it clear in his note that the entire incident be kept as quiet as possible.

The baron continued. "Cursed sorry to hear about the horseflesh, though. Always a sad thing to have to put down your stock."

Annoyance settled on Brice's features with all the look of taking up permanent residence. "What the devil are you going on about? My stable is in better health than you."

The baron blinked his eyes wide. "Don't say? Thought I heard that one of your horses was injured during all the ruckus."

"Did Ashton tell you that?"

"No, picked that up from someone hereabouts." As though trying to remember who had supplied this bit of information, the baron paused, then shrugged and yanked on the cuffs of his jacket when no name came to mind.

"No, Ashton didn't mention anything about horses, he was more interested in getting his governess back. Wasn't a happy man, by God, grumbling about his expecting to have the post filled and all he has to show for it is an empty schoolroom and three children running amok. Inconvenienced by the whole affair, he is." He nudged Brice and made a great show of winking. "Frankly, we know in what direction the wind blows with Ashton. Always has his eyes out for the ladies. I'd wager he had his sights on this little governess of his . . . wouldn't you say?"

Brice didn't say anything. His face set in unyielding lines, he abruptly brushed past the duo and headed for the card room. He never discussed his personal life. However, he knew that avoidance of this issue would only add fuel to the fire. Speculation would blaze, curiosities would ignite and every tongue that wasn't already wagging with misconceptions would have a field day.

Entering the card room, he stopped just inside the doorway and glared about him. The room was nearly full. That in itself was not unusual. At any time of day, there was always someone willing to gamble or gossip. Today he would use that to his own purposes.

He made his way into the midst of gentlemen and one by one, each turned to look his way. Seconds later, the room erupted in a cacophony of male voices, all raised in exclamation and surprise.

Looking for all the world as though he had nothing better to do than entertain the assembled group, he casually took a seat in an oversize chair, leaned back indolently and propped one booted ankle on his knee. Almost immediately, the questions began.

"Is it true, Warrington?" someone asked excitedly. "Did the girl take the shot?"

Brice laced his fingers together, resting his hands against his abdomen. "I will give you the facts but once, gentlemen," he remarked, his voice, as well as his eyes, laced with steel. "Pay close attention so that when you rush off to repeat what I say, you will get the story straight."

No more than thirty minutes later, he was in his phaeton, cursing every member of the *ton*. Their propensity for meddling was ludicrous, and he despised their interference in his life. But at least he had stemmed the tide of erring gossip by doling out the truth with no embellishment of any kind. The would-be murderer was being touted as a cur, and Miss Elora Simmons a guardian angel.

Handling the reins with an enviable skill he took for granted, Brice exhaled an irritated sigh. It had been damned annoying the way the men had focused their attention on Elora. More than one had wanted to know where she came from, while just as many wanted to know what she looked like. Lest he begrudge them the answers they sought, and lay the groundwork for more erroneous speculation, he had been forced to discuss the lady like some common bawdy.

His jaw clenched rigidly. If he didn't miss his guess, James Ashton would like to use Elora in that very way.

Over my dead body.

Instantly he sneered at his own ridiculous thought. Miss

Simmons was tying his life into knots. She needed to get well as quickly as possible and be gone. As he pulled up in front of his house, he irascibly contemplated just how long it took to recover from being shot.

"Good day, my lord," Ambrose Cobb intoned, holding open the front door.

"Enough optimism, Cobb," Brice retorted irritably, stepping into the foyer.

"Yes, my lord." Cobb accepted the hat and gloves Brice thrust his way. "Mr. Quinn is waiting in your study, my lord."

Already turning away, Brice asked over his shoulder, "Anything else?"

Cobb kept pace with his employer. "Dr. Bingham was here to see Miss Simmons."

"And?"

Brice heard the pleasure vibrate in his butler's voice. "And he has diagnosed her condition as better. She is making progress, my lord."

"Good." He entered his study and found Marcus organizing the papers on his desk. "Word is out," he stated without preamble.

"How bad is it?"

"Bad enough," Brice snorted in disgust. "If you should receive any condolences on my death, don't be surprised."

The secretary's lips twitched. "No, my lord. How did you find things at the museum?"

"Old." Brice seated himself behind his desk, and dismissed museums and gossips alike. "What do you have for me, Marcus?"

Standing across the desk from Brice, Marcus got down to business. "I have contacted an investigator, a Bow Street Runner by the name of Mr. Harold Tew."

"I assume he is worthwhile."

"He is purported to be very thorough and very discreet."

Brice glanced up from the paper in front of him and mocked, "I'm glad to hear that someone still is."

"I have explained the matter to him and he is making a preliminary inquiry now. I have scheduled for you to meet with him the day after tomorrow."

"Good." Brice looked back to his desk. "Are these the latest figures from the mining venture in America?"

"Yes, my lord." Marcus made the transition to the next topic without the slightest hitch. "I think you will be pleased."

A knock on the door interrupted the conversation and Cobb came forward. "My lord, Viscountess Redsdale has arrived."

Brice's head shot up, tiny lines of strain forming about his mouth. "Where is she?" he asked curtly.

"In the front salon, my lord."

Grimly, Brice leaned back in the chair, galled to the point of anger. He would prefer that his sister be anywhere other than in his house. Damnably he was quickly coming to realize that his preferences in this entire matter were worthless.

"That will be all for today, Marcus." He shoved himself out from behind the desk and made his way from the room.

As with much of the house, the salon displayed all the signs of Brice's fascination with Eastern cultures. Perhaps that was why, he told himself, his sister looked so out of place sitting on a sofa of oriental design.

She sat still, like a perfect English rose in a pink gown, her dark hair swept up into tight curls.

"I see you got my note," he said in a quiet voice from the doorway. Yes, he thought, she looked extremely out of place.

Vianne Drake came gracefully to her feet, her face pale, her hands clasped tightly together. Automatically, she began to rush across the room, but checked herself, remembering the barriers Brice had erected between them three long years ago. For all that time, he had distanced himself from those whom he had loved.

She had to content herself with searching his face for signs of any changes that might have occurred since their last meeting. He was as handsome as ever, but he appeared older than she remembered, a little tired. And still coldly remote.

"Are you all right?" she beseeched, her voice an aching whisper, her green eyes, so like her brother's, moist with barely contained tears.

Brice slowly made his way to the fireplace. In a conversational tone he asked, "Why does everyone insist on asking me that when it is perfectly obvious that I am fine?"

Vianne's bottom lip quivered. "Nervous reaction, perhaps?"

Standing on the thick hearth rug, his back to the low flames in the grate, Brice shoved his jacket aside, and thrust his hands deep into his pants pockets. "As good an explanation as any."

Nodding, Vianne sighed raggedly, feeling horribly uncomfortable in the presence of a brother who at one time had been her dearest friend. "I . . . didn't quite know what to make of your message. This woman who . . . who saved your life, is she all right, then?"

"Yes. The doctor took care of her."

"And this . . . this person who tried to ki—" Her words choked off. Distressed, she smoothed a hand back over the waves of her deep brown hair and tried again. "Do you have any idea who is responsible?"

Brice shook his head. "No, not yet." Seeing the strained look on her face, he paused. "Why don't you sit, Vianne. You look as though you're about to drop."

Clearly shaken, Vianne sank back to the sofa. "This has all been somewhat taxing. First getting your note and then rushing here."

Brice's mouth pulled downward. "I hope Colin did not mind your coming."

At the mention of her husband, Vianne relaxed slightly and smiled for the first time since entering the house. "No, no, not at all."

"I wouldn't have imposed on you, except that this is an emergency."

"You don't need to apologize, Brice," Vianne said in

earnest. "I'm glad you asked me to help." It was the first time in three years that he had contacted her for any reason. "Colin understands completely."

"Well, it won't be for long. All you need do is act as chaperone while you're here, for propriety's sake."

"Of course, that goes without saying." On an afterthought, she nearly laughed. She found it horribly ironic that she did not need to "say anything" to Brice. Since the death of their parents, she had lost track of the number of times she wished she could have talked to her brother about anything and everything.

A silence fell in the wake of her words, the same kind of stilted hush that resulted every time chance happened to place them together. Finally, his face shuttered, Brice pulled his hands from his pockets. When he spoke, his voice was stark.

"Thank you."

Before she could swallow past the ache in her throat, Vianne watched him walk away, her eyes wide and disbelieving.

A little unsteadily, she rose, stopping in the hall only long enough to ask Mr. Cobb a brief question. Then, supplied with the information she needed, she made her way to the second floor.

Not bothering to knock, she opened the door to Elora's room and stepped within. Silently, she stared at the golden-haired young woman lying in the four-poster, ignoring the look of surprise that entered the blue eyes.

Tension chiseled into her face, Vianne moved toward the bed and implored, "Do you have any idea what you have done?"

Chapter
5

"I BEG YOUR PARDON?" ELORA PROMPTED, HOPING THE WOMAN would stop and explain herself. When she didn't slow her pace, Elora pressed back against the pillows, not knowing what was about to befall her.

Unexpectedly, she found herself drawn into a tender hug.

"You dear, dear woman," the lady whispered, tears coursing a path down her cheeks.

Stunned, Elora gazed about bewilderedly, relieved that she had come to no harm. Still, such startling behavior was most telling. Elora didn't know who this woman was or why she was upset, but it was obvious that she was in need of consolation.

Tenderly, Elora returned the hug, gently patting the woman's back. "Madam, please, whatever is wrong cannot be that terrible."

A strangled laugh was the lady's only response as she levered herself away to sit facing Elora. "Oh, Miss Simmons, you must forgive my impulsiveness. But I am so very grateful to you for saving Brice's life."

Elora carefully regarded the dark brown hair and intense green eyes and noted a marked resemblance to Brice Warfield. "Madam, are you related to the marquess?"

Wiping at her cheeks, a wobbly smile pulling at her

mouth, she answered, "How clumsy of me, this has been a terrible introduction. I am Vianne Drake, Brice's sister."

For some reason, that surprised Elora. She hadn't thought of Brice Warfield in terms of being part of a family. Families were supposed to be a cohesive, loving unit. He seemed so cold and detached from everything and everyone about him.

"How do you do, my lady."

"Wonderfully," Vianne exclaimed. "Better than I have felt in three very long years." Apparently noticing Elora's perplexed look, she shook her head dismissively, and her expression turned poignantly somber. "I didn't come in here to discuss me, I came to thank you for what you did. You are remarkably brave. I will never be able to fully express my appreciation."

Elora heard the utter gratitude in Vianne's voice and looked away, humbled and not a little uncomfortable. No one other than her mother had ever held her in such esteem. Now, she didn't know what to say and it plainly showed.

"Have I embarrassed you?" Vianne asked. She reached out to clasp Elora's hand. "Again, forgive me. If it makes you feel better, we'll talk of something else."

"Thank you," Elora sighed, touched by Vianne's concern.

"How are you feeling?"

"All things considered, quite well."

"Brice said the doctor was in to see you."

"This morning." Elora couldn't help smiling remembering the doctor's diagnosis. "He said I have made remarkable progress."

"That is splendid, but you must take care not to tire yourself out."

Elora didn't mention her excursion to the front door last night. "Dr. Bingham has confined me to this bed."

A worried crease marred Vianne's brow. "Of course he has. You shan't be up and about for weeks, but don't let that upset you. If you need anything, just call on me or Mrs. Cobb for help. After all, I will be here during your recovery."

Elora's blond brows arched in question. "You will?"

"Yes, Brice asked that I act as chaperone, this being a bachelor's household."

Elora did not have to be told of the immodesty of her present situation. An unmarried lady simply did not take up residence in the house of an unmarried man, no matter what the circumstances. However, for the second time in the space of a few short minutes, she was thoroughly bemused.

She had not thought that the Marquess of Warrington would have bothered himself for her sake. Despite his refusal last night to let her leave, he had never said that he didn't resent her presence.

Damn you for ever coming into my life. His words still gnawed at her insides.

Her voice slightly lame, she said, "I am most grateful for your company, my lady."

Vianne gently squeezed Elora's hand. "You can thank me best by getting well. And then by calling me Vianne." She rose to her feet. "Now, is there anything that you need?"

Elora thought that the consideration Vianne had shown her had been more than enough. "No, thank you."

"Very well, but I will have Mrs. Cobb check in on you in a little while. I'm sure Brice would want to make certain that you are being well taken care of."

The smile abruptly dropped from Elora's lips. Memories of the past night drained the color from her face. She looked away uncertainly. How was she to reply? *Lady Drake, your brother has seen to my welfare, but he curses the sight of me?*

She lifted troubled eyes. "Vianne, may I be frank?" At Vianne's startled reaction, Elora knew that her every feeling was, as usual, plainly obvious for all to see.

"Yes, of course," Vianne quickly responded.

"I would not have you misled in any way. I think you should know that the marquess . . . that is, I seem to provoke your brother at every turn. He is not pleased that I am here."

"Oh, dear."

Elora watched Vianne's face fall into a somber mask, and her heart went out to the older woman. "I'm sorry. I did not mean to upset you."

Sighing heavily, Vianne stepped away to the secretary set between the two windows, everything from dismay to embarrassment seeming to weigh her down. "I must apologize for Brice if he has offended you. He is not an easy man to deal with." She rolled her eyes. "Believe me, I have tried."

Elora felt Vianne's distress like a palpable thing. "Please, my lady, do not think I am criticizing the marquess. You have been so kind to me, I only wanted you to know now, before you assumed any differently, how things stood."

"I can well imagine how things are here." Vianne laughed in a hollow tone. "I have to give you credit for bearing up so well."

Elora stilled, confused and not a little surprised. The implication was clear that Brice Warfield's strange behavior toward her was neither unusual nor unexpected. Least of all to his sister.

"I see that I have shocked you," Vianne offered.

"Somewhat."

"Forgive me. It is just that I had hoped that Brice had begun to . . . change."

The pain in the green eyes worried Elora. "I'm afraid I don't understand."

"I know you don't." Evidently talking to herself, Vianne's voice lowered to a whisper and her sight took on a faraway look. "It's been so long since . . . I presumed there might have been a softening in his nature. I thought you might have been the one person . . ."

Before Elora's bewildered gaze, Vianne visibly collected herself, then returned to the bed with what looked to be a resolved smile fixed in place. "Thank you for being so honest with me." She patted Elora's hand. "I'm sure all this talk can't be helping you. I'll leave you to rest, but promise me something."

60

"Yes, if I can."

"Please let me know if there is anything I can do for you."

"You have my promise."

Even before Vianne shut the door behind her, Elora knew that she liked the marquess's sister. She seemed a genuinely compassionate woman who cared deeply for her brother. Sighing, Elora wished that Brice Warfield were as likable. Instead, he was an impersonal cynic, wholly contemptuous and entirely ill-mannered. But why?

She had very little to go by, but he seemed to have a great deal at his disposal. His house showed every sign of incredible wealth. While money wasn't the basis for true joy, it could make life very comfortable. From all appearances, he could afford to be at least a little bit happy.

But he wasn't. She sensed that deep inside her and from what little Vianne had said, he was a cold, hard man. How well she knew that to be true.

Some of the torment he had caused her last night returned now. She wasn't one to normally cry. Her stepfather had abhorred tears, denouncing them as wasteful and useless, so she had learned at an early age to keep such signs of emotion well hidden. But the marquess, with his formidable disdain, had laid bare her feelings. The long hours of the night had seen her struggling with her tears and misery.

She plucked dejectedly at the blue satin coverlet. He was a forbidding man, but if she were totally honest with herself, she had to concede that while his wrath had been terrible, it had not exploded into physical violence. That said something for the man.

Nonetheless, he was still most perplexing. And little good would be accomplished by bemoaning his irascible disposition, for he was bound and determined to have things as he saw fit, whatever that was. She had yet to understand anything he had done since she had first opened her eyes and looked up at him.

Exasperated, she pressed her fingertips to the slight ache in her temple. No, the best she could hope for was to heal

as quickly as possible and then be gone from Brice Warfield's house.

Brice squinted through the veil of smoke curling from the
end of his thin cigar. The tobacco clenched firmly between
his teeth, he leaned back in his chair and studied the Earl of
Stanley.

The man's thick shoulders were hunched over his cards,
and his mouth was as tight a slash as any Brice had ever
seen. A single drop of sweat trickled along the fleshy curve of
the man's cheek while a muscle twitched just beneath his
left eye. It was the demeanor of a man cursing his luck.

Brice sent a look to one of the footmen at Watier's, the
silent command quickly producing a snifter of brandy.
Taking his time, he savored the flavor rolling about his
tongue before he prompted the earl to make his next wager.

"I believe, Stanley, the last bet was eight thousand
pounds." Drawing on his cigar once more, he noted the
subtle trembling in the fist the earl scrubbed against his
corpulent chin.

"I'm good for that," Stanley declared, but to Brice's
experienced eye, the man was wallowing in uncertainty.

Brice settled himself comfortably. "Then what do you say
we raise the stakes, just to make things interesting."

As expected, Stanley's eyes rounded. Patently struggling
to retain his composure, he glared hard across the table. But
Brice felt no sympathy for the man, especially since it had
been Stanley who had insisted on this game.

Brice had to wonder why. Not once in any of the times
they had played cards had the earl ever won. Brice wasn't
keeping an exact record, but over the past months, he had
lightened the man's pockets by at least fifty thousand
pounds.

That was a considerable amount of money. Surely Stanley
had learned by now that he was not a proficient gambler.
Still, no sooner had Brice entered the club only an hour ago
than Stanley had issued his challenge.

Mentally Brice threw up his hands in disgust. If the earl was bent on throwing his money away, then so be it. Brice had no qualms about gaming with the man, particularly since it provided him with the opportunity to assess the man's possible guilt.

"All right," Stanley agreed. "I'll raise the wager to a clean ten thousand pounds."

It was no less than Brice had anticipated, and moments later when he turned his cards over, he was once again the victor. "Damned poor luck, Stanley." Like some tragedy he had seen played out numerous times before, he sat silent and watched the earl inflate with anger.

"God damn you, Warrington!" he decried, jumping to his feet. "The cards should have been with me tonight."

"Perhaps next time," came Brice's cool avowal.

"Except with you there never is a next time, is there?"

"I've had my share of losses."

As though Brice had said nothing, the earl accused, "Some say you have the devil in your back pocket, that there's no besting you. No matter the time or place or circumstances, you always come out on top."

Feeling the ends of his temper begin to ignite, Brice ignored the derision hurled his way. "Are you trying to make a point, Stanley? If not, I expect your settlement on my desk by tomorrow afternoon."

For a second, it seemed the earl would lunge across the table. "I'll see you in hell, Warrington," he spat, then fled the room, but not before Brice had a glimpse of pure, unbridled rage.

Under any other circumstances, he would have found it interesting. Now, such unrestrained anger was cause for serious consideration. Was Stanley behind the shooting? It was possible. Money always had been a powerful motive for any manner of actions. Murder included.

"Look what has arrived for you," Vianne exclaimed the following morning. Carrying an enormous bouquet of lilies, and wearing an excited smile, she glided to Elora's bedside. "They were delivered just this very moment from the Earl and Countess of Ghent."

Elora stared at the beautiful arrangement of flowers nonplussed. "Are you certain there hasn't been some mistake, Vianne? I don't know the Earl and Countess of Ghent." She gave a dubious chuckle. "I don't know anyone in London."

"Well, they know all about you and what you did, and they sent these over." She set the porcelain vase on the nightstand then plucked a crisp vellum note from among the leaves. "Here is the card."

Still staring at the delicate lilies, Elora had to drag her eyes to the small note Vianne placed in her hands. There, written in fluid script, were the words, *Bravo, well done.* And yes, the card had indeed been signed with the names of the earl and countess.

"Why did they send me flowers?"

"Because, silly, they wanted to thank you for your heroics in saving Brice's life. The earl is an associate of Brice's, in fact they are involved in several financial arrangements together, if I remember correctly."

Elora looked back to the note as she tried to digest this. "But they don't even know me."

Vianne's smile turned sympathetic. "Everyone has heard of you. According to a note I received from Lady Kirkland this morning, the other night's incident is the topic of conversation in almost every salon. Whether you wish it or not, Elora, you are all the rage among the *ton.*" She gave the flowers a knowing look. "With the arrival of these, my guess is that more are about to follow."

"Oh?" Elora inquired, feeling well out of her depth.

"Definitely. The earl and countess are the unofficial trendsetters on all matters social. If they have deemed it *à la mode* to bestow flowers on you, then . . ." She finished by lifting her hands in a shrug that said heaven only knew what would happen next.

What happened next was a descent of delivery boys on the

town house the likes of which had never, ever been seen. Elora could not contain her amazement as Mrs. Cobb carried basket after basket of arrangements to her room. Flowers arrived by the dozens and as the morning progressed, Elora watched her room fill to overflowing.

By late afternoon, she thought her room resembled a springtime glade, resplendent in a full array of color. From her place against the pillows, she looked about in wonder. The rich blue and wooden tones of the room itself only added to the sense of being in a secluded glen. The sight was simply beautiful and made her long to be up and about.

Begrudging her confinement to the bed, she caught her lower lip between her teeth. Fuss on what the doctor said. She could not lie there a moment longer.

Carefully, she managed to rise and collect her yellow dressing gown from the armoire. The soft folds flowing about her slender figure, she made her way to the gold inlaid secretary and there examined the stack of cards that had arrived throughout the day. Names of people she did not know, would probably never know, stared back at her: the Earl and Countess of Hempton, the Earl of Stallings, Baroness Blakely, Viscount Haley, Lord and Lady Dunfrey. The stack seemed endless, and not a little awe inspiring.

She was deeply moved by these people who had thought to present her with tokens of their regard. But she was not accustomed to being the recipient of so much attention. It made her decidedly uncomfortable.

A knock came at the door, and she set the cards aside with a disconcerted sigh.

"Come in," she called. Turning away, she tried to locate a vacant spot that could possibly hold another vase. "I don't think there is any more room, Mrs. Cobb."

"Tell me horticulture is your hobby," came the smooth-voiced reply.

Elora's head spun toward the doorway, the sudden move sending her unbound hair over her right shoulder. Startled, she found Brice standing just inside the room, an imposing figure in a dark blue jacket and buckskin riding breeches. As usual, he seemed remotely detached, the green of his eyes a dead cold as he returned her look. Slowly a look of exasperated amazement knitted his brow, the expression incongruous with the vase of wild flowers he held.

In an instinctive gesture, she reached to the secretary for her glasses. It was an old habit; putting her spectacles on when she felt unsure of herself. There was a certain amount of security to be found in clear vision, and she needed all the confidence she could get while she was in Brice's company.

As quickly as she could, she collected her wits. She had not seen him since the night she had attempted to leave and he had carried her back to this room. Her chin came up at the thought of how his chillingly impersonal manner had reduced her to tears.

"I would have you know that this is not of my doing," she stated briskly, feeling the need to defend herself.

He pinned her with a taunting gaze. "Ah, then we shall have to lay the blame on your scores of admirers."

"You know very well that I don't have any admirers. The blame is to be laid on your friends."

He didn't comment on the use of the word *friends,* although he turned it over in his mind and came up scoffing. "You don't sound pleased. Don't you like flowers?"

"Yes, I love flowers, but . . ." She spread her hands wide in a helpless gesture. "But I am overwhelmed."

"Such is the price of fame." He shrugged, then advanced with the vase he held. "When I returned home just now, it was to discover from Cobb that some flowers had been delivered to you today. I would say that my butler is a master of understatement." He removed the card from the arrangement and unceremoniously plunked it in her hands. "These arrived at the same time I did. Where do you want them?" He turned away in search of a space.

Elora ignored the card and moved to clear a spot on a low table by the fireplace. "I suppose here."

She watched him set the flowers beside the others and noted that he was exceedingly careful of the blossoms, despite his less than enthusiastic manner. It was very much the same attitude he applied to her. Although he wished her gone, he was mindful of her recovery.

Not meaning to, she let her eyes stray. A shock of black hair fell negligently over his forehead. The white of his cravat was a soft contrast to the hard edge of his jaw. His jacket stretched with his movements, delineating his powerful arms and tapering waist.

He straightened and awareness rushed back to her. Flustered, she sat in the tufted chair.

"Who are they from?" he asked, bracing a forearm against the mantel.

Forcing her attention to the card, she said, "Lady Barbara Richmond."

"I'm impressed."

The sincerity in his voice drew her gaze. "Are you?"

"Yes, Lady Barbara is the *grand dame* of all the dowagers. She just also happens to be my godmother and takes her duties as such quite seriously. Consider yourself lucky that she has even deigned to acknowledge you."

Elora looked back to the card, and some of her earlier uneasiness returned. "I shall write her a thank-you note straightaway."

"That would be wise. She can be irritatingly proprietary where I am concerned."

"I certainly appreciate her thoughtfulness. I am grateful to everyone for their kindness." She waved a hand to indicate the entire room. "But none of this was necessary."

"You think not?" he asked, watching her intently.

"No." She knew that sounded petulant and she hastened to explain. "Please do not think that I am ungrateful for the courtesy everyone has afforded me, but I imagine these people have better things to do with their money than to send flowers to a total stranger."

"Consider it a whim on their part if it makes you feel better."

"What would make me feel better is to be well and gone." She fingered the white card, and gave him a challenging look. "I hope to do so in a few days."

His mouth quirked with the shadow of a smile. "You thought yourself well enough two nights ago."

She ignored his comment. "Be that as it may, I have a position waiting for me. Lord Ashton will be patient for only so long."

James Ashton, Brice silently vowed, would wait for as long as he was told. "You will leave when the doctor says you are fit."

His stubbornness was annoying, posing a host of problems. She had promised the creditors that she would begin to make good on her stepfather's debts in a matter of weeks. She could not afford to lie about not earning her salary.

"My lord," she began, trying to make him see reason. "This position was very difficult to come by."

Brice straightened and came within arm's reach of her. "There are always others."

"No, there are not. It was only through the efforts of Reverend Platt that Lord Ashton found me suitable."

"Who is Reverend Platt?" he asked in a lordly voice.

"He is the minister in the town where I lived. It was he who found me the post."

Brice considered that on a jaundiced note. The Reverend Platt wasn't a very astute man to have placed someone as beautiful as Elora Simmons beneath the nose of a lecher like Ashton.

He examined the graceful contours of her face. She was indeed breathtaking. Eyes the color of a rare sky, skin as smooth and flawless as oriental silk. He looked lower. The curves of her body were defined by the soft fabric of her dressing gown. In his mind's eye, he saw her as he had that first night, standing in nearly that very place; full breasts, narrow waist and trim legs, all gilded by the flames in the hearth and all bared to his view.

Elora felt his stare, and debts and governesses were dashed from her mind. His look made her feel overwhelmingly female and she didn't know why. All she knew was that no one had ever looked at her as he did.

"My lord."

His eyes came up and their gazes locked. Acting on some undefined, inner impulse, he reached down and carefully removed her glasses, letting them drop into her lap. Exhilarating currents of awareness shot between them. In a flash, Brice was gifted with a sure knowledge.

"You don't remember," he averred, lured by the undiluted blue orbs.

"Remember what?" came her strangled whisper.

"That night."

"What . . ."

"You, standing here by the fireplace."

"No . . ."

Hot, shimmering radiance threatened to inundate him, but he forced his eyes shut, blocking her from view in time to spare himself being engulfed. *I refuse to let this happen again.*

His voice harsh, he grated, "It is best that you don't remember."

Elora sucked in a labored breath, shaken by their exchange. She didn't know to what he had been referring. More significantly, she did *not* understand what had passed between them. He had looked into her eyes and she had felt exposed, both in body and mind. Somehow, she had felt intimately united with him.

His unyielding face provided no explanations, and even long after he left her sitting by herself, she could not make sense of what had transpired.

Mystified, she took her questions to bed with her, but found the matter completely illogical. Considering his ill-temper, there was no reason for her to feel anything more than politeness in his company. But as the night progressed and darkness enveloped the far corners of her room, she could again feel his eyes coursing over her and there was no denying or ignoring the impression of familiarity that assailed her once more.

Sleep proved to be elusive. Even with one of her windows

opened, as she preferred, her mind continued to examine the situation. When the clock chimed one, she gave up on sleep in sheer frustration.

Her movements cautious, she eased from bed, experiencing a sharp reprimand from her side. However, she was determined to make her way to the chair at the hearth and perhaps there find some peace of mind.

Pressing a hand against her bandaged ribs, she prepared to cross the room when a peculiar sound checked her movements. She tilted her head and found the noise coming from outside her window. Curiously, she headed there instead of the cozy fireside setting.

The scratching grew louder as she peered into the darkness of the sculpted garden; however, the sound was not emanating from the bushes, but rather from directly below her window. Against the house. Leaning forward just the smallest bit, she could make out the indistinct shape of a man.

A nervous tremor raced through her. There was no plausible reason for someone to be down there, tampering with the house, in the middle of the night.

She straightened . . . too quickly. Clenching her teeth against the pain, she fought back the cry that came to her lips. She spared herself only that one instant for recovery. Arms wrapped protectively about her aching side, she hurried to the door connecting to Brice's room.

"My lord," she whispered as she headed for his bed. By the light of the smoldering embers in the fireplace, she saw him rise to a sitting position in one lithe movement.

"Elora?" His deep voice came from deep within the shadows.

As rapidly as her body would allow, she made her way toward that voice. "My lord, something is wrong." Exhaustion and fear crumpled her knees. She sank down beside him, her hands reaching out in unconscious appeal.

"There is a man outside, below my window. I heard him scratching at the house." Her words came out in a quaking rush and her palms flattened on the sturdy wall of his bare chest. "I saw him standing there meddling with a window or perhaps a door."

Brice eased her away, then jerked back the covers.

"When?"

"Just now." Before she knew it, Brice stood and she had fleeting glimpses of broad shoulders, tightened buttocks and long solid legs. Hastily, she averted her eyes.

He disappeared into a darkened corner of the room and was back in seconds, black pants securely in place. Picking her up, he set her in his bed.

"Stay put," he ordered.

Eyes wide, she pulled the covers to her chin and nodded. Even if she had been tempted to disobey, she couldn't have moved very far. Her limbs had been reduced to a quaking pulp.

"Please, be careful," she implored, but he was already out the door, leaving her in ominous silence.

Seconds became hours and minutes stretched into days. Flickering shadows, cast by the low fire, danced across the room, creating menacing forms that played havoc with her composure. She could not dismiss this incident as coincidental, especially in light of the attack on the marquess's life. She might not be versed in city life, but even she knew that it was rare that one became the target for nefarious doings twice in a matter of days. She knew with a certainty that whoever was outside was the same person who had fired the pistol and that he wanted very much to finish what he had begun.

A horrible dread assailed her and whatever differences lay between herself and Brice Warfield evaporated. Despite his difficult temperament, she did not want him to come to harm.

The muted sound of the door opening captured her attention and her gaze. Profoundly relieved, she saw Brice shut the door and return to the bed.

"Are you all right?" she asked, drinking in the sight of him. Unconsciously, she searched the chiseled planes of his chest for evidence of injury.

"Yes, yes, I'm fine," he uttered, but he sounded provoked to the point of anger.

"Did you discover who was there?"

"No. The bas—" He exhaled sharply. "There was someone outside the doors on the terrace, but he fled the minute I entered the study. He was gone before I could see him clearly."

"What did he want?" Elora's anxiety was escalating. "Do you think he meant to rob your house?"

The muscles of his shoulders flexed into a shrug. "Possibly."

"Or possibly he was the same man who tried to kill you, and he came back to try again." Voicing her fears only enhanced the distress that had besieged her. She pressed cold hands to her lips, oblivious to the fact that every ounce of her dismay was plainly visible for Brice to see.

"Elora?" he questioned carefully.

"I don't understand," she softly wailed. "Why would someone want to kill you?"

"I don't know, but there is no need for you to fret. The man is gone."

"For now, but what if he comes back?"

"Then I will deal with him."

"Will you be safe? What are you going to do?"

Brice knew exactly what he was going to do, but that wasn't the issue he considered now. More pertinent was Elora Simmons. That she would worry herself to such a degree amazed him.

Sitting beside her, he took her hands in his own. Twice now, she had come to his rescue, and both times her motives had been pure. She had acted solely for his benefit, dismissing any thought to herself.

"You really are my little protector," he breathed in astonishment, brushing his thumbs over her knuckles. He searched her face. Fear, concern and confusion flashed freely. But in her eyes, behind the brilliant indigo, was something else he dared not name.

The surge hit him with a devastating force that jolted him

to his marrow. Unprepared, he stiffened in self-defense as his world narrowed to the blue of her eyes. Crazily, the room twisted, curving about him like warped silver, reflecting a glowing, heated image of Elora.

She was fire. In an attempt at rational thought, his mind struggled furiously to understand, but she swept into his consciousness, pervading his body with her flame. She touched, seared and finally . . . against his will . . . ignited a flame that he claimed as his own.

He burned. There was no escaping the blaze emanating from his chest and spreading outward. Every inch of his skin was sensitized. To the most infinitesimal fiber, his nerves quaked.

Some part of his mind told him to fill his lungs. The moment he did, an overpowering compulsion to take her in his arms engulfed him. His blood pounded under the urgency to capture her mouth. His body ached to make her his.

How and why were meaningless, reason ceased to exist. All he could do was react.

Groaning low in his throat, he thrust his hands back through her hair. He urged her head up and brought his mouth down on hers, possessively, hungrily, as though his life were dependent on drinking in her sweetness. And in that second, in the coldly remote hollows of his heart, the imperishable flame sparked a small, steady ember.

Too stunned to move, Elora clung helplessly to his shoulders, striving to gain some kind of equilibrium. She had never been kissed and the hard pressure of his mouth made coherent thinking impossible.

Wondrous glimmers of heat inundated her. They coursed through her body in a new and exotic force, igniting glitters along her nerves and giving rise to a silken heat in the depths of her. The sensation was foreign, but consuming in its intensity, turning her insides to liquid.

The fears that had brought her to his side fell away, and if she could have dreaded anything at all it would have been that this delight would cease. Her breath quickened and her hands tightened about his corded neck. Beneath her fingers, she could feel the power of him luring her closer and she leaned against him.

Brice absorbed her softness like a desert sand consuming water. The feel of her breasts against his chest, her hands about his neck sent his already abused senses reeling out of control. Whether it was because she had saved his life or because of the strange, unearthly link that bound them, he knew only that he could not hold her close enough.

He lowered one arm to the small of her back and gathered her to him, relishing every inch of her. Frustratingly, the touch only created a need for more. Desperately, he parted her lips and thrust his tongue into the sweet recesses of her mouth, exploring, savoring. Of its own accord, her head came to rest on his shoulder. His mouth followed, never relinquishing its claim, while he cradled her in his arms, turned slightly and eased her down to the bed.

The shift brought Elora's eyes open. She was floating in a dreamlike bliss, but seeing Brice looming over her shocked her into awareness.

"My lord . . . Brice," she choked out, not certain how she had come to be in such a position.

He heard her softly spoken words as though through a thick shroud, and paid them little heed. For the first time in three dark, anguished years, he felt whole. He could think of nothing but making her his own. Bracing his weight on one forearm, he bent one leg over her thighs. His lips sought the silken column of her throat while his hand eased her nightgown from her shoulder.

Elora's world fractured. His firm mouth was sending delicious tremors down her neck, but air touching her breasts filled her with dismay.

"No," she exclaimed, trying to pull her nightgown back into place. "No, you mustn't."

Yes, he thought, *I must. My life is here, in this woman.*

Her resistance barely registered on his intoxicated mind. He tugged the fabric free of her fingers and lowered his head to her breasts. But panicked hands gripped his hair, staying his movements.

"No, oh, please stop," Elora cried. She was mortified by her behavior. In good conscience, she could accept his kissing her, but there was no excuse for the fact that she was in his arms, flat on her back, half-naked. "Please, let me up," she demanded, although her words were barely more than a whisper.

It was the tearful catch in Elora's voice that penetrated Brice's fervor. Tremulous and alarmed, it affected him as no strident shout ever could have.

His head snapped up. One look at her trembling lips and the fire was extinguished. Sanity rushed back. He bolted to his feet and drew in one strained breath after another. His back to the bed, he jammed both hands through his hair and gripped his head.

"What are you doing to me?" he ground out, clenching his eyes shut in a bid for the self-control that had come to be his armor.

That part of Elora's mind that wasn't in frantic chaos wanted to ask the same of him. At the touch of his lips, he had commanded her senses. Effortlessly, he had stripped her of all logical thought while her body had been swamped by the most luxuriant sensations.

Well, she was in complete possession of herself now and she could not remain where she was, lying abed like a wanton. Unfortunately, her position allowed her no leverage and she was capable of little movement that was free of pain.

Pulling her nightgown back into place, she gripped the fabric about her neck like a feeble shield. "Would you please help me?"

Brice turned at her low, stiff tone and leveled her with a look that was as implacable as his temper. Who was this woman that she kindled in him a spirit that soared free and unburdened? What was it about her that she took his dispassionate life of order and reduced it to a fervent tempest?

Green eyes blazing with accusation, he again bit out, "What are you doing to me?"

Stung by the fire in his gaze, her humiliation was joined by a certain degree of trepidation. "I haven't done—"

"What mystical power do you possess?"

"I don't have any power." A tremor of fright skittered down her back at the raw intensity in his bearing. Ingrained fear of angry men clutched her hard. "I don't know what you're talking about."

"Don't you?"

She shook her head in frantic denial. "No, no, I—"

"Like some fey thing, you threw yourself into my life . . . and then ripped it asunder." He leaned forward, grasped her by the shoulders and carefully pulled her to her feet. But he didn't release her. Instead, he lowered his head and stared directly into her eyes. *"Who are you? What do you want of me?"*

His embittered anguish buffeted her. In self-defense, her arms crossed over her breasts as she tried to define his manner. He was held in the grips of a terrible ire that had him charging her with witchery and the like.

She wanted to flee, but knew it was useless. As strong as he was, she could only remain within his hold and pray that, as before, he would ride out his anger without hurting her.

"My lord, I am not endowed with any singular powers." Her voice shook with her apprehension. "And I do not want anything from you. But if the truth be told, I am frightened and confused by everything that has occurred."

"Frightened. By the attempted murder."

"Yes."

"And by this miscreant outside tonight."

"Yes. And by you."

His black brows slashed downward and his hands tightened about her shoulders. "Me?"

"Yes." She winced at the pressure of his fingers. "Let me go."

She waited expectantly, not knowing what he would do. When he did not resort to raising a fist, she would have sighed in relief, but part of her was still afraid that he would pull her back to the bed and continue where he had left off. She didn't know where that would lead, but it was definitely beyond anything she could handle.

Chancing a look at his face, she nearly cried out when his lips drew into a fierce line and his jaw clenched. But he dropped his hands from her shoulders and stepped back.

Her eyes drifted shut. A wavering sigh escaped her lips. Arms still crossed before her, she stepped away and headed for the door, determined to be gone from this house, from Brice Warfield, first thing in the morning.

Brice watched her make her way back to her room. Suddenly he knew he would never let her go.

Chapter

6

"MISS SIMMONS, WHERE ARE YOU GOING?"

Startled, Elora turned from the armoire as Mary Cobb entered her room. Quickly, she found her poise. "Good morning, Mrs. Cobb." Fastening the last button on the front of her bodice, she watched the housekeeper bustle forward, the woman's round face lined with amazement.

"Miss Simmons, you shouldn't be up. It's a wonder you haven't injured yourself."

Elora slipped her feet into low-heeled shoes that matched her pale blue muslin gown. "I am feeling much improved, Mrs. Cobb."

In truth she was. Despite a sleepless night, her mind was clear and her side ached just slightly. Her only incapacity lay in her lack of stamina. Twice since she had risen that morning, she had had to rest. Still, she was determined.

"As you can see, I am fit enough to have even dressed."

Mrs. Cobb's gaze traveled from the empty armoire to Elora's clothes case by the foot of the bed. "You can't be leaving?"

Elora nodded. "I'm afraid I am."

"But his lordship didn't mention anything to me about this."

Elora worked the button on one of her cuffs. "I have not yet informed his lordship."

The housekeeper pressed a plump hand to her chest, her look of astonishment giving way to one of dismay. "Miss, do you think that this is wise?"

Seeing Mary's worried frown, Elora smiled gently. "Do not fret, Mrs. Cobb. I assure you, I know what I am doing."

An air of utter misgiving seemed to act on Mrs. Cobb's nerves. She wrung her hands and gave Elora a stare of such appeal that Elora paused.

"Oh, Miss Simmons, the marquess has given strict orders that you are to follow the doctor's prescription to the letter, and Dr. Bingham has most definitely not released you from your sickbed." An uncertain looking smile wobbled at her lips. "Perhaps, you should discuss this with his lordship."

Elora's head came up in a rebellious angle. She had no intention of discussing anything with Brice Warfield. She wanted only to get as far from him as possible. And quickly.

"That won't be necessary, Mrs. Cobb." For once, Elora was glad that her face was as readable as it was, for Mrs. Cobb obviously saw her unshakable conviction.

"Very well, miss," the older woman conceded reluctantly. "Is there anything that you'll be needing?"

Elora squinted slightly as she looked about. "I seem to have misplaced my spectacles. If you should happen to find them, I would appreciate you forwarding them to Lord Ashton's."

"Of course, miss. Will there be anything else?"

Elora paused to consider the best course of action. As though Mrs. Cobb's face would provide the answer, she carefully peered at the round countenance.

"Perhaps there is something you might do for me, Mrs. Cobb." Stepping to the secretary, she picked up an envelope containing a letter she had penned earlier.

She studied the thick paper that bore Brice's name. During the night, she had thought long and hard on how best to take her leave. Under normal circumstances, she would personally offer her respects to both his lordship and his sister for their hospitality. But the situation was a far cry from normal, especially after last night.

Her stomach lurched. The scene that had unfolded in the next room . . . the next bed . . . played through her mind. Oh, the things she had allowed him to do. His lips on hers, his powerful thighs pressed intimately to her own. She had never given any man leave to so much as hold her hand, yet she had nearly offered him *carte blanche* to do as he wished and she had shamelessly reciprocated.

She had felt the crisp mat of hair on his chest, tasted the faint remnants of brandy on his tongue, clung to the hardened muscles of his back, and had been utterly helpless against the torrent of emotions that he had aroused. What had possessed her?

Her face brightened with a furious blush. She had never thought that a kiss was placed anywhere other than on the lips. But his mouth had been everywhere, scalding a path from her neck to her shoulders and . . . Helplessly, she shut her eyes. If she had not restrained him, he would have placed his mouth to her breasts.

By will alone, she suppressed a low moan. She felt so utterly embarrassed. And ignorant. She hadn't known what men and women did together, and she suspected that she still didn't know the half of it. As incredible as his every kiss and touch had been, she sensed that they were only a prelude to something more, but none of her knowledge told her what that could be. Apparently, young, unmarried women were not supposed to know, or else her schooling had been horribly neglected. In any event, she did know that young, unmarried women did not engage in this sort of behavior with men.

Then why had she done so with Brice? But she already knew the answer. Brice Warfield was a rare man. In all her life she had never met anyone like him. Even as mercurial as his temperament was, she was undeniably attracted to him. True, he never smiled and there was that aura of detachment about him most of the time. But she sensed that there was a great reserve within him that beckoned to her.

She responded to that force in spite of a temper that could flare so hotly. More precisely, because of the way he restrained that temper. Last night he had been furious, but he had not turned into a cruel brute intent on inflicting pain as her stepfather had.

She took great comfort in that, although she was still a long way from feeling prepared to deal with Brice, for the onslaught of his passion and the fury that had followed.

The color staining her face drained away. Even now with the bright light of day to shed reason on the matter, she could not understand what had happened to the marquess. He had been like a man possessed, caught up in some horrible inner turmoil where she became the target for his wrath.

What had she done? She admitted that her behavior had been beyond the bounds of propriety, but certainly that shouldn't have provoked him to such heights of anger.

"Miss Simmons?" Mary voiced quietly.

Elora blinked. The letter was still clutched in her hand giving her world focus once more. No, this way would be best. His lordship was adamantly determined to keep her there for the duration of her recovery. But it was impossible for her to remain.

She placed the letter in the housekeeper's hand. "Please see that his lordship receives this after I have gone."

Mrs. Cobb's gaze dropped to the thick paper, then flew back to Elora. "You're leaving without a word?"

Nodding quickly, Elora explained, "I know this appears odd, but it is what I wish." She stood unwavering beneath the woman's intense regard, practically feeling the concern and trepidation in the kindly stare.

"Very well, miss," Mrs. Cobb relented, her voice laced with regret. "I'll see that he gets this. Your bag will be sent on."

"Thank you," Elora breathed in relief. "And thank you

for everything you have done for me. I will never be able to repay your kindness."

Mrs. Cobb squared her shoulders with what appeared to be a grand measure of pride. "It has been my honor to serve you, miss." With that, she took her leave.

Elora gathered her cloak from the bed before giving the room one last look. The array of flowers brought a smile to her lips, but the smile faltered when she glanced to Brice's door. An inexplicable sadness descended on her. Hastily, she shook off the melancholy and hurried from the room as quickly as her body would allow.

Her exit from the house was witnessed by no one, and in a few minutes, she walked the short distance to Lord Ashton's residence. Unfortunately, what limited strength she had was rapidly depleted, and by the time she was seated in the Ashtons' small, dark sitting room, she was clutching the arm of a massive sofa, trying to will away the throbbing in her side.

In a concerted effort, she restored her breathing to a regular pattern and slowly some fortitude returned, and not a moment too soon for her peace of mind. She did not want his lordship to enter and find her less than capable of her duties.

Feeling better, she took in her new surroundings. The walls were covered in a ponderous pattern of gray and green flowers, and heavy moss-colored drapes were fitted with intricately twisted swags. Chairs and tables alike were bulky pieces, fashioned from deeply stained mahogany that nearly blended into the black marble-tiled floor.

Elora viewed it all a little uncertainly. The atmosphere created was dismal and so darkly oppressive as to be depressing. Secretly, she hoped that the rest of the house was not quite so intimidating. From what Josiah Platt had told her, Lord Ashton was purported to be a pleasant enough man. Unfortunately his household decorations did not reflect that particular bend of character.

At the thought of the Reverend Platt, Elora felt a twinge of homesickness. She missed Josiah and his mother. For the past ten years, they had been dear friends. On more than one occasion, she had turned to them for comfort; after her mother died and during those times when her stepfather's drinking or gambling had become unbearable. Josiah, especially, had offered solace when she had been most in need.

Mentally, she thanked the stars above for his friendship. She shuddered to think what might have become of her if he hadn't arranged for this position for her. The prospects were not encouraging, but before she could speculate on the matter further, the door swung open and Lord Ashton entered the room.

Elora's first impression of the man was that he was not at all what she had expected. In her mind she had pictured a man well into his middle years, portly, and perhaps balding. This tall, dark-haired man with his lean, muscular build and arrogant face bore no resemblance to the man she had imagined.

Her opinion of him continued to shift as he sauntered forward, his pace marked by a predatory kind of grace that she found unnerving. As he took his seat in a chair directly before her, she couldn't help noticing that his brown gaze traveled the length of her body with great deliberateness.

Squinting slightly, she came to her feet, her rise slightly unsteady. "Good day, my lord," she offered, quelling the odd desire to step back to a safe distance. Out of habit, she wished for the security of her spectacles.

"I was beginning to wonder when, or possibly even if, you were going to make an appearance, Miss Simmons," he drawled, stretching one long leg out before him.

"I believe Lord Warrington sent a note of explanation, my lord." She chanced a quick look down at his foot grazing her dress and realized that the hem was trapped beneath his boot. Again, she wanted to step back, but to do so might possibly offend his lordship. She stood perfectly still. "I hope you have not been put out by this delay in my arrival."

Ashton propped his elbow against the arm of the chair and raised his hand to idly trace a finger along his lower lip.

Disregarding all subtleties, he fastened his gaze on Elora's mouth.

"That is a pretty little speech, Miss Simmons, but I have been put out. In the extreme." Peering directly into her eyes, a dissolute smile stretched his lips.

Elora swallowed with difficulty, her insides twisting nervously at Ashton's manner. There was something about him that made her distinctly uncomfortable. "I can only apologize, my lord. But I am here now and ready to take up my post."

"Not quite so fast, my dear. We have barely had any time to become acquainted." He made a slow and thorough inspection of the generous contours of her breasts. "Sit down."

An overwhelming desire to run swept along Elora's nerves. She did not like the looks he was giving her. Unfortunately, she was faced with no other option than to do as she was told. Carefully, her nerves prickling cautiously, she perched on the edge of the sofa.

"So," he mused aloud, "you seem to be in perfect health."

"I am feeling much improved, my lord."

"No ill effects from your little foray with pistols and such?"

"Very few, my lord. Lord Warrington was most solicitous of my health."

"I can well imagine," he mocked in a tone that Elora thought rude. Abruptly, he stood and walked away to one of the windows. "You have never been a governess before, have you, Miss Simmons?"

"No, my lord."

"Then you know relatively little of what will be expected of you?"

"Reverend Platt did explain some of the responsibilities."

"Ah, yes, the Reverend Platt. That good man of the cloth. What did he have to say?"

"He said that I would be seeing to the needs of your children."

"Aptly put, this matter of needs." He left the window and returned to stand at Elora's knees. "Yes, your duties will most definitely deal with needs, my dear."

Elora tilted her head back in order to look directly up at him. The moment she did, she wished she hadn't. He reached out and caught her chin in one hand. A knowing, ugly grin played across his lips, while his gaze roved over her bodice as though to strip the muslin away.

Her skin crawled with fear, the same kind of fear she had felt when her stepfather had bellowed in rage. Like Harmen Gillet, she sensed that James Ashton possessed a ruthlessness that would take a physical means of expression.

She pulled away, sinking as far against the back of the sofa as she could. "My lord," she whispered, her alarm visible in the trembling of her lips and the darkening of her eyes.

Her gesture made him laugh. "Modesty becomes you, Miss Simmons. But that suits my purposes quite well, I think." On a remnant chuckle, he moved to the far wall to give the bellpull a firm tug. "The children are about on their riding lessons, at the present, Miss Simmons. My wife has not yet risen for the day. When she does, she will instruct you on the children." He removed his watch from the pocket of his waistcoat. "I myself have several engagements this morning"—he pocketed the timepiece and stared straight at her—"but we shall resume our discussion tonight after you are settled in."

Disregarding any possible strain to her wound, Elora came to her feet, feeling very much like a cornered animal. Her every instinct urged her to flee right then, but looming over her head lay her stepfather's debts and the promises she had made to his creditors. She needed this position and the money it would bring.

A dour-faced maid appeared in the doorway and Ashton flicked a hand in Elora's direction. "Show Miss Simmons to her room."

Elora hesitated briefly, struggling with her need to rush out the front door, but where would she go?

Her heart whispered, *Brice.*
Not saying a word, she followed the maid.

Brice sat at his desk, the deep slant of his brows and the glitter in his green eyes attesting to his dangerous irritation. Coldly, he stared at Mr. Harold Tew as the squat Bow Street Runner cocked his head to one side and peered out of his one good eye.

"I don't mean any disrespect, my lord, but in cases such as this, where someone would stand to gain considerably from your death, I have to consider every avenue."

Brice clamped his teeth down hard on a thin roll of tobacco and exhaled a fine stream of smoke. For the better part of an hour, they had been discussing the matter of the attempt on his life and any possible suspects. Mr. Tew had been most thorough in his preliminary inquiry and like Brice, could not rule out the Duke of Westford or the Earl of Stanley. But Tew's last suggestion that one of Brice's relatives might be responsible stretched Brice's frayed temper.

The scenario of a disgruntled relative killing the titled lord in order to inherit had all the feel of a shabby one act play, making him want to scoff at the nonsense of it. Unfortunately, as the investigator had so succinctly pointed out, the possibility could not be ignored.

His cousin Thorbon was the next in line to inherit, but the man was nearing seventy and had always made it clear that he had never wanted the title or its responsibilities. The old codger was happy as long as he had a good bottle of port and a willing serving wench to dally with every now and then. No, Thorbon was out of the question.

The only other male relative who stood to gain from his death was a very distant cousin all of the age of six. The child in this case would be quite blameless, but not so his mother if she sought the title of marquess for her son. Unlike some designations that were hollow distinctions, Warrington was backed by an immense fortune that stretched from one end of the realm to the other. Even a portion of that fortune could be the motive for murder if one was greedy enough.

Brice easily recalled the boy's mother, Katherine. She was the widow of his second cousin on the paternal side of the family. It had been several years since he had laid eyes on her, but he remembered her as a shrewd, avaricious woman, covetous of nearly everyone. Her late husband had left her in comfortable financial straits, although she was not wealthy by any stretch of the imagination. But neither was she one step from debtor's prison.

Brice's lips thinned. Katherine's greed could very well be behind the whole matter, but it was sheer speculation. For all he knew, she could be entirely innocent and someone else was to blame.

"Do you honestly think a member of my own family might be responsible?"

Harold Tew's one good eye widened into a bulging sphere. "I'm not saying that is the case, my lord, only something I intend to look into, just as I will probe deeper into the Earl of Stanley's affairs." The investigator scrunched up his face. "I don't like these threats he has been making at you."

"Given recent events, I have no great fondness for them myself," Brice remarked blandly.

"Do you know the man to be vengeful?"

"The only opinion I have of the man is that he isn't particularly bright."

"How so?"

"Mr. Tew, after losing to me as often as he has, the man should have figured out by now that he is most likely the world's worst gambler."

"As you say, he may not be particularly bright, but he could still be out for revenge. It certainly fits. Last week, he lost a great sum of money to you and within twenty-four hours, you were nearly shot dead. Now, just a day ago, he loses to you yet again, and last night someone attempts to break into your house."

It was certainly logical enough, and so galling that Brice

ground out his cigar in one jabbing move. "All right, Mr. Tew, do what you must. Investigate to your heart's content, but I do not . . . do you understand . . . *do not* want wind of this to reach the ears of anyone outside of this room."

"That goes without saying, my lord. For the sake of this investigation, it is best that your servants, including your secretary, not know the extent or direction of my inquiry."

Brice sent him a narrow-eyed look. "Do you suspect Marcus Quinn?"

"No, my lord, I do not. But if he knows nothing of my investigation, then there is no chance that he will inadvertently say something he shouldn't."

It made sense, as much as anything in the entire mad affair could possibly make sense. "All right," Brice agreed. "I will wait to hear from you next week."

"Very good, my lord. You know how to reach me, should anything else untoward occur."

"Yes, yes," Brice snapped, impatient for this interview to conclude.

Bowing slightly, Mr. Tew departed, leaving Brice to the solitude he craved just then. But his privacy was cut short by Ambrose Cobb's discreet entrance into the study.

"I beg your pardon, my lord," the butler said, coming forward with his words. "Miss Simmons asked that this be delivered to you."

Brice stiffened, then swore beneath his breath. That's all it took, the mere mention of her name and his insides twisted into knots.

He mentally swore again, cursing Elora, cursing himself. He could not forget, would *never* forget, what had happened last night. Never in all his life had he wanted a woman the way he had wanted Elora. He had felt scorched from the inside out, burned with a need that made him want her to the ends of the universe and back again. Then again, and again, and he doubted that *that* would have even been enough.

He stabbed a chilling look to the envelope resting on the small silver tray Cobb held. His name was neatly scribed across the note. He lifted the envelope, oblivious to Cobb's exit, and withdrew the single sheet of paper contained within. Scanning the lines of delicate script, his teeth ground together when he reached Elora's signature.

"Damn you, Elora Simmons," he snarled. Balling the missive tightly, he flung it away. *"Damn you!"*

Lady Ashton's summons came an hour after Elora had been led to her room off the nursery on the third floor. Hastily, she rose from the bed on which she had been resting, smoothed several errant curls into their place in a tidy knot and followed the same dour-faced maid back to the drawing room.

Her descent was gilded with an anxiety that stripped all color from her cheeks. She could not put Lord Ashton's unwanted attentions from her mind and meeting his wife only intensified her distress over the matter.

Some part of her dared to hope that Lady Ashton might serve as a shield to somehow deter her husband's actions. But in her heart, she saw that prospect as a folly born of desperation. No, she alone was going to have to contend with Lord Ashton.

Lady Judith Ashton, like her husband, was a source of surprise for Elora. The lady, seated regally on the sofa, was a statuesque brunette with a beautiful, if haughty, face.

"Stand here, Miss Simmons," she stated, pointing a ringed finger to a spot several feet in front of her.

The imperious tone widened Elora's eyes, but she crossed to the designated place and stood under the lady's close scrutiny. Silence ensued, a thick unnerving hush that increased Elora's tension tenfold, especially when Lady Ashton's expression became one of extreme displeasure.

"My husband made arrangements for your position here, Miss Simmons. Not I."

"Yes, my lady."

"I can now see why." Her perfectly plucked brows arched disdainfully. "Personally, I do not think you will suit at all."

Elora's lips parted in dismay. "My lady, I do not understand."

"Oh, don't you?" Lady Ashton rhythmically clenched and unclenched one hand resting on her lap. "You have no experience as a governess. But even if you had, your reputation precedes you."

"My reputation?"

"Do not cast that innocent air on me, miss. You have become notorious since your arrival in London. Your name is known in every household in the city."

"By no choice of my own, my lady," Elora reasoned.

"Whatever. I will not have my children influenced by a person of such notoriety."

Elora saw her future rapidly crumbling into a disastrous heap. "My lady, I'm sure the furor will die down."

"Of that I have no doubt. That still does not eliminate your more serious flaws, Miss Simmons."

"My . . . what flaws?"

Judith Ashton's humorless laugh scraped over Elora's nerves. "Oh, yes, I see why my husband wants you here. He's had a penchant for innocence ever since he took mine." Doing nothing to hide her animosity, she surged to her feet.

"You are a conniving little slut, to think that you could dally with the Marquess of Warrington and then blithely take up here." She dragged a contemptuous glare down the length of Elora. "I'm sure he spread your legs and used your little alley quite well."

Elora's face burned with humiliation and shame. Her behavior in Lord Warrington's arms had been improper, but this other thing Lady Ashton was accusing her of . . . what did she mean?

"My lady, please," she began in her own defense.

"Save your entreaties. Take them, and your whorish behavior, back to the marquess for you won't be using them here on my husband."

"Utter one more word, Lady Ashton, and I will be forced to shove it down your viperous throat."

The deadly cold voice jerked Elora and Judith's attention

90

toward the door. Stunned, they found Brice Warfield standing just inside the room, a harried-looking butler behind him.

Her eyes glazed by churning emotions, Elora watched Brice advance, an imposing, dangerous figure in black. His face seemed that of some grim being, the very lack of expression painfully menacing, the iciness in his eyes akin to a feral gleam.

"I tried to stop him, my lady," the butler cried, rushing forward while keeping a healthy distance from Brice.

Brice ignored the butler, advancing like a dark jungle beast intent on its prey. Elora unconsciously stepped back, but she needn't have moved, for two paces off, Brice stopped and leveled his lethal gaze on Judith Ashton.

"You dare much, lady. Do not abuse my future wife again. *Ever.*"

Chapter
7

"WIFE?!" JUDITH'S CRY WAS TORN FROM HER MOUTH.

Too shocked to utter a sound, too stunned to even move, Elora stared at Brice in a disbelief so profound that she actually thought she had lost part of her sanity. His wife. He had referred to her as his future *wife!*

Her breath came out in short gasps, her lungs striving valiantly to sustain her suddenly racing heart. The air around her grew thick, the atmosphere took on a bizarre quality, and all she could think was that he was mad. Quite, quite mad.

The "mad" man placed a hand to her elbow and, before Lady Ashton's incredulous eyes, escorted Elora from the room and out the front door. But Elora's weakened body and already flayed nerves had endured enough for one day. Halfway back to Brice's house, her legs refused to take any further commands that her brain issued and, unexpectedly, her knees buckled.

Brice's arms shot out to steady her before swinging her up against his chest. "This is becoming a habit, madam."

Elora didn't know if she had heard his voice or if she had imagined it. In either case, she was simply too bewildered to care. She let her head rest against his shoulder for the short distance to the house.

A worried-looking Cobb was standing at the ready, door opened wide. "Should I call for the physician, my lord?"

"I don't think that will be necessary," Brice said, making his way to his study. Cobb rushed ahead to open the study door, closing it quietly as Brice gently placed Elora on the sofa.

Stepping back, he stared intently at her pale face. "Are you all right?"

Elora briefly studied her hands in her lap, trying to make sense of what had just occurred. It was beyond her comprehension.

The blue of her eyes reflecting every ounce of her bewilderment, she lifted her gaze to his. "Why?"

Brice returned her look for a long moment, then swung around toward the French doors, giving her his back as he wrestled with her question. Irritably, he scrubbed a hand across his chin. He should be held in the grips of a mighty stupefication, like Elora shocked by his declaration. But he wasn't. Bloody hell, he wasn't. All he knew was that something was happening, she had some hold on him. The pistol had been fired and he had somehow, in some way . . . become linked with her.

As soon as the thought entered his mind, he viciously shoved it away, denying it completely as the ramblings of a fool. He was behaving like an ass, letting himself be caught up in the stuff of fairy tales when the simple truth was that today's situation was a matter of honor. Nothing more. Nothing, *nothing* more.

He had done his damnedest . . . had even gone out of his way . . . to ensure that Elora's reputation remained intact. Unfortunately, his efforts hadn't been good enough for the likes of Judith Ashton. Remembering how she had spewed her putrid accusations, his anger rose again.

Declaring Elora to be his future wife had been the logical and noble means of rectifying a situation that she could have never won. With the benefit of his name, no one would dare to insult her further. For those who did question her virtue, marriage was the only accepted stamp of approval to save her from ruin.

Carefully, he weighed his decision. Marriage had not been a conscious thought when he had stormed from his house. His only purpose, he rationalized, had been to return Elora's stubborn little hide until he was convinced she was fully recuperated. Nevertheless, he did not regret his actions. He had always planned to take a wife some day. That day had just come a little sooner than he had expected.

Elora as his wife. The notion was becoming more appealing with each moment that passed. She was bright and spirited, her manner good-humored, and there was no overlooking her extraordinary beauty. Or his desire for her. Yes, marrying Elora would suit him very well, despite the peculiar effect she sometimes had on him.

Turning, he found her staring at him and he half expected to be caught by her gaze, assailed as he had been so many times in the past days. But her eyes revealed only amazement and a blatant misgiving. Slowly he came to stand before her.

"Are you feeling better?"

Elora nearly choked on a hysterical bubble of laughter. "How can you ask me that?"

"Elora . . ."

"Tell me I have imagined all of this," she cut him off, pressing shaking fingers to her forehead. "Tell me I am caught in a dream."

"You're not."

That was *not* what she wanted to hear. She searched his face in hopes that the answers she wanted would be there. All she saw was an unrelenting determination. "How could you? How could you have told Lady Ashton that I am to be your wife?"

Brice eased his jacket aside and shoved one hand into the pocket of his trousers. "Because that is what I plan."

Elora stared wide-eyed at him. "You might have thought to include me in this decision."

"Circumstances being what they were, there was no time.

94

Lady . . . and I use the word loosely . . . Ashton was already well on her way to ruining you."

It was a truth that Elora could not escape. But for him to offer, no, *decree,* marriage was astounding. "My lord, this is impossible."

"No, it isn't."

"We hardly know each other."

"That can be rectified."

His answers were too nonchalant, too unperturbed for such an emotional subject. She nearly groaned in frustration. "Need I point out that our stations in life are horribly dissimilar? You, my lord, are a peer of the realm while I am the daughter of a schoolteacher. You should be marrying a viscountess or at the very least the daughter of an earl."

He dismissed her objections with an upward flick of his brows. "Very well, if it makes you feel better, then I can tell you that the class difference means nothing to mc."

She briefly squeezed her eyes shut. Somehow she had to make him see reason. "My lord, we share no basis for a marriage."

"Marriages occur for any number of reasons," he returned with a shrug. "Convenience, combining of estates, the insurance of lines."

His rationale stung. "No one knows that better than I, my lord. My own mother married my stepfather for the sake of security, and it brought her nothing but misery." Some of that misery inundated Elora now and her pained gaze dropped to her lap. "Mama was the most lovely woman. Like a flower, she blossomed and thrived under my father's love. Her life was filled with joy and laughter. Until Papa died."

As the memories continued, her dejection increased. Rubbing her palms together, her voice lowered. "It is difficult for the widow of a teacher with a small child to make do in the world. Mama married Mr. Gillet out of necessity, believing she was doing the right thing. But no love existed between them." She could still hear Harmen Gillet's harsh, bitter words. "My stepfather is a cruel, heartless man. Mama couldn't bear up and she just withered; before my very eyes she lost her joy for life and died heartbroken."

Realizing the extent of her disclosures, she flushed in embarrassment, but raised her head and gave Brice a direct look. "I don't want that kind of marriage."

Brice's brows snapped into angry slashes. "You think to compare me to your stepfather?"

"No, my lord." She was coming to realize Brice was not a cruel man. So far he had not mistreated her in any way. But she had hoped, in her deepest heart of hearts, for a marriage like her parents'. "People should marry for love and you don't love"—her lips trembled "—you don't love me, my lord."

He stiffened at her words. Long ago he had harbored such convictions about love and marriage. At one time, he had wanted both of those, but he had learned that such hopes were only a weak tenet meant to undermine a person's sanity.

Coolly, he looked down into her pure blue eyes. "Many marriages have been known to survive without love. In fact, that is more the case than not."

"Of that I have no doubt, my lord. But you do not even like me."

Insulted by her words, he demanded, "Where did you get that idea?"

"From you. You have been angry with me from the very start, although I do not know why. I have done my best not to inconvenience you in any way, but"—she looked down at her lap, humiliated and bewildered—"but you have made it very clear that I provoke you no matter what I do."

Brice ground his teeth. *Bloody hell.* He was doing his damnedest to make the best of the situation and she was reacting as though he were offering her some vile sentence. He clamped his fist behind his back, controlling his temper with a scrap of logic and a shred of patience.

Long seconds passed as he considered his actions of the past week. Reluctantly he had to admit that based on all that had occurred between them, she could have been led to think the way she did, but it had never been a matter of his not liking her.

Dragging forward a Chinese armchair from beside the sofa, he placed it directly before Elora and sat, spreading his legs wide to encompass her own in between. He leaned forward, bracing his forearms against his thighs and gently smoothed the fabric of her dress over her knees. "I assure you that I do not dislike you."

In dreadful fascination, Elora sat immobile, staring at his hands on her knees. Stunned by his unexpected closeness, she instantly forsook their conversation. A part of her mind screamed warnings about proprieties and acceptable behavior of a gentleman. But a quiet steady voice inside her said that *nothing* between them had ever been normal or even remotely proper.

The warmth from his fingers soaked into her legs. Dazed, she realized that she was as vulnerable to his touch now as she had been last night when he had held her against the heated expanse of his chest and kissed her.

A blush stole up her neck as she became increasingly aware of his body practically surrounding her. His torso was directly in front of her, filling her vision with impressions of broad shoulders and strong arms. His head was only a hand's breadth from hers, his lips formed into a firm line. The insides of his muscled thighs pressed the outer edge of her own, the shocking contact irresistibly drawing her eyes down to where their legs touched. Encompassing everything was the muskiness of his cologne, the scent filling her senses with the essence of him.

Helplessly, she looked up, confused by the sensations he was making her feel. She found him watching her with an intensity that made her blink self-consciously, and suddenly remember that they had been in the middle of a discussion.

A little frantically, her mind dragged up the remnants of their conversation. He had stated that he did not dislike her. Forcing herself to concentrate, she lifted her chin, fully prepared to dispute the issue . . . for two reasons. One, she didn't believe him and two, she needed something to distract her from his disturbing presence.

She stared straight into his eyes, formed her words, then stopped abruptly. For once, mixed with the icy remoteness in the green depths, she saw a hint of human vitality that seemed oddly out of place. That glimpse of spirit was barely discernible, but it was all too real and enough to convince her of the sincerity of his words. That was reassuring. But only to a small degree.

Her voice slightly choked, she murmured, "There are other reasons we cannot marry, my lord."

"What could those be?"

Studiously ignoring the fact that her knees were almost snuggled into the juncture of his legs, she said, "I have obligations to a great many creditors."

"You're in debt?"

"Not personally, no. The debts belong to my stepfather."

"Then let him pay."

She nearly laughed, but there was no humor to be had in the situation. "If it were only that simple. I do not know where my stepfather is, and I am bound by my own word to repay the monies he owes."

Brice's eyes narrowed as he digested her words. "Am I to take it that your stepfather disappeared to parts unknown and left you to face his creditors?"

"That is essentially the matter summed up. I have no claim to his debts, but neither could I allow these people to be cheated out of their due."

"So you thought to earn back the money by taking the post as governess."

Elora nodded. "So you see, my lord, I have no dowry to bring to a marriage. Only responsibilities that I do not expect you or anyone else to assume."

"Consider it paid."

"What?"

"I will settle the debt."

Her mouth fell into an astonished *O*. "You can't do that."

"I just did. How much does he owe?"

"My lord, you . . ."

"How much?"

She swallowed past her tightened throat.

"How much?"

"Nearly five thousand pounds."

Brice scoffed in disbelief. "And you thought to settle that amount on a governess's salary?" He sat back and regarded her in dubious wonder. For a man of his means, the sum was paltry, but in her circumstances, the amount was astronomical. "Madam, you would have been working for the rest of your life."

Settling her shoulders, she averred quietly, "I am well aware of that."

Her honest pride struck the skepticism from his face. He had to admire her noble intentions. "As it is you don't have a position any longer. What happened?"

Elora gripped her hands tightly as she remembered Lady Ashton's slurs about her reputation. "I don't know. I did nothing more than walk into the parlor and Lady Ashton insisted that I would not suit as her governess."

But Brice had overheard the majority of Judith Ashton's contemptuous accusations. He understood only too well that jealousy and a vile, selfish character had been hard at work. "It doesn't surprise me that she found you unsuitable," he said, taking in the beauty of her face.

Startled and not a little insulted, Elora frowned sharply. "I am no monster, my lord. I am well educated, well mannered and I happen to love children."

"You are also incredibly naive." Seeing her wounded look, he explained. "Your qualifications could have been sterling, but you possess one merit that Lady Ashton will forever hold against you."

"What is that?"

"You're a beautiful woman."

Elora's heart lurched in her chest. All her hard won efforts to hang on to her composure disintegrated and once again she was excruciatingly conscious of the intimacy of their seated positions. Feeling her entire face heat up, she glanced away from the knowing glint in Brice's eyes.

He studied the rosy hue in her cheeks, thinking that if possible she looked all the more beautiful for it. "No woman in her right mind is going to place a governess or a nanny or a maid who looks like you beneath her husband's very nose. Especially when that husband has predilections that run toward the dissolute. Be thankful that you did not have the dubious pleasure of meeting his lordship."

Before she could even think, Elora's gaze flew to Brice's. Almost immediately, she glanced away, but not before Brice saw the unspoken disclosure.

He surged forward in his seat, his hand reaching out to take hold of her chin and tilt her face back to his. "What did he do?" he demanded in a rough whisper.

She shook her head, unable to meet his eyes.

His fingers tightened ever so slightly. "Look at me."

The command in his voice could not be denied. She lifted her gaze to his. Amazed, she found his face drawn tight.

"What happened?"

"Nothing, my lord."

"What did he say to you?"

"Nothing really. I just . . ." She paused, seeking the best way to define what there had been about Lord Ashton that had upset her so. "It wasn't what he said, but how he said it."

The green of Brice's eyes chilled dangerously. He knew James Ashton well enough to know that had the bastard offered her a cup of tea, the suggestion would have had all the connotations of a lewd proposition. Not surprisingly Elora was too innocent to fully understand the underlying intent.

She was guileless. Nothing could have pointed that out more clearly than the way she had responded in his arms last night. Her passion had been artless, untutored. But so erotically tempting that he had been completely swept away. She was capable of stirring up consuming desires, yet she did so unknowingly, not out of design. Incredibly, he wondered if she was even aware of the effect she had on men. He doubted it seriously, and that kind of naiveté could be dangerous when dealing with someone like James Ashton.

"He didn't do anything else, did he?"

For all the sharp intensity of his query, she found the touch of his fingers against her chin tender, and not unwelcome. Where Lord Ashton's touch had been repulsive, the contact of Brice's warm hand was more of a caress.

"No, my lord, he did nothing else."

As though to weigh her words, he nodded slowly. An odd silence fell between them, a stillness that could have been comforting. But the predicament in which Elora found herself loomed over her head.

He had countered her every objection to their marriage with calm reasoning. She was without a position, and thanks to Lady Ashton not likely to receive another. She had no means of providing for herself while creditors lurked one step behind her. He may not love her, but he at least liked her. He was willing to go to great lengths to give her a respectable future even though he was not in any way responsible for her welfare.

Realistically, she should be overjoyed. The most handsome, compelling man she had ever met, the only man to have ever stirred her passion, wanted to marry her. However, she could not ignore the yearnings of her heart. Staring earnestly into his eyes, she whispered, "I beseech you, put this notion of marriage aside."

His fingers still at her chin, Brice steadily returned her look. This may not have been the way he would have gone about choosing a wife, and she might be as hesitant as all hell about taking him as a husband, but he *knew* with absolute assurance that he could not let her go . . . not to the James Ashtons of the world. Not to anyone.

"I can't put this notion aside." In his mind he had claimed her as his own. It was only a formality that church and state sanction that to which he was already committed.

His thumb lightly stroked from the delicate line of her jaw to the sweet curve of her lips. "I want you as my wife, Elora."

Her eyelids drifted shut, blocking his fiercely resolved face from view. "My lord, perhaps you are allowing gratitude to affect your better judgment."

"Gratitude?" It had never entered his mind.

"Yes." She opened her eyes and regarded him sadly. "For my saving your life."

His hand left her chin and slipped back along her neck. His other hand joined in until he cradled her head and tilted her face up toward his. Lowering his mouth to hers, he stopped just short of kissing her. "This has nothing to do with gratitude."

Elora would have drawn in her breath, but Brice closed the space separating their mouths and any gasp that escaped her lips was captured by his. His tongue slipped into the warmth of her mouth and thoughts of gratitude flew out of her mind.

He had kissed her so last night, but she was still unprepared for the feel of his tongue gliding over hers. It thrust forward then retreated, only to do so again and send a wondrous heat coursing through her body. Of their own accord, her hands rose to grasp his jacket as his mouth slanted feverishly over hers.

"You are mine," he vowed fiercely, when he lifted his head. His green eyes inflamed with a rare, burning light, he insisted, "Marry me." As though to prevent any word of denial she might have uttered, he kissed her again, demandingly, possessively, making her head swirl.

"My lord," she whispered around ragged little pants.

"Say yes."

Her gaze locked with his. His eyes, usually so cold and remote, glowed with an inner fire that startled her. Staring past the fine lines of green and varying hues of gold, she beheld a near desperate need, a yearning that hinted at some inner torment that burdened his soul. The sight wrenched her heart.

That this strong, indomitable man would want her to such

depths was overwhelming, and so heartbreakingly touching that tears clogged her throat.

She sobered at her own reaction and levered away slightly. Resolutely she faced the issue of marriage, not because of all of his logical arguments, but because of the pain she sensed he held inside of him. She could only wonder what had put that icy resolve in his manner, who had stricken the humor from his eyes. Whatever the case, his torment was real and in some way it beckoned to her.

It wasn't easy for her to forsake her dream of having a marriage such as her parents'. But perhaps that was all it was, a dream best held close to her heart where it wouldn't be trampled on by harsh reality. And if she couldn't have love, what then? Marriage to a man she liked, despite his mercurial temperament, marriage to a man who in turn liked her. One who needed her, not as in a cherished dream or hope, but in true stark reality.

"Promise me you'll never hurt me." She saw his confusion and pique. "Promise me."

"Of course," he averred, wondering why in the devil she would need to exact such a pledge.

He was not offering her love, but she felt that in his own way, he was giving her all he was capable of giving.

Staring once again into his eyes, she vowed, "Yes, I will marry you."

Chapter

8

"EXCUSE ME, MISS."

Elora looked up from her breakfast. "Yes, Mr. Cobb."

The butler approached the dining room table where Elora sat alone. "I beg your pardon, miss, but are you home to callers?"

The question brought Elora up short. "Callers?"

"Yes, miss. Lady Barbara Richmond wishes a word with you."

The blue of Elora's eyes darkened at the mention of the woman's name. Brice had referred to her as the *grand dame* of all dowagers. She was his godmother, and from his description, a woman to be reckoned with.

"Me? Are you sure she isn't here to see Lady Vianne?"

Cobb dipped his head in a nod. "Quite certain, miss."

Elora blinked in amazement, then looked just beyond her plate to that morning's issue of *The Times*. It wasn't all that difficult to figure out why she would be receiving callers. The answer lay in the third-page announcement of her engagement to the Marquess of Warrington.

The thought shortened her breath. It was all happening so fast. Brice had asked her to marry him yesterday and by this morning it was official news, complete with its tangle of social obligations. Unfortunately she didn't have a blessed clue as to how she was supposed to handle those obligations.

Her upbringing had been a modest country affair. Under her father, she had been well educated, while her mother had overseen lessons in deportment and social niceties. But the dark years with her stepfather had allowed her little time or money for keeping company with anyone, least of all the gentry.

She didn't know what was expected of her as a future marchioness. Up until yesterday it wasn't something she would have ever considered. Now, she was having to behave accordingly by mingling with a member of the very same class that she had only the day before been fully prepared to serve. It was a daunting prospect, made even more so by the fact that she was completely on her own. Brice was out of the house and Vianne was abed with a headache.

Taking a fortifying breath, she gathered her resolve. When she had agreed to marry Brice, she had committed herself not only to him, but to his way of life as well. Their marriage might be based on respect and friendship rather than love, but she would do everything in her power to make the marriage all that it could possibly be. She would try her best to make Brice happy.

She laid aside her napkin and rose stiffly, trying not to grimace.

"Are you all right, miss?" Cobb asked, reaching out an assisting hand.

Elora waited for the twinge in her side to abate before answering. "Yes, thank you. I seem to be less than graceful this morning." She took another breath, this one for good measure. "Where is Lady Barbara?"

"I put her in the morning room, miss."

Fingers tightly entwined, Elora made her way to the door, but there she stopped. "Mr. Cobb, is it unusual for someone to visit at this hour?"

"Yes, miss, it is."

Elora hesitated, considering what sort of person would

knowingly call on a stranger at an inconvenient time. The answer she got was not reassuring. "Is she terribly fierce?"

"Not terribly, miss."

She tried to smile. "Good, because I would hate to make a fool of myself. I don't want to do anything that would reflect badly on his lordship."

"No, miss."

She followed the butler down the hall, grateful for his slow pace. After only several steps, she halted their progress again.

"Mr. Cobb, could you please bring us chocolate?"

"Of course, miss."

She nodded slowly, feeling a little better. She didn't know if offering chocolate at this hour was *correct* or *quite the thing,* but it was polite. She may not know the first thing about being a marchioness, but she knew everything there was about courtesy.

Bolstered by that thought, she entered the morning room with a pleasant smile, determined to make Lady Barbara welcome.

"Good morning, my lady," she commented, carefully crossing to the settee. She squinted slightly in an effort to gain a clear view of this dowager among dowagers.

Silently, she wished for her glasses as she gained her first good look at Brice's godmother. Lady Barbara sat regally in unrelieved black, her thin shoulders squared, shriveled lips pursed and brown eyes sparkling in blatant examination. Elora had the distinct impression that the woman noted everything from her simply arranged curls to the modest cut of her plain gray dress.

"Do you know who I am, young lady?" came the crackly, imperious voice.

"Yes, ma'am. His lordship has told me of your relationship."

"Good." The tip of her head, by a huge exaggeration, might have been considered a nod of approval. "So you are the young woman who saved my godson's life. Everyone is talking about you."

"So I have been told, my lady."

"Ha! Is that supposed to impress me?" Lady Barbara jabbed a gnarled finger at the air.

Elora took the brunt of the gray-haired matron's scrutiny, understanding immediately the critical tone this interview would take.

"To impress was never my intent, ma'am." Elora resisted the urge to clench her hands together. Instead, she cautiously lowered herself to the settee, bracing her right hand on the cushioned arm for support. The telltale movement did not go unnoticed.

"Now *that* is impressive," Lady Barbara declared.

"My lady?"

The sharp brown gaze scoured Elora's face as though seeking hidden clues to some mystery. "Is that modesty or stupidity?" Her aged mouth twisted to one side before she grumbled, "Probably a dose of each. After all, that's what makes up courage, isn't it? Just enough idiocy and humility not to be concerned for yourself." The boney finger jabbed at her knee in an urgent staccato. "I'm talking about your injury, missy, your injury. Most impressive."

The delicate curve of Elora's blond brows arched skeptically. "I would not call it that, my lady."

"Don't disagree with me, gel. If I say it's impressive, then it is." Her narrow chin came up majestically as once again she searched Elora's face. Finally she announced, "You've created quite a stir. What do you have to say for yourself?"

Feeling very much like she was expected to pass muster, Elora raised her own chin. "I am glad that I was able to save his lordship's life," she returned in a voice laden with an elegant dignity.

"No doubt you are." Something close to anger contorted her face. "You saved the man's life and wound up as the next Marchioness of Warrington."

Elora stiffened. The implication was clear. While Lady Barbara might applaud her for saving Brice, she had all but

107

called her a scheming adventuress who had used her injuries to gain a proposal.

"My lady," she stated rigidly, her ever expressive face registering her affront. "I see no reason why I should have to sit idly for your insinuation. Nonetheless, I will remember that my mother raised me to respect my elders." She ignored the increasing scowl directed at her. "I can only assume that as godmother to his lordship, you believe you are entitled to explanations. But I can say nothing that will alter your opinion of me. You will believe what you will. Anything that might convince you is a private matter between his lordship and myself. While others might not respect my privacy, I most definitely respect his."

Lady Barbara reared back in her chair, wearing her shock as badly as she wore her black satin hat with its outrageous ostrich plumes. Her lips worked for several seconds then quickly parted with the sounds of wicked laughter.

"Well-done, well-done," she crowed, slapping her knee in glee.

Nonplussed, Elora stared wide-eyed, trying to catch up with the sudden shift in mood.

Lady Barbara reined in on her humor. "Gave as good as you got, that's the way. Although, you'll have to curb the edges of that temper if you're going to go about with any style at all."

It finally dawned on Elora that she had somehow won the lady's approval. Not that it truly mattered, but she would much rather have this lady as her friend than not.

A shaming smile curved the corners of her mouth. "I was worried, my lady, that I would not be able to deal with English society. Something tells me that my fears are no longer necessary."

"True, I'm the worst of the worst. Or the best of the best, however you wish to view the thing."

"I think it would be prudent of me to choose the latter."

"Smart girl. Now, let's have a look at you."

"I thought you already had," Elora reminded her.

"Don't be impertinent with me, gel. Save that saucy

mouth for Warrington. Lord knows he'll know what to do with it."

It took several seconds for the meaning of Lady Barbara's words to sink in. When they did, Elora could not contain her embarrassment.

"There's no need for blushes, my dear," the elderly lady advised. "Every featherheaded miss that litters the *ton* would give her right front tooth to be in your shoes. Warrington's a man worth having."

Elora silently agreed, but she was saved from making a suitable comment by the arrival of Cobb. The stately butler entered the room carrying a tray bearing cups and a pot of steaming chocolate.

"As you ordered, miss," he intoned, placing the service on the low table between Elora and Lady Barbara.

His subtle hint that it was Elora who was responsible for the refreshments was not missed by the dowager. She gave the man a speculative look as he asked, "Do you wish me to pour, miss?"

But Lady Barbara was quick to answer. "No, no, we'll handle it ourselves, man."

Cobb stood unmoving, his gaze resting unwaveringly on Elora until she realized that he was respectfully waiting for *her* to reply.

"Thank you, Mr. Cobb, but I'll pour," she stated quietly, hiding a grateful smile.

Nodding, Cobb took his leave. The moment he did, Lady Barbara erupted with a shout that widened Elora's eyes. "Ha! I knew I was right."

"About what, ma'am?"

"About you. That man"—she pointed toward the door to indicate Cobb—"proves it."

"Mr. Cobb?"

"Yes, Cobb, uppity butler that he is. Without saying a word, he made certain that I deferred to you. My dear, if you've received a stamp of approval from Warrington's staff, then you are as good as gold. I was right in thinking that you're up to scratch."

Elora had trouble containing her dubious humor. Lady

Barbara had been far from supportive upon her arrival. "Would you care for some chocolate, ma'am?"

"No, none for me, my dear, although I appreciate the thought. I've overstayed my welcome as it is." She rose to her full five foot one inch of height. "When Warrington returns tell him I expect to see the two of you at my house four days from now. I plan to have a party in honor of your betrothal."

Coming to her feet, Elora stood amazed for a moment, touched that Lady Barbara would go out of her way to such a degree. "Thank you, my lady. I'll be sure and tell his lordship."

"Yes, yes, but I'll send an announcement around all the same." She adjusted her hat before she headed for the door. "Now, I'm off. I expect you will do just fine. You've already set the *ton* on its ear, and Warrington never was any better. Especially so after yesterday."

"Yesterday?" Elora asked, escorting Lady Barbara on her way.

"No fewer than ten people saw him carrying you into this very house, and in broad daylight at that. That kind of behavior is the stuff of audacity."

Her cackling laughter followed her from the room, and embedded itself in Elora's mind. More than once during the day, Elora recalled the lady's dry chuckles. The resulting smile that came to her lips added a sparkle to her blue eyes and a hint of color to her cheeks.

Seated on a cushioned bench in the garden behind the house, she looked at the tall boxwoods surrounding her. The hedge that shielded her from view of the house was a majestic affair, imposing and stately and she couldn't help but compare it to Lady Barbara. Once again, she smiled at the memory of the elderly lady's laugh . . . until she noticed Brice striding up the path toward her. All thoughts of amusement fled and her heart lurched into her throat. Immediately, she reached into her pocket for her missing glasses and wished she knew where she had misplaced them.

"Hello," she said, not knowing what else to say to this

impossibly handsome, intricately complex man who would soon be her husband.

"Good afternoon," he said, coming to stand before her.

Helplessly, Elora let her gaze stray along the long length of him. He was dressed formally. An impeccably tailored gray jacket outlined the breadth of his shoulders, the folds of his pristine cravat framing the hard edge of his jaw. But it wasn't the clothes that held her attention. It was the man.

A multitude of impressions hit her simultaneously: the remembered warmth of his muscular chest beneath her fingers, the unmovable strength of his arms, the feel of his mouth on hers. A little frantically, she wondered why she was besieged by the sensations now. Perhaps it was because she had agreed to marry him, or because he had relieved her of all her burdens. Or it might be because of the way he had kissed her the day before, searing her lips until he had snatched away her breath. For whatever reasons, her heart now pounded wildly and a fine trembling began in her fingers.

He radiated some kind of energy that disarmed her. She had sensed it the first morning she had awakened and discovered him standing in her doorway. She had been struck then by his aura of stark masculinity. That essence had only increased with time.

"Did you have a nice day?" Her voice sounded too thick.

His dark brows quirked upward. "Reasonably so. And you?"

She shrugged with her hands, then clasped them together to hide their shaking. "Lady Barbara called this morning."

He muttered something nasty under his breath. "So Cobb has informed me. That old harridan is a plague to mankind. I'm sorry I wasn't here to deflect the worst of her barbs."

His concern surprised her as much as it touched her. "Oh, there wasn't any need, really. We got along quite well after the first few moments." She gave him a hesitant smile. "But thank you for wanting to be here."

He worked his jaw. He had most definitely wanted to be here. Annoyingly he had spent the better portion of the day fighting the urge to return home and seek her out. For no apparent reason.

"Well, you don't look any worse for your time spent with her."

"No injuries, I promise."

Staring intently at her curving lips, his voice lowered. "How are you feeling?"

"Tired, a little stiff, but no real pain."

That pleased him. He could recall all too clearly the agony she had suffered.

In a quicksilver instant, he recalled other, more distracting images. His mind pictured her generous breasts, smoothly curved legs and the soft thatch of golden curls at the juncture of her thighs.

He drew in a sharp breath and could not release it. Once again his control slipped in a manner least expected. Damn it, he wasn't some untried youth. He was a man well accustomed to women, a man in full command of his sexual appetite. Still the blood was pounding into his loins, making him want to reach down, pull her up into his arms and kiss her until they were both senseless and he was buried deep inside her body.

He stepped away to one of the tall boxwoods that blocked the house from sight, using the time and distance to still his desire. After several frustratingly long seconds, he wasn't sure which was worse, getting assailed by the sorcery of her eyes or being beset by this raging hunger.

"I've made arrangements for you to be fitted with a new wardrobe."

His hard tone as well as his words brought Elora's head up sharply. Dismayed, she stared at his rigidly set face. She drew breath to protest, then abruptly clamped her lips together.

Her gaze dropped to her gray dress. It was the same dress she had worn that morning to meet Lady Barbara. Made of muslin, it was well constructed with a lace edging around the modest neckline. As dresses went, it was one of her best, but compared to the expensively cut and detailed dress Lady Barbara had worn, it was sadly lacking.

She fingered the fabric of her skirt dejectedly. She couldn't deny that she needed gowns more appropriate to her new position as Brice's wife. She only wished that she could afford to purchase them herself without having to rely on his generosity. It was humiliating enough that he had insisted on paying her stepfather's debts. The added expense of a new wardrobe only made her realize just what a charity case she really was.

Judging by the caustic sound of Brice's voice, he realized it, too. "Thank you." Her voice was low with regret.

Green eyes narrowed in irritation. "You don't sound pleased."

She lifted her chin to return his look. "Neither do you."

"What the devil do you mean?"

"I am sorry that you have to incur yet another financial burden on my behalf." Having said that, her composure failed. She glanced away from his cold, all too penetrating eyes.

He returned to where she sat, his face drawn into bewildered lines. "Would you mind telling me what this is about?"

Her eyes shut briefly. "I think you already know."

But he truly didn't. Impatiently, he crossed his arms over his chest and said, "For the sake of this discussion, why don't you enlighten me."

She exhaled in mounting frustration, her embarrassment tripling at having to explain. "My lord, do you think that just because I am without a penny that I am also without some pride? How do you think it makes me feel knowing that all I am bringing to this marriage is bills and more bills?"

He grunted a sound of annoyance. "I thought we settled this yesterday."

"I thought we had, too."

"Then why are you making an issue of it?"

"Because you obviously resent this matter of a wardrobe."

He stared at her as though she were demented. "You are mistaken."

"Am I? Then why did you sound so angry when you said that you had arranged for a new wardrobe? Why are you so angry with me right now?"

Of their own accord, his hands did exactly what he had imagined them doing earlier. They reached down and pulled her to her feet, imprisoning her against his chest.

"I don't give a bloody good damn about your clothes, other than I'd prefer you not wearing any at all."

She gasped, her eyes rounding enormously, but he stepped all over her shock and muttered, "What you heard in my voice wasn't anger. It was this."

Like a black raven swooping down from the clouds, his dark head lowered. His mouth captured hers precisely as his hands had captured her body, urgently and with little warning.

His lips savored hers, molding, caressing, rediscovering their shape as though it had been years since he had last tasted her. He held her tightly, feeling her along every starving inch of him. She was soft and warm . . . everywhere; her trembling lips beneath his, her full breasts pressed to his chest, the gentle curve of her belly against his hardened length.

"This is what you heard, Elora," he groaned against the corner of her mouth. "This need that you instill in me until I don't have a mind." His mouth came back to hers, shaping her lips to the contours of his own, parting them for his tongue.

A low moan sounded deep in Elora's throat at the searing invasion that stripped her defenses to nothing. She trembled with a desire that she had come to know in his arms alone. When ingrained proprieties would have tugged at her conscience, she turned them away, responding to Brice's need as she responded to her own.

Yes, her heart whispered.

She gave herself up to the kiss without reservation or thought, her limbs melting with a sweet lassitude. His tongue swept over hers, withdrew then repeated the pattern until instinctively she returned the caress.

Yes, her heart cried.

At the feel of her tongue sliding over his lips, Brice thought he would drop to his knees. Her response was all that he could have wanted, more than he had hoped for. She was giving herself to him with an honesty that was elemental to her nature, the same kind of sincerity that made her face shine with every emotion she felt. She could no more hide her need for him than she could hide a lie.

The quintessential maleness in him gloried in the fact that he affected her as much as she did him. It was a heady reality that sent one of his hands to the small of her back to press her tightly against his thighs.

His breath stopped in his lungs. Agonizingly sweet vibrations spread out in every direction, assuaging the raging need for a brief, blissful moment. But all too soon, the need was back, more fervently intense than it had been just seconds before.

He tore his mouth from hers, kissing a path to her ear. Her name escaped his lips like a ragged caress as he released the row of buttons that ran down the front of her bodice. Long masculine fingers slipped beneath her chemise and stroked the sweet flesh within.

Elora managed no more than a strained sigh. She was perched on the edge of a precipice of desire and fear. Once before she had stopped him at this very point . . . and she had been left yearning to discover . . . What? She didn't know. Now she held her breath, anticipating, fearing only that she would be left wanting again.

Brice dipped his head and kissed the first swell of her breast, pulling more and more of her chemise aside until her sweet fullness was bared to his view. Gently, he took the rosy crest into his mouth and she cried out softly.

Whatever she could have imagined in her innocent confusion, nothing could have prepared her for the feel of his tongue and lips. Wondrous shivers raced down to the core of her, turning her legs to water.

"Brice," she choked out, clasping her hands together behind his neck. But his arms tightened about her, supporting her weight effortlessly. All the while, his mouth seared her breast with a consuming heat, his hand urging her dress and chemise down over her shoulder.

I don't give a bloody good damn about your clothes, other than I'd prefer you not wearing any at all.

His words came back to her, fighting for space in her passion-drugged mind. Her eyes opened, their indigo depths reflecting her puzzlement. This wasn't the first time he wanted her out of her clothing.

"Brice?"

Hearing her whisper his head came up. He saw her candid bewilderment and his brows lowered.

"No," she said, soothing her fingertips over the lines of his frown. "No, don't be angry . . . it's just that I . . . don't . . . ." She searched his gaze for answers. "I'm so ignorant in these matters."

Her words froze as she tried to make sense of only half-formed suspicions. Blinking rapidly, she glanced away, then peered up into his green gaze again. "That night in your bed, you wanted to remove my nightgown. Now again, my clothes . . ." She swallowed. "I don't . . . I mean . . . I think you should know that if there is something that I should have been taught, I wasn't."

Through the haze of desire clenching at his insides, Brice stared into her painfully expectant face, shocked. "Elora," he groaned, struggling with his body's demands as he tried to make sense of her words.

"Well," she said, seeing his disbelief. "I'm not so stupid that I don't know why you want me naked."

Straining against the blood surging in his loins, he demanded, "Why are you even bringing this up?"

Her face fell, the curve of her lips turning downward in dismay. "Because like my lack of a dowry and my lack of suitable clothing, I am also apparently lacking a certain . . .

understanding of precisely what occurs between men and women." Sighing, she looked away. "I thought you should know."

Brice could scarcely believe his ears. She was actually apologizing for an ignorance that was part and parcel of her virtue.

He shut his eyes, sobering to the magnitude of what had just transpired. He had been well on his way to taking her, with no thought to her virtue or her ignorance. If she hadn't said a word, he wouldn't have stopped until they were both replete and exhausted.

He needed to cool his blood. Now. If not for her honor than his own sanity. But that was impossible with her soft curves pressed against him. He swore beneath his breath, and released her so suddenly that she had to steady herself against the bench.

Elora's fingers flew to her breasts, restoring order to her bodice. Her wide gaze was fastened on Brice's back as he stalked to an ancient-looking sundial. For long seconds he seemed to calmly study the patina on the bronze piece, but even through the space between them she could feel the waves of his anger.

Habit urged her to be wary, but her experience with Brice thus far had taught her not to judge him by her stepfather's behavior. She very much wanted to trust him.

"Brice? What's wrong?"

What was wrong? He was standing there in an agony of desire so great that his muscles were shaking, all because she again somehow, someway managed to make him lose control. Damn her. He knew when he had pulled her off that bench that she was a virgin, but the second he kissed her, that fact had vanished from his mind. Hell, he hadn't even been left with a mind. She had snatched that away and left him with a body that had a will of its own.

Damn her. He did not lose control of himself, not for any reason. Ever. Mentally, he laughed in jeering contempt at that notion. All he had done since she had fallen into his arms was lose control. He detested that. Immensely.

Swinging back abruptly, he pinned her with a gaze that was chilling. "Get into the house."

Trembling, Elora stared at the fury on his face. "Brice, what have I done?"

"Get upstairs," he bit out, *before I lose control and take you right here on the ground.*

She didn't wait to be told again. On shaking legs, she hurried up the path, alarm and dread chasing her all the way to her room.

Brice watched her retreat through narrowed eyes, not really seeing her fleeing figure at all. His mind and body were locked in a struggle for mastery and it was all he could do not to bellow at the cloudy sky.

Long moments passed before he could take a steady breath. Even longer moments elapsed before he stalked into the house and entered his study. Stirred to a savage restlessness, he paced the room until he at last found himself by a glass cabinet containing some of his most prized possessions.

He stared at the ancient artifacts, forcing himself to be distracted by their aura of permanence. It was just the diversion he needed to take his mind from Elora and the effects she had on him.

Unfortunately, among the treasures lay the Sennedjem Papyrus. The Egyptian scroll brought to mind another problem that plagued his life of late.

A bitter resentment billowed to full glory within him. The entire business of someone trying to kill him was galling. Damnably as the minutes crawled by, he could not prevent himself from picturing each suspect plotting with hired murderers.

He credited the Duke of Westford with enough finesse not to actually meet with his henchman. His grace was worldly enough to employ a second or even third party as a buffer to such a nefarious plot.

The Earl of Stanley, on the other hand, was a much more blunt person, one who was more prone to actually pulling the trigger himself. The likelihood of that was possible, especially given his lordship's blatant need for revenge.

Like the earl, Katherine Warfield was not at all subtle. She had never made any pretenses about her coveting his title and wealth for her son. But he could not see her aiming a pistol, nor mingling with killers and miscreants. As disdainful as she was, she would make sure that she was as removed from the situation as she could get.

Such discretion was something to which his cousin Thorbon paid little heed in his private life. The old codger was as flagrant about taking a wench as he was about overindulging in Madeira. But how he would go about arranging a murder was a mystery.

Pressing his hand to the cabinet's glass, Brice flexed his fingers rhythmically as he examined the situation from all directions. No, he didn't think any of the four had personally pulled the trigger. Or had tried to break into the house. Each in his or her own way had too much to lose by actually getting caught red-handed: the duke, his reputation and position; the earl, his pride; Katherine and Thorbon, the security of a possible inheritance. No, each needed to be as removed from possible exposure as possible.

His gaze focused on the papyrus once more. It irritated him to no end that he was forced to dwell on this. But until he had his answers as to who wanted him dead, he knew that his thoughts would be fully occupied with the matter.

"My lord?"

Brice turned at the sound of Marcus Quinn's polite interruption. He gave the man a testy look. "What are you doing here, Marcus? We don't have a meeting scheduled until tomorrow morning."

"Yes, my lord," the stout secretary apologized. "But you told me to get this to you as soon as the jeweler had it finished." He handed Brice a small velvet box.

Brice flipped open the lid. Twinkling back at him was a flawless blue sapphire set in intricate twists of gold. Elora's betrothal ring.

"I hope it meets with your approval, my lord," Marcus prompted. "The jeweler said that the stone is one of a kind. He has never seen that particular shade of blue."

Brice nodded, thinking that the sapphire was the exact same blue of Elora's eyes. "Yes," he retorted tightly, "this is fine."

"I am glad you find the ring acceptable, my lord."

Brice merely nodded, but he could see Marcus gathering himself. "Yes?"

"May I take this moment to congratulate you on your upcoming nuptials, my lord."

Brice gripped the box tightly. "That will be all for today." He ignored the secretary's discomfited grimace and his quick exit.

With the closing of the door, he sighed heavily. The lonely sound echoed off the book-lined walls, only to return as a discordant sneer, mocking him for a fool. Irritably, he took a seat behind his desk, setting the jeweler's box on the flat surface before him.

Silence was his companion. Silence and the steady gleam of the sapphire. His gaze strayed to the ring. Almost reluctantly, he removed it from its bed of velvet.

It was perfect. The cut and clarity of the stone was superb, while the gold filigree was delicately wrought into a deceptively strong setting. The ring was both beautiful and unique.

It was supposed to be a symbol of his affections.

He shied away from the thought and tried the ring on the smallest finger of his left hand. It barely slipped past his nail. It would fit Elora well.

"Elora." He whispered her name, slowly shaking his head in self-disgust. His conscience pricked him with an unfamiliar twinge of regret. He hadn't meant to take his anger out on her, but it seemed he did that. Often. It was no wonder she had been reluctant as all hell to marry him.

Mentally he squirmed at the admission and cursed soundly. He didn't normally give a tinker's damn what anyone thought of him. But he could not deny that Elora's opinion did matter. At that moment, she was probably thinking him the worst sort of boor, and he couldn't blame her. He had lashed out at her for his own ungovernable reactions to her. Unfortunately as innocent as she was, she couldn't even begin to comprehend that, not when she didn't fully comprehend why he would want to remove her clothes.

He looked back to the ring and saw the same clear, honest color that shone in Elora's eyes. That kind of sincerity couldn't be ignored and it didn't deserve to be trampled.

Shoving out from behind the desk, he left the room and climbed the curving stairway to her door. He rapped twice and her muffled call bade him enter.

He found her standing at one of the windows, staring down to the garden below, her arms wrapped tightly about her waist.

"Elora."

She turned her head sharply, surprise widening her eyes. Unconsciously she took a step back, drawing Brice's immediate attention.

He muffled the curse that came to his lips; his mouth thinned to a bitter line. Closing the space separating them, he stood within arm's reach. He could tell that she had been crying.

"Elora." Now that he was here, he didn't even know where to start. The sight of a remnant tear caressing her cheek gave him some direction. Reaching out, he traced the path the tear had taken.

The feel of her skin warmed his palm. Instantly, he yanked his hand back, scrubbing his fist against his chin. "You need to know that my anger was not directed at you. I was angry with myself."

Her face remained impassive, neither believing nor condemning his words. "Why?"

Because I allow you to break down barriers that I have fought long and hard to erect. "Because you made me want you more than was safe," he said, giving her an answer he knew would suffice. But the minute he spoke the words, he knew she wouldn't understand. Her baffled look confirmed that.

He raked a hand through his hair as he searched his mind for the best way to explain this to her. "You said you don't understand what occurs between men and women. You don't need to fret over that. Once we're married, I'll show you all there is to know about making love."

She gave a huge sigh, relieved that she wasn't as inadequately prepared to be his wife as she had thought, and also because he had once again proven himself to be a man unlike her stepfather. He had not resorted to violence as a means of expressing his rage.

A very real affection flowed about her heart, bringing a soft smile to her lips. "Thank you for telling me. I'm glad that I wasn't the cause of your anger." She frowned delicately, her eyes filling with concern. "I know that I was hesitant to come to this marriage, but now that I have, I want to do everything I can to make you happy."

Staring into her eyes, Brice's guard came up. He waited tensely for some overwhelming surge to inundate him. The seconds ticked by and all he saw was a serene, pure blue so like the sapphire.

He reached to his left hand and removed the ring, then slipped it onto her finger. "Every betrothal starts this way."

Elora's lips parted. "Oh, Brice, this is lovely," she breathed in wonder, staring at the stone that was at least as large as her fingernail. "Thank you."

"You're welcome."

Overwhelmed by his thoughtfulness that had prompted such a magnificent gift, she acted on impulse and rose to her toes. Before Brice knew what she was about, she pressed her lips to his. The kiss was poignantly sweet, touchingly shy . . . and arousing enough to fan every flame of desire Brice thought had been tamped down.

Stiffening, he turned for his room, furious with her once more for slipping past his every defense.

Chapter
9

"WELL, WHAT DO YOU THINK?" VIANNE ASKED, WAVING A SLEN-
der hand toward the numerous shops lining Oxford Street.

"I think," Elora replied in awe, "that I have never seen the
likes. We only have a handful of shops in Yately, where I
grew up. Certainly nothing to compare to this."

Vianne laughed gaily, elated by Elora's delight. For the
better part of the morning, they had been strolling along one
of London's most fashionable shop districts, and Elora had
been like a child at Christmas.

The assortment of wares displayed in finely decorated
windows drew her enthusiastic acclaim. Items that Vianne
took for granted gave Elora pause. Bonnets and books, silks
and prints all captured her attention, and more than once
lured her into a particular store for a closer look.

But look was all Elora did, Vianne noticed. No amount of
prompting on Vianne's part could convince Elora to purchase a single item. Elora simply shook her head, thanked
the shopkeeper politely and departed for the next store. It
was rather baffling, especially since Brice had given Elora
carte blanche to purchase whatever she desired.

"Oh, Elora, look at that necklace." Vianne stopped to
view the display in a jeweler's window. "Those pearls would
look lovely with your white crepe evening dress."

From the rounding of Elora's eyes behind her spectacles, Vianne could tell that her soon-to-be sister-in-law agreed that the double strand of pearls was stunning in its simplicity. Vianne also noted from the hesitancy marring Elora's brow that she was uncomfortable with the idea of buying the necklace.

"It would even complement the gown you're wearing now," Vianne urged.

Looking thoroughly amazed, Elora took in her fashionable dress of pale yellow muslin, complemented with a dark blue spencer and matching bonnet.

"You're right, of course, Vianne, but . . ."

"But what?"

"Brice has spent too much as it is. Just thinking about the countless gowns, shawls, shoes, hats and underclothing takes my breath away."

"It shouldn't. Brice was more than willing to see you dressed as befitting your new position."

"Yes, I know," Elora said, unable to hide the uneasiness she was obviously feeling. "He went to such pains. I didn't think it was possible for dressmakers to work so quickly."

Vianne could not contain her laughter. "It was rather amazing. But you have to realize that when Brice sets his mind to something, he usually gets his way." She shrugged prettily. "He wanted the clothes within a week, and that's what you got."

"Regardless of the cost."

Vianne's humor came to a startled pause. "Is that what's bothering you? The thought of Brice spending his money?"

"A rather exorbitant amount of money."

Vianne beamed a smile that knew no bounds. Disregarding any curious stares she might receive from passersby, she gave Elora a fierce little hug. "Oh, you silly goose. Do you know how long it's been since Brice has taken this much interest in anything other than his relics? Years, Elora, years. I am just so thankful that you came along. Not only did you save him from being killed, but you saved him from himself."

"Why do you say that?"

A touch of melancholy dulled the gleam in Vianne's eyes. "I think you know why. You've come to know my brother. You know what he can be like."

"Yes. I don't think he's happy."

"He hasn't been."

"Why is that?"

Why indeed? Vianne knew the answers only too well, but she hesitated in telling the whole of it, for nothing she said could possibly do justice to the anguish Brice had been living with. The explanations, if and when they came, should come from Brice. Only then could Elora fully understand the depths of his suffering.

"Despite the outward impressions he gives, my brother is an extremely sensitive man. Sadly, he has had to endure bitter grief in his life." She took Elora's hand in her own. "But now that he has you, I can hope that he will put that all in the past." It was a wonderful thought that brightened Vianne's mood at once.

"I really do think we should go in for a closer look at the pearls," she coaxed, all too willing to ride the buoyancy produced from her newfound faith in Brice.

Elora looked back at the necklace, and shook her head. "No, I don't think so."

"But you don't have any jewelry, and you're going to need at least a few baubles."

Smiling, Elora countered, "I need air and food and water. I don't *need* jewelry."

"But it just isn't *chic* to go about with nothing."

"You said it wasn't *chic* to go about with my spectacles either, but here I am."

"Yes, and throwing my words back at me. It almost makes me wish we hadn't found the blasted things." The spectacles had finally been located beneath Elora's bed, and Elora had insisted on wearing them despite Vianne's suggestions to the contrary. "Well, I have to admit that only you could turn wearing glasses into a matter of style. But I still wish you would at least consider the pearls."

Elora gazed to her left hand and a soft light entered her eyes. "With this ring I don't need any other jewelry."

Vianne's gaze followed Elora's and all her arguments ceased momentarily. The ring was magnificent, its solitary sapphire sparkling in its intricate gold setting. But more importantly, it was inspiring. For too long, she had feared that Brice would never take a wife, that he would spend the rest of his life alone.

"It is a beautiful ring," she agreed, a well of happiness choking off her voice.

One of Elora's shoulders rose in a small shrug. "It is more than I ever dreamed of."

Vianne reached out and gently clasped Elora's hand. "I think it's wonderful that you're going to marry Brice."

"Thank you. It means so much to me to know that you approve. I only hope that I can make Brice happy."

Vianne hoped so too. For Elora's sake as well as Brice's. "Everything will be just fine," she said with more confidence than she felt. "Now, why don't we go speak to the jeweler?"

Elora's laugh was one of good-natured stubbornness. "I'm not going to let you talk me into purchasing the pearls, Vianne. I will let you talk me into going home for tea."

Vianne gave in graciously. "All right, but only because we've been out for hours. I don't want you tiring yourself for tomorrow night."

The reminder of Lady Barbara's party made Elora shudder. "Oh, Vianne, I'm frightfully nervous about this party."

"It's just going to be a small affair."

"Large or small," Elora countered uneasily, "I so dislike the idea of being the focus of everyone's attention. My hands will be shaking so hard, I'll probably spill soup down the front of one of my new gowns."

Laughing, Vianne shook her head. "Don't worry about a thing. Brice will be with you, and so will Colin and I."

At the mention of Vianne's husband, Elora gave in to a chuckle. As soon as Vianne had been told of the engagement, she had sent word to her husband immediately, requesting that he join her in London. Invitations to balls and parties, all in honor of the betrothal, had begun to pour in, and she had no intention of attending any of the functions without her husband.

But beyond that, Vianne missed Colin. Pure and simple and she made no pretenses about it at all.

"I will be grateful for any extra support I can get," Elora confessed. "When is he expected to arrive?"

"His note promised he would be here this afternoon sometime. I can't wait for you to meet him." Vianne's face beamed. "He is too dear for words."

On the tail of her avowal, a woman's chilling voice sounded from nearby. "You can only be talking of the viscount, Cousin Vianne."

Elora and Vianne turned as one to discover a tall, austere woman behind them. Dressed in a dark carriage dress, the severity of her clothes seemed a perfect complement to her sharp features.

"Cousin Katherine," Vianne declared in surprise. "I didn't know you were in London."

Katherine Warfield hitched her pointed chin up several notches. "There's a great deal you don't know about me or my doings. But no need for wonder. I do manage to come to town upon occasion . . . when I can afford to do so." She snapped her head toward Elora. "Who is this?"

Common courtesy prevented Vianne from saying what she thought of the irascible woman. As amiably as she could, she made the introductions.

"So you're the little amazon I read about in the paper," Katherine remarked, giving Elora a bland look. "I thought it was an interesting touch the way the papers recounted your heroics along with the announcement of your engagement." Her gray gaze scratched over Elora's figure before she sighed pityingly. "One can only hope that Brice is happy."

Elora felt the distinct need to defend herself, but before she could say anything, Vianne interrupted. "Brice is delirious. Not that it should be any concern of yours."

A travesty of a smile soured Katherine's face, barely

camouflaging the disdain and jealousy roiling through her. "Didn't you know, Vianne, that everything even remotely concerning Brice is of interest to me?" She made a show of nodding politely. "I will see you both tomorrow night at Lady Barbara's. Make sure you give my best to Brice. I cannot wait to see him." Without another word, she swept past, leaving the two women to stare in shock.

"What on earth did I do to offend her?" Elora asked in amazement, trying to find an explanation for the woman's rude behavior.

"Katherine was born offended. She is envious and spiteful, always crying poor when she is in fact very well off. I'm only sorry that you had to meet her, but I suppose it was bound to happen sooner or later. She comes out of the woodwork every now and then." She paused to roll her eyes. "Usually she's home doting on her only son to an almost fanatical degree. It's positively frightening at times the way she carries on about him."

"You say she is your cousin?"

"By marriage, to be exact. We don't see much of her, just often enough for no one to forget that her son is the Warrington heir." She held up a hand in a bid to restore her humor. "I don't want to think about her anymore. It's time for you and I to have our tea."

Elora was only too glad to follow Vianne's suggestion, and moments later they were ensconced in Brice's carriage. All thoughts of Katherine Warfield were left behind, and the conversation that ensued on the way back to the town house was both light and jovial.

"I shall have to tell Brice that you are a penny-pincher of the highest degree." Vianne laughed as she stepped down from the carriage. "It is just unheard of to go shopping and not spend a farthing."

Climbing the stairs to the front door, Elora teased back. "It was in your mind that we were shopping, Vianne. I never once suggested that we were out to buy anything. I already have more than enough."

Cobb opened the front door, and Vianne glided into the

foyer. "Whatever you do, Elora, don't mention such a thing within earshot of anyone. Women will think you're crazed and men will want to kiss your feet."

Elora laughed as she, too, stepped into the foyer. "Hello, Mr. Cobb," she said around her chuckles.

"Good afternoon, miss."

"Have you had a pleasant morning?"

"Yes, thank you, miss."

Her laughter dwindled to an expectant sigh. "Is his lordship in?"

"Yes, miss. He and Viscount Redsdale are in his study."

Vianne's eyes widened. "Colin is here already?" Not waiting for an answer, she spun about and rushed down the hall.

Elora followed at a slower pace. When she entered the study, it was to find Vianne in the arms of a tall, blond gentleman whom Elora could only assume was Colin Drake.

"Oh, Colin, how I've missed you," Vianne declared, her radiant gaze drinking in the sight of her husband.

Colin cupped her chin in one hand. "The sentiment is returned tenfold, my sweet." Lowering his head to hers, he kissed her with a tender passion.

Elora stood rooted where she was, feeling as though she were intruding on a private moment. It was obvious that Vianne and Colin had missed each other terribly. It was also apparent that they were very much in love.

Unbidden, a wistful yearning tugged at Elora's heart. The couple shared the kind of love that she had always hoped to have in a marriage. The kind of love that sprang unburdened from the heart to transcend time and distance.

Her gaze burnished with a poignant longing, she looked away only to find Brice staring at her from beside the fireplace, his green eyes boring into her. Her pulse skipped a beat.

Quickly, she stared down at her clasped hands, putting her hopes and dreams away. She hadn't meant to pull them forth, but the visible proof of Vianne and Colin's love had caught her unawares.

She stood awkwardly, not knowing whether she should make a hasty departure or simply wait as discreetly as possible. In a flustered gesture, she loosened the satin ribbons beneath her chin and removed her bonnet just as Colin and Vianne stepped apart.

"I should leave you alone more often," Vianne suggested, looking adoringly up into Colin's face.

"I admit, there is something to be said about the re-unions," Colin answered with a wicked smile.

Brice shoved away from the fireplace. "Are you two just about finished?" His voice was as dry as centuries-old parchment.

"For now," Colin said, from all appearances unperturbed by his brother-in-law's chiding.

Vianne tried to hide her shameless smile, but she wasn't very successful. "I don't feel the need to apologize to anyone for giving my husband a warm welcome." She did, however, step out from under Colin's arm and hold out a hand to Elora in invitation. "Elora, do come meet Colin."

Elora glided toward Vianne's tall, broad-shouldered husband. He was a handsome man, possessing an angular face with a wide mouth and a strong chin. Deep-set, dark brown eyes studied her kindly.

"It is a pleasure to meet you, Miss Simmons."

Elora felt an instant liking for the man. "Thank you, my lord."

Vianne chuckled. "That was nicely done, but please let us put the formality aside. We are, after all, going to be one happy family." She enthusiastically looked to Elora and then Colin for their agreement. Her gaze slid more reluctantly to Brice. "Did you have a good trip?" she asked, turning back to Colin.

"No problems to speak of. We made good time. My trunks should arrive shortly."

Elora felt as much as saw Vianne's uncertainty. She studied Brice's sister, wondering at the abrupt shift in the woman's mood.

"Brice," Vianne began slowly. "My stay here was supposed to have been short, and not worth the bother of having our town house opened. If you would prefer that we not remain here, I will have our things sent over as quickly as possible."

With those few words, Elora understood the reasons for Vianne's unease. Now that she was joined by her husband, Vianne apparently was doubtful of her continued welcome in Brice's house. It was a horrible notion.

Dismayed, Elora looked up into Brice's shuttered face and discovered him staring straight at her with eyes so empty that it sent a chill over her skin.

"Of course, Elora will join us," Vianne was saying.

Unbelievably, Elora saw a sudden flash of emotion flare for an instant in Brice's gaze. Its unexpected appearance caught her off guard, prompting her to search the green orbs for more of the same. All she found was the return of the habitual coldness that she had come to know so well.

A trick of the light, she told herself, turning her attention to the fireplace. More likely, wishful thinking on her part.

"I see no reason why you can't stay," Brice uttered stiffly.

Elora's head came up, her gaze flying to Brice's. Just as she had felt Vianne's discomfort, she now felt her fiancé's. His tension was like a hand clenching her lungs, but there was no telling from his inscrutable face what he was thinking. Unfortunately, she could not shake the sensation that whatever it was, she was to blame.

She was never more grateful to hear Vianne's voice break the silence.

"Why don't I order tea, if that is all right with everyone."

"That sounds wonderful," Elora agreed.

Conversation drifted from that point. The group settled into the sofa and chairs by the French doors, and tea was served within moments. Brice was his usual taciturn self. It was obvious to Elora that he was not in an agreeable frame of mind. His penetrating gaze would stray to her face, linger, then snap away, only to have the pattern repeat itself again and again. By the time everyone finished with tea, and Colin escorted Vianne to their rooms, Elora was unnerved. She was greatly relieved when Cobb entered the study.

"Excuse me, miss, but there is a Reverend Platt to see you."

Elora started visibly. "Josiah? Here?" Shock and pleasure mixed freely in her voice. "Oh, yes, Mr. Cobb, please show him in."

"Am I to take it," Brice inquired in precise tones, "that this is the same Reverend Platt that arranged for your position as governess?"

"Yes, and I can hardly believe that he is here, in London of all places." Completely distracted, she missed the criticism saturating Brice's voice. Coming to her feet, she explained, "He and his mother have always been dear friends."

His eyes narrowing, Brice watched the dear friend in question walk in. A short, middle-aged man with thinning brown hair, the Reverend Platt was in Brice's estimation as weak and worthless as his receding chin suggested. Any man who would send a woman as artless and trusting as Elora into the world to face someone like James Ashton was deserving of nothing less than contempt.

Unaware of Brice's cold, unwavering glare, Josiah Platt crossed to Elora, his round stomach leading the way. "Oh, what a relief to find you well," he fretted.

"Josiah, what a surprise," Elora exclaimed. She took his hands in her own, a full, dazzling smile lighting her face.

"I can well imagine that my calling has taken you aback, but when I read of your mishap in the paper, I was beside myself with worry." He stepped away and surveyed her in gladdened awe, scanning first her face and then the rest of her. "But I can see that you are recovered."

"Yes, fully."

"For that, I thank the Lord above." His pale, round face seemed to whiten even more, and his thin lips curved into a crooked line. "I count myself responsible for your being here, and the danger you have encountered."

"Oh, Josiah, you mustn't. You and I both know that it was my decision to come to London."

"Yes, but I could not forgive myself if you had come to harm."

Deeply moved by his concern, her gaze turned wistful. "I am fine, Josiah, I promise. I was well looked after by his lordship." She turned to Brice where he sat opposite her, drawing Josiah's gaze along. "May I introduce to you the Marquess of Warrington."

Josiah bowed effusively. "My lord, a pleasure, I assure you."

Rising, Brice intoned coolly, "Reverend."

Still amazed by Josiah's arrival, Elora shook her head. She hadn't realized until she had seen his wonderfully familiar face just how much she missed her friends from home. "Oh, Josiah, I'm so glad to see you. Please, sit down. Can I pour you some tea?" Her words bubbling, she sank onto the sofa.

He waved away her offer as he sat in the chair vacated by Colin. "No, thank you. I cannot stay. I meant only to convince myself of your welfare."

"I am quite all right, truly."

"I can see that now."

"What brings you here to London? I never thought to see you again."

Under bushy brows, his limpid brown eyes rolled heavenward. "Ecclesiastical matters. A meeting with the bishops, but I vowed to check on you before all else."

"Now that you have, you can set your mind at ease."

"Mother's as well."

Elora's expression softened. "How is she?"

"Fine. She's gone off to live with her sister for a while."

Elora remembered the sweet elderly woman and her sister with fondness. "And Mrs. Drew? Is she still fussing over finding husbands for her daughters?"

"Of course."

"And Mr. Philpot, did he finally recover from the cough?"

The reverend chuckled at the barrage of questions. "Elora, London hasn't changed you a bit."

133

"Did you think it would?"

Some of Josiah's humor fled. "Nothing ever stays the same. People change, situations change." He looked to Brice in all seriousness. "You are to be congratulated on your betrothal, my lord. I have known Elora for nigh on ten years and I have never met a more generous heart nor a more divine soul."

Brice refused all consideration of the possibilities of souls, but he would agree to the matter of generosity. Elora was the most unselfish person he had ever known. "I regard myself a most fortunate man, Reverend."

"It does my heart good to hear that, my lord. Elora has always been very special."

With deceptive nonchalance, Brice rested his elbow on the chair and lifted a hand to stroke his chin. "Is that why you agreed to help her obtain a situation here in London?"

Josiah's narrow mouth puckered with a lopsided grin. "It was the least I could do. She was left in terrible straits." He fidgeted uneasily in his seat. "I assume Elora did inform you of the problems her stepfather created."

"She told me."

"Then you can see that there was little else for her to do. She was determined to repay the debts, and the only place she could possibly earn enough money was here in London."

Brice thought it would have been a reasonable explanation, if he had been in a reasonable mood. As it was, he wanted to smash the minister's face for his cavalier attitude toward Elora. "How did you manage to arrange for her to be in Lord Ashton's household?"

His scrupulously controlled voice gave Josiah pause. Platt appeared glad for the truth of his answer. "I consider that nothing short of a miracle, my lord. His lordship's solicitor posted notices to charitable institutions, churches and the like, for a governess, and one of those notices landed upon my desk."

"Then you have never actually met Lord Ashton."

"No, I have never had the pleasure."

The statement only confirmed in Brice's mind just how atrociously stupid he found Josiah Platt. If Elora weren't so obviously glad to see the man, he would take great pleasure in having him thrown out on his ear.

He scanned her beautiful face, and was reminded of the blinding smile she had bestowed on Josiah Platt at his entrance into the room.

Mentally, Brice cursed. He had not seen her give into such unrestrained delight since that evening he had entered her bedroom and found that she had fallen asleep reading. She had awakened and asked him to sit beside her, and even wracked with pain as she had been, she had given him a beaming smile.

Then he had gotten snared by the blue of her eyes and he had cursed her soundly. From that moment on, he had seen no further displays of her joy. Until now.

Josiah hefted his weight from the chair, giving Elora a fond look. "Now that I have seen with my own eyes that you are indeed well, I believe it is time I took my leave."

"So soon?" Elora queried in disappointment. She understood that there were other matters that needed his attention, but she was sorry to see him leave.

"I am afraid so. I have come all this way to London to listen to the most learned minds discuss the problems of the church." He scratched the back of his head. "I suppose I should be about listening."

Elora rose and gave him her hand. "Thank you for coming to see me, Josiah."

"To see you happy and well is thanks enough. Praise be to God above that He has blessed you with His goodness, Elora Simmons." He looked to Brice benevolently. "God bless you both. I wish you every happiness together." Patting Elora's shoulder, he turned and walked briskly from the room.

Elora watched until the door closed behind him with a soft click. Then she turned back to Brice only to find that he had risen and moved away to face her from the French doors.

She regarded him curiously. "I hope it was not an inconvenience for Josiah to visit."

"You miss your home," he said. It was both a statement and a question.

Concern flickered across Elora's face. She could sense a rise in the tension that had claimed him earlier. "Since my mother's death, I had no home to speak of, my lord. Not a true home with a loving family around me. But there are people I have known for many years who are very dear to me."

"Josiah Platt being one of them."

The cold edge in his voice drew her brow into a deep frown. She hesitated to think why Brice would sound so terse about Josiah. Still, an inner voice told her to tread carefully with her reply.

"He and his mother both befriended me after my mother's death. They were kind when I most needed kindness."

He fixed her with a piercing look. "You find no such kindness here in London."

"Brice . . ." She shook her head for emphasis, wondering how he could possibly think such a thing. "There are no words to describe how wonderful you have been to me."

"It apparently isn't enough."

"Why do you say that? I am more than content here."

He threw a hand wide before clenching it at his side. "So content that you carry on as though you have been away from your friends for years instead of only two weeks."

Elora blinked in amazement. Had it only been two weeks since that fateful night when the pistol had been fired? It felt like a lifetime.

"My lord, do not think that I am unhappy here with you. It is just that I am not accustomed to this way of life. I grew up quietly, expecting no more than the love my mother gave me. My wants and needs were simple, most of the people I knew, honest and caring. I do not know what to make of the violence and animosity I have encountered since my arrival." Her fingers slowly linked together in an unconsciously vulnerable gesture, and when she spoke again it was more to herself than to Brice. "Lady Ashton accuses me of terrible things, Lady Barbara of deviousness." She scoffed lightly. "Even your cousin finds me sadly lacking."

"My cousin?" Brice scowled. "Who are you talking about?"

Realizing that she may have offended Brice by criticizing Katherine, Elora instantly regretted her words. "I beg your pardon. I meant no disrespect. I only sought to explain that I will need time to adjust to my new life. But that is not a criticism of you or all that you have done for me. Oh, my lord, you have been kindness itself."

Her words skimmed over his senses, inexplicably diffusing his ire. He wouldn't have thought that she would hold him in such regard, yet she did and he admitted that it pleased him.

His reaction gave him pause, but he did not ignore it as habit dictated he do. In fact, he gave it greater attention and decided that if he was going to admit things to himself, he might as well confess that the idea of her leaving his house to stay with Vianne had been like a blow to his chest. He had already begun to think of Elora as belonging with him, which was one reason, he decided, he so greatly resented Josiah Platt.

Not stopping to examine why, he conceded that it was important to him that Elora not regret her decision to marry him. A pent-up breath escaped him. "You will have to forgive my temper."

Her lips curved gently as the blue of her eyes softened to a plush velvet. "You will have to forgive my quick tongue in mentioning your cousin as I did."

"Elora, what cousin do you mean?" he queried, puzzled.

"Your cousin Katherine."

Every nerve and muscle in Brice's body jumped reflexively. As though he hadn't heard correctly, he asked, "Katherine Warfield?"

"Yes. I didn't mean to upset you with my comment about her."

"When did you see Katherine?" he snapped.

"Today," she said uncertainly.

"Where?"

"In front of one of the shops. We met by chance."

Brice quickly thought of all the ramifications of Katherine's presence in London. It could be an accident that her rare emergence from her remote country home coincided with his adversities of late. Or it could very well mean that she wanted to be close at hand when he met his death and the inheritance was passed to her son. Then again, he could very well be letting his suspicions run away with him. Katherine could be in town simply for the festivities that would accompany his betrothal.

"Brice?" Elora asked gently. The atmosphere surrounding him seemed to change too rapidly for her to follow. He exuded anger one moment, forgiveness the next, then a tense kind of urgency at the mention of his cousin. Again, she wondered if she would ever understand him. She desperately wanted to, as much as she wanted to make him happy.

Brice collected himself and gave her his full attention. "I was just thinking on Katherine. It has been some time since I have seen her."

"Well, that will be rectified tomorrow night."

"How?"

"Katherine mentioned that she will be at Lady Barbara's party. She specifically mentioned that she can not wait to see you."

Chapter
10

IN SOMETHING CLOSE TO DISBELIEF, BRICE WONDERED IF LADY Barbara wasn't somehow in league with the devil. Standing in her music room, half listening to the lady's niece warble her lungs out, he looked about at the assembled group and realized that every person who could possibly want him dead was within twenty feet.

Silently he cursed the edicts of polite society. It was patently obvious that Lady Barbara had invited only a select few to honor his engagement to Elora; family members and the *crème de la crème* of the *ton*. Hence, not only was his cousin Thorbon present, and his dead cousin's widow, Katherine, but the Duke of Westford and the Earl of Stanley as well.

The young woman's singing came to an end and Brice clapped distractedly. Around him, voices rose and amiable chatter ensued, but he remained silent as he gave each of the possible suspects a searching look. Not one appeared capable of murder. Thorbon was cozily ensconced in a soft cushioned chair, his jowls quivering at some inanity made by one of his cronies. Katherine, for all her sour disposition, was on her best behavior and wore a face right out of a book on etiquette. The duke stood beside his wife, his head tipped attentively to catch her whispers, while just beyond them the earl was doing his utmost to flatter the women surrounding him.

Each seemed harmless enough, but looks always had been and always would be deceptive. Unfortunately, in this case such deception could very well see him dead. It almost had.

His gaze swerved to Elora, his fierce little protector. The corner of his mouth twitched upward. She was seated among a group of women, poised and serenely elegant. No one looking at her could possibly tell that she had spent the better part of the day battling a nervousness she claimed put butterflies in her stomach. Or that on the coach ride over, she had removed and replaced her spectacles so often, he had finally had to pluck them from her hands and tuck them into one of his pockets.

Mentally he shook his head. It was astonishing that this very same woman who had risked death was unnerved by the prospect of meeting thirty or so of his acquaintances. Apparently she didn't know that she could teach everyone of them the meaning of the word *courage*.

"She's not going to grow a second head, Warrington," Lady Barbara muttered teasingly. She sidled up beside him, a challenging glint in her brown eyes. "But I suppose you can be forgiven since this betrothal business is new to you. Go ahead, stare all you want."

Mockery settled on Brice's face, pulling his brows upward. "Thank you, Lady Barbara. I wasn't aware I needed your permission."

"Don't take that tone of voice with me, wicked boy. You always were too droll for your own good."

Towering over her diminutive height, he leaned down for his rejoinder. "If I have taken any tone at all, my lady, it has been out of sheer self-defense. Experience has taught me to be on my guard whenever you are within speaking range."

"Ha!" Her cackling laughter rent the air. "It's about time you acknowledged that I am a person to be reckoned with." She sent an encompassing glance around the room, waving her blue-veined hand in a careless arc. "Now if I can only get the rest of these mutton-headed fools to do the same."

Brice swallowed a sound that was between a laugh and a groan. She was audacious down to her bones. "Careful, my lady, your cynicism is showing."

"It's all right, I'm allowed. It's one of the pleasures of being old. You can say what you please. And it pleases me to say that I am glad you have finally decided to settle down."

Despite the fact that he didn't think his private life was anyone's concern, Brice acknowledged her comment with a patience he hadn't thought he possessed. "I take it you believe my trip down the aisle is long overdue."

"Entirely. But your wait was well worth it." She flicked a peek at Elora. "She's a beauty, there's no doubt about it. Charming to boot." Her face took on a haughty cast. "I liked her from the start."

Brice gave her a pointed stare. "From the start?"

The task of arranging the drapes of her shawl seemed to distract Lady Barbara as she answered. "Very nearly from the start, and you are quite impertinent to make an issue of the matter." She sniffed disdainfully, the shawl forgotten. "All that truly signifies is that Elora will make you a good wife, and you are to be congratulated."

Katherine Warfield's voice cut in unexpectedly. "Yes, you are to be congratulated, my lord."

Brice turned, his face instantly wiped clean of all expression. "Katherine," he intoned levelly. "It's been some time, has it not?"

"There is little chance or reason for our paths to cross, my lord. After all, we do not run in the same circles."

Lady Barbara's back straightened. "I have heard tell that is by your own choice, Katherine. No one forces you to spend your life in the wilds of the country. Or am I too blind to see the twist marks on your arm?"

Katherine's lips formed a shallow smile. "You have such a wit about you, my lady. But you are right, I choose not to live in London. If it were only me, perhaps I might feel differently, but I have my son . . . and his future to consider."

Brice found her reminder annoyingly transparent. No one

141

knew better than he who his own heir was. Leave it to Katherine to make a subtle mention of the fact whenever she was about. Normally, he shrugged off her remarks as tedious harpings, but given recent events, her comments took on entirely new dimensions.

He could well imagine what she thought of his upcoming marriage. She could not be pleased, not when the natural outcome of his taking a wife resulted in children. In this case, an heir who would strip a coveted title from her son.

"I trust your son is well." His voice was studiously polite.

"Very, but only because I guard his health. There is no telling what horrible illness he could contract here in London."

"It's a wonder I haven't cocked my toes up yet. Are you in London for an extended stay?"

Katherine tilted her head ever so slightly with her reply. "That remains to be seen. Now if you will excuse me, I promised a word to Lord Welton."

Through narrowed eyes, Brice watched Katherine move away until Lady Barbara gestured urgently for him to lend her an ear.

"If you ask me," she whispered for him alone, "her stay in London has already lasted one day too long." She laughed richly at her own irreverence.

Something close to a grunt caught in Brice's throat. "I believe I will rescue Elora from the gossips. I hope you can manage to stay out of trouble, my lady."

She snorted indelicately. "Where is the fun in that?"

He offered a respectful nod, then turned and made his way across the room. His gaze fell on Elora at once and an unexpected tranquillity seemed to bathe his senses, making him forget shrewd old women and attempted murder.

Not giving a damn if it was acceptable or not, he continued to stare at her, surprised to discover that he didn't want to look anywhere else. She was achingly beautiful, and with each step he took, he felt increasingly drawn to that beauty.

A fine trembling skittered through his nerves, and a wry

laugh worked its way up from his chest. Perhaps this was more of her "sorcery," but for once, he accepted it without protest, for the sensation sweeping through him was too appealing to deny.

Reaching Elora's side, he held out his hand. "Ladies, if you will excuse me, I am going to steal my fianceé away for a moment."

Twittering assurances and sly giggles floated around Elora as she let Brice draw her from the settee. She was deeply grateful for his arrival. As much as she enjoyed talking to the myriad women, she was rapidly tiring of making idle chatter.

She came to her feet, willing to go wherever Brice would lead her, but try as she may, she could not prevent the tight pull at her side. Her lips thinned ever so slightly and a hesitation marred her progress.

Brice cast her a curious look. "Are you all right?"

Glad to have her hand tucked into the crook of his elbow, Elora nodded. "Yes, a little stiff is all. That happens when I sit for too long and then get up quickly."

On the verge of entering the dining room, Brice stopped abruptly, wearing a dark frown directed at himself. He should have realized that physically she was still weak. But damn, she went about so effortlessly that he hadn't given her injury a thought in days.

Guilt unsettled him, twisting his gut with a sad truth. He rarely, if ever, allowed himself to be concerned with others, not any more than he accepted others' concern for him.

There had been a time when that hadn't been so.

It was a sobering admission, and one that he wasn't proud of. Especially for Elora's sake.

"I'll take you home at once."

"Oh, no, Brice," she protested. "I'm fine, really."

"You shouldn't be tiring yourself out."

"Brice, how can I possibly be tired? I have done nothing but sit for the past three hours. I feel better for simply having stood and walked." She laid a hand on his chest, and coaxed, "Please, there is no need to leave on my account."

Studying her intently, he finally relented, having no defense against the velvet softness of her gaze. "All right." He sighed heavily. "But the very second you feel too tired to continue, you had damn well better tell me."

Despite the severity of his voice and the fierceness shining in his eyes, she couldn't help but smile. It was heartwarming that he should be so concerned for her welfare, even if he did appear rather grim about the whole thing.

She slipped her hand into the crook of his arm again. "I promise."

They entered the dining room where a sumptuous supper buffet was spread out in a magnificent culinary display. Not for the first time, Elora was amazed, and she could only marvel at how sheltered a life she had lived.

The evening was unlike anything she had ever experienced. She had been introduced to so many people that she feared forgetting which name went with which face. She had curtsied and shaken hands, nodded and smiled, all the while frantically trying to remember Vianne's instructions on how to properly address a particular earl or duchess.

She had listened to a round of gossip she couldn't even begin to make heads or tails of. She had accepted countless congratulations on her betrothal, as well as accolades for preventing Brice's death. It had all been enough to make her head spin, and her nerves quake.

But Brice had never been far from her side the entire time.

She gazed at his profile as he filled a plate for the two of them. It was compellingly dynamic, reflecting the strength of the man himself. Whether he realized it or not, she had drawn heavily on that strength all night, deriving much of her composure from his presence.

"Thank you," she told him tenderly.

Brice looked up from a tray of lobster pâté. "For what?"

"For helping me get through all of this." A slight flush stained her cheeks. "I can't tell you how grateful I am."

Had anyone other than Elora made such a comment, he would have thought the matter a farce. But if he had learned anything about his future wife at all, it was that she was

144

hopelessly guileless. She wouldn't know how to lie if she tried.

Her gratitude was genuine and it brought him up short. "Elora, I didn't do anything." With the exception of pushing her past her physical endurance.

Pleasure brightened her face. "Yes, you did. You just don't know it, which makes it all the more wonderful."

He narrowed his eyes, wanting to ask what she meant, but his cousin Thorbon chose that moment to interrupt.

"Warrington," the elderly peer mumbled in a cantankerous voice. "Miss Simmons."

Elora looked up at the portly old man. They had been introduced earlier and she remembered him instantly. His florid face and white hair were notable only because of the startling contrast each provided for the other. Privately she was thankful she could recall his name because she had the most disturbing feeling that he would be the one person here tonight who would take great exception to being forgotten.

"My lord," she said with measured pleasantry.

"Thorbon," Brice stated in a chillingly neutral voice that pricked Elora's curiosity.

"I've been meaning to speak to you all evening." Thorbon paused, then added, "Privately." Quickly he turned an ingratiating grin on Elora. "I hope my timing is not inconvenient, Miss Simmons, but you can understand how things are with family matters, I'm sure."

"There is no need for her to understand," Brice quietly snapped. "Say what is on your mind."

Hearing the annoyance in Brice's tone, Elora clamped her lower lip between her teeth. Something had set Brice on edge, but she could not imagine why he was so obviously antagonistic to his own cousin.

"As you wish," Thorbon consented. "I was surprised to read about your engagement."

"Why? You knew it was bound to happen sooner or later."

"That is not my point," Thorbon announced in a sudden near shout that widened Elora's eyes. Hastily, he glanced about. "That is not my point," he repeated more calmly.

"Then what is?"

"Only that I resent learning about this development by having to read the papers. I don't like being kept in the dark like some old goat."

"Then I suggest you stop behaving like one."

Thorbon sputtered to catch his breath. "I may be sixty-eight, but I'm not old."

"May I remind you, *cousin,*" Brice ground out in a thinly veiled command, "of where you are. You are about to cause a scene."

The admonition hit its mark with visible results. Thorbon collected himself. When he spoke again, his voice was low, even if it was belligerent. "That's just like you, Brice, to treat everyone with that impersonal manner of yours. It's enough to make a body feel second class." His jowls shook as he adjusted his waistcoat about his paunch of a stomach. "Well, I'm a man still in my prime. And by God, Warrington, you and everyone else will remember that."

Before Elora could think better of it, she said, "Brice has a wonderful memory."

She wasn't wearing her glasses, but she would have had to be blind not to see the astonishment on both men's faces. *Let them stare,* she thought. She had no idea of what undercurrents were responsible for their mutual antagonism, but now was not the time nor the place to vent their animosity.

"He is wonderfully attentive, too," she explained, trying her best to alleviate the air of unease surrounding them. "I think it's because he is afraid that in my shortsightedness I will mistake a pillar for one of the footmen."

Her remark drew laughter from several people standing nearby.

"Are you really shortsighted?" a Lady Smithson asked, stepping into the tight circle formed by Brice, Elora and Thorbon.

"Oh, indeed," Elora confirmed. She welcomed the distraction the woman's company provided. "In fact, I spent

146

considerable time tonight deciding whether I should wear my spectacles or not."

Lady Smithson pressed a beringed hand to her cheek. "Did you really? How absolutely unusual."

"What is this about 'unusual'?" The question came from the Earl of Stanley. The man sauntered up and planted himself at Elora's elbow.

"Miss Simmons wears spectacles," Lady Smithson announced, clearly believing the notion delightful.

"Is that a fact?" Stanley directed his words to Elora, but she could not shake off the unsettling impression that his words were not meant for her. "I always was one for clear vision. Know what you want, take sight of it, and then go after it." He raised one brow. "I got nearly everything I ever wanted that way."

Giving Elora no warning, Brice set down the plate he had been holding and took her elbow. "It has been a pleasure. Now if you will all excuse us, it is time I saw Elora home."

Elora wasn't certain who was more surprised. Those around them or herself. Still, she managed to make a polite exit from the room, assured that Brice must have some purpose for their hasty departure. Intuitively, she knew it had everything to do with the air of tension that emanated from him like a prickling aura.

They made their farewells to Lady Barbara, blaming Elora's recent ill health for their early departure. Their coach was summoned, and in a matter of moments, they were on their way home.

Elora sat opposite Brice, using her time to steady her pulse. She wasn't out of breath, nor was she afraid. Nonetheless, her heart beat at a frantic rate, a purely involuntary reaction to Brice himself.

By the subdued light of a moon intent on playing games with the clouds, she tried to determine his mood. There were no emotions that she could detect. No anger or anxiety, nor compassion or hatred. Nothing, not even the cool detachment that was so much a part of him.

"Brice."

He heard the question beneath the utterance of his name and swallowed a string of pithy curses. She wanted an explanation for his behavior. But how could he tell her that he had had his fill of trying to second-guess the most innocuous of statements.

Dealing with Thorbon had been bad enough, but Stanley's presence had pointed out the indisputable fact that his life had been reduced to a vile game of conjecture, where he was forced to suspect those around him. And, even if he wanted to tell Elora as much, he couldn't, not without involving her in the entire madness any more than she already was.

His gaze cut through the space separating them. "I can only take so much of the social game at one time." Like his face, his voice lacked all emotion.

Worry etched a delicate line across Elora's brow. "Does your cousin Thorbon have anything to do with your dislike?"

"Why?" His question was so casual as to be somehow menacing.

"Because the two of you made no secret of the fact that you are at odds with each other."

Brice lifted a shoulder into a sketch of a shrug. "I don't know what prompted his behavior tonight."

"I think it is obvious."

"Do you?"

"Of course. He's terribly insecure about his position in life."

"What makes you think that?"

"The things he said, the way he said them. I believe he's frightened of being old."

Brice turned the notion over in his head. Thorbon was getting on in years. It was plausible that his cousin had reached this point in his life and looked back with regret and ahead with fear.

Like envy and greed, fear was a powerful force. It could be

just as likely a motive for murder if taken to the extreme. Thorbon's behavior tonight had definitely been immoderate.

"Perhaps you are right."

Elora released a sad sigh. "I'm sorry if I am. It's a shame that there should be such rancor between you."

"I won't lose sleep over the matter."

She tilted her head to one side and gave him a discerning look. "Do you lose sleep because the Earl of Stanley hates you?"

Shocked, Brice stared at her for a full five seconds. "Where did you get that idea?"

"I don't really know." She squinted trying to put clearly into words what she could only sense deep inside her. "It's just something I felt when he spoke to me. And because of your reaction to him."

"He barely said anything, and if I remember correctly, I did not react at all."

"But you did react, by hastening our departure. Not that I blame you. There was something about him that I found disturbing."

Her appraisal of the situation was almost more than Brice could credit. How could she have been so accurate in so short a time? Then again, how could she do half the things she did? He had yet to fully understand her, but he realized suddenly that he wanted to.

She was an intrepid little thing, full of honor and a wisdom beyond her years. She had braved his temper as well as death and still managed to sit there looking supremely soft and feminine. The edge of his jaw yielded to dubious humor and for once he didn't seem to mind sharing his private thoughts.

"I'm not sure hate is the right word, but you are correct in that Stanley does not, shall we say, hold me in the highest esteem."

"Why?" The query came out before she could think. He had not, either by word or action, given her leave to pry into his private affairs. True, they were engaged, but what she knew about him personally could fit into the split shell of a walnut. He seemed to prefer it that way.

"If you would rather not tell me, I will understand," she continued. "But it would help me considerably if I am to be watchful whenever we should meet him in public."

He dismissed her distress with a raised hand. "It is no secret, Elora. I would have told you sooner had I known Stanley was to be present tonight. The simple truth revolves around money."

"Money?" Her eyes rounded. She wouldn't have ever laid the cause there.

"That's right. The earl and I have at times sat down to the same card table. The night before the shooting, and even since then, we have played. Stanley has lost a small fortune to me."

Understanding bloomed in Elora. She remembered well her stepfather's losses at the gambling tables. He would return home, drunk and enraged, swearing retribution for having been cheated out of his money. But there had never been any cheating involved. Harmen Gillet had simply lost his money in hand after hand, game after game to a compulsive habit that could not be broken. With each new loss, his accusations had become wilder and angrier, and everyone on earth was to blame but himself.

She could not identify with such warped thinking. But then, she did not understand why people would care to gamble. It seemed that most men did. Her stepfather, the scores of men with whom he played. Even Brice, and logically those he played with. It was not a comforting thought. Harmen Gillet's propensity for gambling had been directly and indirectly responsible for most of the pain in her life.

"Do . . . do you play often?"

Even in the darkened coach, Brice could read the anxiety on Elora's face. "No." Then because he wanted to know what had put the apprehension in her voice, he asked, "Why?"

She gave into a shaky sigh of relief before she answered. "My stepfather gambled. Badly. When he ran out of money, he sold whatever he could. Or borrowed from someone." She scrubbed her palms over her knees. "In the meantime, my mother died because there wasn't enough money to pay for a doctor or medicine or treatment. It still didn't stop him. Even after . . . after Mother was buried he kept on until there was nothing left but debts." She didn't need to tell Brice that those were the very same debts he had paid.

Without realizing it, Brice searched her face. She wore her anguish like she wore all her emotions, clearly visible and for all to see. Nonetheless he was caught off guard by the sight of an unrelenting ache in the blue depths of her eyes.

He leaned forward and took her chin in his hand. "Elora, you don't have to worry about me gambling us into debtors prison. I play infrequently. When I do, I know when to stop." His thumb stroked the satin texture of her cheek and he saw himself galloping recklessly along on forgotten instincts. "But if it makes you feel any better, I will promise you now never to wager so much as a shilling again."

Elora's breath came in and stopped. That he would make such a vow for her filled her with a joy so unbelievable that she thought she would melt where she was.

"Brice, I don't know what to say." In her heart, she knew exactly what she would never *have* to say. She would never have to ask him to keep his promise. The fact that he had made it was promise enough for her.

A blinding smile lit her face, obliterating all signs of distress. Her hand rose to caress his lean cheek, but the night suddenly erupted crazily around them.

The coach bumped wildly accompanied by a cacophony of men's shouts and shrieks from frightened horses. Brice's hands automatically caught Elora as she was thrown from the seat.

"What the devil?" he snarled, righting Elora across his lap.

On the heels of his exclamation came a man's startled yell and then the loud shot of a pistol. Muffled thumps crashed against the outside of the coach, rocking it alarmingly before another shout ended too abruptly. The crack of a whip burst overhead and the coach lurched forward, racing through the darkened London streets.

"Brice, what is happening?" Elora gasped as he set her on the seat beside him.

Brice didn't bother with a reply. A feral gleam turned the green of his eyes to shards of splintering emerald glass. Every muscle and nerve tensed as he glared out through the window of the door. The buildings raced past in a blur.

The coach careened around a street corner, and Elora could barely contain her cry.

"It's him again, isn't it?" Staring desperately at Brice, her hands clung tightly to the leather strap as she tried to brace herself into the corner. "The man who tried to kill you."

Brice blocked out her question, all his attention focused on the window near his left shoulder. He examined the space directly above and outside the door.

"Brice, what . . ." The motion of the coach veered haphazardly to the right, forcing Elora's words into a muffled groan of fright. "What are you going to do?"

He shifted so that his back was flush to the coach's side wall and he peered out the window toward the roof.

It took Elora several seconds to realize that Brice meant to go out the door. "Oh, no, Brice, you can't." She lifted her arms in a gesture meant to draw him back and hold him safe, but the coach took another corner at breakneck speed.

Brice's hand shot out to keep Elora from toppling forward, all the while her tempestuous words poured forth. "You can't go! You don't know how many men are out there, they have guns, they could shoot you. *You could get killed.*"

He jerked off his jacket and threw it aside. "I'm sure as hell not going to sit and wait for whoever is out there to make his move."

"Oh, Brice, please . . ."

In the next instant, he grasped the handle, shoved open the door and thrust himself out of the coach. Instantly, he grabbed onto the molding above the door and swung outward, Elora's alarmed cry following him into the night.

He sucked in his breath at the cold air whipping over him. The muscles of his arms bunched and strained to retain his hold as the ground sped past just inches below his feet.

Battling the dangerous rocking of the vehicle, he hauled himself upward, his foot finding purchase on a lacquered rail. His leg gave a mighty thrust and his shoulders and head cleared the roof of the coach. Instantly he took sight of two unknown men seated in the driver's box. There was no sight of either his driver, Holloway, or his footman, Rafferty.

The coach wheel caught a rut as it entered Hyde Park. Any light that had accompanied the city was left behind. Brice was left in an enshrouding darkness and a wildly shifting world.

Gritting his teeth, he gave a mighty shove and hoisted himself onto the roof. His move gave him the leverage he needed. It also caught the attention of the men.

"God damn," the driver snarled, glancing over his shoulder.

His burly partner lurched about, his grizzled face contorted in rage. One look at Brice crouched on the roof behind him and he threw himself out of his seat.

Brice saw the man ready himself to attack and braced for the impact. The man's massive shoulder caught him in the chest and knocked the air from his lungs. Together they slid precariously close to the edge of the roof, twisting, turning, each struggling to gain hold of anything that would prevent falling.

Brice rolled to his side and in the same second shoved his hand toward the driver's box. His fingers closed about the cold metal rail. It was all he needed.

Anchored to the metal by one hand, he pulled himself forward to his knees. Muscles straining, breath hissing, he released his grasp only long enough to take the bastard's neck in both hands, forcing him onto his back.

A weighty fist swung upward. Brice leaned to the left in

that instant before it would have connected with his face. The swing went wide, carrying with it a powerful momentum. Bracing his feet, Brice yanked his hands away and let the man's own motion carry him over the edge of the roof.

A guttural cry rent the air. In the next instant the coach lurched upward as it struck the man's body, crushing it with hooves and wheels. The driver cursed loudly, hauling on the reins in a vicious effort to keep the vehicle righted.

The jarring motion sent Brice to his knees, his hands gripping the flat surface of the roof. Still, he allowed himself only a moment to regain his balance and then he launched himself at the driver.

His right arm clamped about the man's neck and wrenched backward. Garbled curses spewed from the driver's mouth and the reins dropped free as he scrambled for his life.

The man twisted violently, gasping for air, digging his filthy hands into the flesh that gave no quarter. Suddenly, he grabbed for a knife sheathed in his boot and slashed upward.

Pain erupted in Brice's left shoulder. The gleaming metal sank into his body, ripping downward along his arm. His hold loosened under the torturous assault, but still he would not relinquish his grasp. Instinctively he knew that this would be a fight to the death and if he didn't win, Elora would be dead also.

Eyes glazed with black fire, he struggled to keep his right arm firmly locked about the thick neck. But the pain shooting out from his left shoulder was nearly blinding in its intensity. His vision blurred, sweat ran down his face. He gritted his teeth and tightened his arm.

Without warning the coach swerved crazily, the motion throwing Brice in one direction, the driver in the other. The pitch wrenched Brice's arm from its hold and he crashed backward onto the roof.

Pain exploded everywhere, bright lights flashing before his tightly clenched eyes. He cursed and shoved onto his elbow . . . just in time to see the driver get tossed over the side at the coach's sudden jarring motion.

Relief, rage, frustration, pain; all raced through Brice as he eased himself carefully into the driver's box. Hampered by the night's darkness and his near useless left arm, he grabbed for the reins. Using his last reserves of strength, he hauled back savagely on the leather straps, fighting against the power of the horses that had been running scared and without direction.

On her knees, her forehead pressed to her hands gripping the seat, Elora didn't take note of the coach's gradual slowing. Dragging in labored breaths, she prayed for Brice's safety, appealing to God that He spare Brice. Tears filled her eyes and hoarse, strangled sobs tangled with her entreaties.

Brice was a good man, she pleaded in a silent invocation. He had treated her kindly, generously, assuming responsibilities that a lesser man would have ignored. Despite his mercurial temperament, he had shown her great consideration. He didn't deserve to die. Not this way. Not now.

She wasn't aware that the coach had come to a stop until the door was flung open and Brice's strained voice cut into her misery.

"Elora?"

Her head came up, and through her tears, she saw him standing just outside the door, his tall, powerful figure outlined by the moon's light.

"*Brice!*" Joy and relief and disbelief blended together, straining her voice to a feathery whisper. "Oh, Brice, are you all right?" Heedless of anything other than reaching him, she scrambled across the floor until she could reach out and touch him. "Are you all right? Are you hurt?"

Brice caught her against him as she toppled into his arms, her hands skimming over his shoulders, his face, his neck. His movements tempered, he lowered her until her feet reached the ground.

"It's all right, sweet," he told her, sucking in a sharp breath.

155

But her hands continued their search, as though discrediting the evidence before her eyes. Her fingers skimmed over his tightened jaw, down to his heaving chest then out to his arms, her gaze following closely behind.

She lifted her right hand to his face, but it came away from his arm warm and sticky with blood. In the next instant, Brice fell to the ground.

Chapter
11

"OH, MY GOD! *BRICE!*"

Elora sank to her knees at Brice's side, heart-wrenching fear making her limbs quake. Quickly, she cupped his face between icy hands.

"Brice. Brice. Oh, you can't die. *You can't die.*" Desperately, she forced her hands away, realizing she was doing nothing to help him with her pleading.

Frantically she looked beyond the coach and steaming horses, seeing the darkened shadows of trees and little more. Nothing looked familiar. The light wind tossed branches overhead, and moonlight and black voids consorted eerily with the ashen mist swirling at the cold ground.

She had no idea where they were, or how far they had come from Lady Barbara's. The driver and footman were nowhere in sight. If she thought she could run for help she would, but leaving Brice was the last thing she wanted to do.

She examined the dark stain on his white shirt, barely choking back a sob when she felt the warm blood saturating the fabric. Tears came to her eyes, and she damned whoever had done this to him.

Veins teeming with anger and fear, she swiped at the moisture on her cheeks. As carefully as possible, she untied his cravat, her frustration escalating at the neck-cloth's stubborn ties and folds. Fingers trembling fiercely, she finally removed the cloth and saw to the buttons on Brice's waistcoat and shirt.

She eased the garments away until his shoulder was bared to her view. Instantly, a hoarse cry was wrenched from her lips. A ragged tear ripped his flesh open, and blood seeped freely from the wound that began in his shoulder and ran down the corded muscles of his arm.

The cravat she had flung aside just seconds ago was hastily pressed to the bleeding cut.

"Brice, wake up. Please wake up." As hard as she tried, she could not contain the tears that flooded her eyes again. "I won't let you die. Do you hear me? I won't. I love you. I love you and I don't know if I could stand to live if you die."

The words were torn from her choking throat, but she wouldn't have recalled them for anything on earth. How it happened or when, she didn't know, but to the very marrow of her bones she had come to love Brice. He meant everything to her.

Horribly she could be losing him even as he lay there before her.

"No!" Keeping one hand pressed to the cloth on his shoulder, she lifted her other hand to his face. In a tender caress, she stroked his forehead. "If you die now, I won't be able to love you. You'll go on without ever having known what it was like for me to hold you close and give you my love. If you die, I'll be left behind to spend the rest of my life regretting."

A low murmur sounded deep in Brice's chest. Elora's heart pounded and she frantically searched his face.

"Brice." Her voice was a chorus of hope. She laid her hand along his cold cheek, repeating his name again and again until finally his dark lashes stirred and he looked into her eyes.

Reality came back to Brice in a rush of pain and the sight of Elora's pale face. Memory was instant and razor sharp. Gritting his teeth, he tried to sit up, but his shoulder protested viciously.

"The driver . . ."

"There's no one, Brice," she assured him, ecstatic to hear his voice again.

"He fell over the side . . ." Once again he attempted to rise, this time with better results. Ignoring the shards of fire shooting into his chest, he struggled into a sitting position.

"There is no one here but us." She gazed steadily at him, memorizing his beloved features as though to commit them to the keeping of her heart. Her hand fumbled to hold the bloodied cravat in place. "You shouldn't move. You've already lost a great deal of blood."

He reached for the makeshift bandage and pressed it firmly in place, clenching his muscles against the resulting pain. "Help me up," he uttered in a rasping voice.

Elora began to protest, but she had only to look at his fierce expression to know that with or without her assistance, he was going to stand.

Kneeling, she levered her shoulder under his right arm, one hand bracing his chest, the other circling behind his waist. Slowly, awkwardly, they came to their feet, Elora stumbling slightly beneath his weight.

He relieved her of the burden at once. Impelled by nothing but a brutal determination, he removed his arm from about her shoulders and stepped away. The ground tipped precariously, but he blinked at the distortion, clearing his vision.

Beside him, Elora urged, "Brice, please sit down."

He ignored the plea. Standing on legs locked by sheer will alone, he scanned the blackened surroundings. There was no sign of the bloody bastard with the knife. Either he had been knocked unconscious from the fall or he had run off. No doubt to report to whoever had paid for his services.

He swore softly. He had had the man in his hands only to have him escape.

"Are you all right?" He gave Elora a quick but thorough inspection.

"Yes, I'm fine. It's you who . . ."

"Which park is this?"

"I don't know . . ."

"How long was I unconscious?"

His rapid-fire questions were unnerving her. "A few minutes, no more." Although it had felt like forever. "Oh, please, Brice, you must take care."

A fresh wave of pain swept outward from his shoulder, making him fight back a moan in silent defense. He clamped down on the agony, turned it inward where he could absorb it with clenched muscles and a string of curses too foul to utter.

"Brice," Elora cried, holding him with shaking hands. "You have to lie down."

He drew a deep breath, then another, as the surge dissipated. Finally, he opened his eyes and turned his attention to more pragmatic matters.

"Get in the coach, Elora," he ordered.

"What?"

"You heard me, so don't waste my time by asking me to repeat myself. I'm fresh out of patience."

"What are you going to do?"

He glanced over to the horses. "I'm going to get us out of here."

She couldn't believe what she had heard. He could barely stand, he was bleeding profusely, and he intended to climb up onto the coach and drive them back.

"Brice, you can't." She clasped the loose ends of his shirt. "You'll kill yourself."

"What do you suggest, madam? That we stand here for the rest of the night and wait for every miscreant in the city to come our way?"

She flinched as his harsh words scored her flayed nerves. "No, but surely we can walk to the nearest house and send for help."

His jaw tightened. "I will not leave my prime horseflesh."

Her head shook slowly from side to side in amazement. "You care more for your horses than you do for yourself."

"Damn it, Elora, I will not argue this with you."

The sound of running feet arrested their heated words. Before Brice could even consider whether they were being approached by friend or foe, Holloway raced up, disheveled and winded.

"My lord, my lord, are you . . ."

Even by the light of a fickle moon, Brice could see the coachman's gaze take in the hastily applied bandage.

"Good God Almighty," Holloway burst out. "We have to get you back. I got here as quick as me legs could go, my lord. I seen the coach come this way and . . ." The poor man's voice tripped to a sudden halt, only to start up again, this time sounding even more agitated. "I'll get you back to the house quicklike, my lord. Do you need any help, my lord? Can I . . . do you need a hand, my lord?"

Brice didn't say a word, but the piercing look he leveled on Holloway clearly told the man, *shut the hell up*.

"Yes, my lord. Right away, my lord." Holloway scrambled up to his driver's box and took the reins firmly in hand.

The exchange between the two men brought a worried crease to Elora's brow. Holloway was nearly stumbling over himself in his efforts to give Brice the assistance he so clearly needed, but Brice had rejected the driver's offer with a brittle coldness.

"Brice, let me help." Stepping to his side, her arms went about him, and she felt him stiffen. For a second she had the distinct impression that he would refuse her aid as he had Holloway's, but for the little time it took to steady his short progress into the coach, he remained silent and allowed her support.

Holloway sent the team into motion as soon as Elora shut the coach door. The same ground they had covered in such haste was now retraced at a more sane if not brisk speed.

Sitting to Brice's left, Elora examined his wound as best she could. In the coach's dim interior, it was difficult to accurately judge if the bleeding had slowed or stopped. Either way, the cravat was nearly soaked with blood.

"We'll need to send for Dr. Bingham." She studied Brice

carefully. His head lay back against the deep blue squabs, his eyes shut. "I don't know how serious it is, but there is too much bleeding."

She tucked a clean edge of the cravat closer to the cut, drawing a grunt from Brice.

"Damn it, Elora, will you stop fussing."

His harsh words were like a slap in the face. Eyes rounding, she leaned away. She hadn't meant to hurt him. She had only tried to help in whatever way she could.

The coach came to a stop and she relinquished her hurt. As the door was thrown open and she stepped down, she told herself she had no business giving into emotionalism when Brice was in such pain.

"My lord," Cobb exclaimed, his face a mask of apprehension. "Miss Simmons. Are you all right? Rafferty arrived here to tell us how he and Holloway were accosted. We sent out search parties." He automatically reached out to help Brice descend from the coach, but Brice yanked his right arm away.

"Get out of the way, man." His snarl was just precise enough, the intonation just controlled enough to tell everyone within earshot that he was in a dangerous frame of mind.

Elora scowled at his caustic manner. She understood only too well how pain could shorten one's forbearance, but Brice was treating his servants abominably, especially so in light of the fact that they only wished to help him.

She lifted her chin, pulling her patience about her like a much used cloak. She had learned a great many things about Brice tonight, not the least of which was that he was extraordinarily stubborn. Setting her shoulders, she decided it was time for a dash of her own stubbornness.

"Mr. Cobb," she said in a voice gilded with steel. "Would you please help me get his lordship into the house?"

Cobb looked between Brice and Elora, evidently wanting to offer what assistance he could, but not daring to do anything that might displease Brice in any way.

Elora took the decision out of the butler's hand.

"Mr. Cobb."

As gently as he could, Cobb took much of Brice's weight against him.

"Damn it," Brice growled, gritting his teeth against the pain.

"I beg your pardon, my lord."

Elora ducked her head around Brice's chest in time to see Cobb swallow with difficulty. "Don't worry, Mr. Cobb," she told the butler, hoping to alleviate his distress. "He has been swearing at me for the better part of the past half hour."

"Yes, miss."

Vianne and Mary Cobb were waiting in the foyer. As soon as Elora and Brice entered the house, they gasped in horror.

Vianne rushed to Elora's side. "What happened? Oh, my God, Brice, you've been hurt."

"A very astute observation, Vianne," he muttered. Looking past his sister to his housekeeper, he bit out, "Get me a brandy, Mrs. Cobb."

Mary Cobb hastened into his study to do as she was bid, looking as though she had been shaken to the roots of her hair.

Elora glanced to Vianne. "We need to send for the doctor."

"No," Brice declared.

Exasperation threatened Elora's tolerance. The man was impossible to help, and with every step they took into his study, she was sorely tempted to shake some sense into him. "My lord, I think we should have a look at your injury before we make that decision."

Mrs. Cobb bustled forward with a snifter of brandy. Brice took the glass and drained the liquor in one deep swallow.

"Elora, this is a decision that I shall make, not *we* as in a committee of five."

"Mrs. Cobb." Elora proceeded as though Brice had not spoken. "We will need a basin of water and some bandages until Dr. Bingham arrives."

"Yes, miss." The housekeeper took her order and scurried out of the room.

"Damn it, Elora," Brice snapped.

Like most of the expletives he had hurled at her, this one rolled off Elora's back. She had more important matters to concern her, like tending to Brice's injury as quickly as possible.

With Cobb's help, they maneuvered Brice to the fireplace, then removed his shirt. Ignoring the hands outstretched to aid him into the leather chair, Brice carefully lowered himself, refusing to give in to the fierce burning in his arm.

He jerked his gaze from the orange flames in the iron grate only to look up and find Vianne, hovering just beyond the fireplace, staring at him. Her face was contorted in what he assumed was fear and anguish.

"Brice, we've been so worried. Colin and I left the party just shortly after you did. But you never arrived." Visibly, she tried to control her erratic breathing. "When your footman arrived to tell us all that happened, Colin sent the servants to search. He's out there, too."

Helplessly, her gaze fell to his shoulder as Elora pulled the cravat away. She pressed her clasped hands to her neck in horror.

The extent of the angry wound brought a gasp to Elora's lips. Kneeling close to Brice's left thigh, she gazed at the long cut that ran from his inner elbow to his shoulder, slicing through the skin in a ragged tear. Blood seeped through areas that had not crusted over and trickled down the dark mat of hair on his chest.

"Oh, Brice." The sight of his blood made her want to weep.

He stared hard at her golden head bent so close to the mess of his arm. Strands of her hair hung haphazardly about her face, her dress was torn and smeared with blood. Her hands were pale and trembled almost as much as her lips, and her blue eyes were darkened with emotions he refused to name.

"Cobb," he declared brusquely, "send someone out to find the viscount."

"Yes, my lord." Cobb gathered up Brice's clothes, but

instead of quitting the room, stood and stared at Brice's arm as though hesitant to leave. "Is there anything else you require?"

"No."

"Perhaps . . ."

"Just do as I asked," Brice snarled.

Cobb hastened away, passing his wife as she entered.

"Here you are, miss," Mary Cobb said.

Elora gratefully accepted the warm water and strips of linen. Carefully she began to clean the torn and bloodied flesh. With Vianne's help, the cloths were repeatedly dipped and rinsed. By the time Elora had wiped away as much blood as possible, dots of sweat glistened Brice's forehead. He hadn't uttered so much as a sharp breath, had not flinched the smallest degree, but the cost to his self-control was evident.

"Brice." She lay a tender hand along his clenched jaw. "That is all I can do until the doctor arrives."

To call a doctor implied a certain helplessness that twisted at Brice's gut. The sensation was all too similar to the powerless feelings he had experienced at the death of his parents and brother.

His green eyes blazing, he stabbed Mrs. Cobb with a burning look. "I want Marcus Quinn here within the hour." He turned his glare on Vianne. "Get out there and make some order of the servants."

Elora came to her feet at Brice's knee, blue eyes snapping. She watched both women rush from the room as though chased by horrid demons.

"Would you please tell me what in the world is the matter with you," she burst out, his contemptuous manner pushing her to the end of her patience.

Her indignant tone brought a silent curse to his lips. "Not a thing, other than this." He indicated his shoulder with a tip of his head.

"Not a thing? How can you say that? Why are you treating everyone this way?" She pointed to the door. "You are surrounded by all these wonderful people who only want to help, yet you rebuff their honest efforts and to your own expense."

"If you are referring to my staff, they do what they are paid to do."

She gasped in disbelief. "How can you be so blind? Poor Mr. Holloway was so worried about you when he found us in the park, he could hardly get a word out. Do you pay him for that kind of concern? And do you think Mr. Cobb rushed out to meet us and helped you into the house, looking like he had aged five years, because he is adequately compensated?" Her face flushed with the heat of her ire, her knee pressed along his thigh trembled. Still, the stare she leveled on Brice was unwavering.

"What about Vianne? She's not paid to be your sister and worry herself into tears. Although from the way you treat her, I don't know why she would even bother." She flung a hand wide, too irate to care about the black scowl darkening Brice's face. "There isn't enough money on earth for you to purchase the loyalty and love these people feel for you. If you weren't so wrapped up in your own crippled sense of detachment you would see that they genuinely care about you. And whether you like it or not you need them."

His right hand shot out and clamped around on the fragile bones of her wrist, pulling her down across his legs and chest. Abruptly his fingers clenched, his reflexes struggling as though to keep her from tearing him apart. A pain to exceed that in his arm gleamed in his eyes as he stared into the brilliant sapphire orbs regarding him so diligently.

The first tremors began in his chest, rippling out to his limbs. Brice felt the waves, one on top of another like an insidious undertow drawing at him from deep in his gut. She was doing it to him again. There was something in her eyes, catching him, holding him, refusing to let him go. But it was different this time; no heat or light or shifting reality. Just a real and unrelenting force that demanded he feel what he did not want to feel, and remember what he had spent years in hell trying to forget.

He had *needed* his parents. He had *needed* his brother. *He had loved them.* And they him. But nothing he had done had been able to save them from Napoleon's madness. The money he had spent to secrete them out of France had been useless. All the political power at his disposal had fallen on deaf ears. The bribes, the letters, the prayers to God above . . . all of it had been sickeningly worthless.

In the end he had been left with nothing but his need to have them back, to love them. For years he had nearly strangled on that need, and on a torment of the mind that called to him from the past, reminding him that he had not been able to save those whom he loved.

Elora watched Brice's face harden until she thought it would crack. Horrified, she saw pain there, but not the kind produced with blood. His pain was from the soul, harsh, cruel and eating him alive.

She could feel his torment like a band around her lungs. "Brice." His name trembled over her lips in a desolate whisper. "Oh, Brice, what has caused this hurt in you? What has happened to make you so bitter?" Wanting to ease his suffering, she pressed her cheek against his and hugged him close, giving him her warmth. Giving him her love.

Sitting like stone, he absorbed the feel of her, fighting off the sweet, pleasurable ache of simply being held, not in passion or lust, but for the sake of the comfort to be found in holding. Out of habit, he nearly gave into the impulse to push the sensation away, to thrust her away. But he couldn't. He could not lift his hand and deny himself this. Her arms about him felt too good.

He gave in, telling himself that it was only for a brief second. He would take what she was offering and then restore his life to normal. He would take control of his emotions and forget this one unthinkable instance. But the moment his right arm circled Elora's waist, he knew he was lying to himself.

His hand held her securely, pressing her close, letting the heat from her body melt the chill that had become so much a part of him. He could feel her pulse against his chest and it echoed his own heart's cadence. Nothing in his life had ever felt so right.

Knowing he shouldn't, he turned his head, wanting to see what it was about this woman that she could stir him as no person ever had. His shift brought her head up and their eyes met.

"Don't push me away, Brice," she murmured against his lips. "Let me help."

He knew she was talking about more than just his arm. But to admit to that kind of need was to step into the realm he had forsaken at the graveside of his parents and brother. It was a realm where vulnerability led to anger and love ultimately coursed a path to pain.

Nonetheless he could not bring himself to tell her no.

He closed his eyes, forcing himself to regain control. His mind heard only a transient whisper for the demand for self-discipline. She had breached all his carefully constructed defenses, and there wasn't a damn thing he could do about it.

"Summon your doctor." He forced the words out, knowing that from this moment on, there would be no going back.

Chapter

12

BRICE IGNORED THE UNCOMFORTABLE PRESSURE IN HIS SHOULDER as he came down the curving stairway. Not bothering to look about, he walked past Cobb who was at attention at the front door, and Mary who stood waiting near the hallway. Three paces toward his study he stopped, feeling two pairs of eyes boring into him from behind.

"Well?" He gave them each an exasperated look, irked by the astonishment so plainly visible on their faces.

"Mr. Tew is waiting in your study, my lord," Cobb informed him.

"Is that all?"

"Yes, my lord."

"Good." But it bloody well was not. His housekeeper was observing him like a mother hen over a chick with a broken wing. No doubt she thought he should still be abed resting and sipping broth. "Was there something you required, Mrs. Cobb?"

Mary's pristine mobcap dipped and fluttered as she shook her head in a manner that could have meant both yes and no. "I trust you are well, my lord."

It was the most tactful way that someone had inquired after the state of his health. Brice had to give the woman credit. Not only for her diplomacy, but also for broaching the subject at all.

Heaving a sigh, he searched the ceiling before he replied with extreme self-restraint. "I have been better, Mrs. Cobb. Thank you . . . for inquiring."

Striding to his study, he missed the incredulous look that went from Mary to Cobb and back again. That was most fortunate for the couple because Brice did not feel inclined to have his behavior analyzed by anyone, least of all his staff.

"Mr. Tew."

The stocky, short-legged investigator came to his feet as Brice entered the book-lined study. "My lord."

"I see you received my message." In movements as concise as his statements, Brice sat behind his desk. "Mr. Quinn has informed you of the latest?"

"I'm afraid so."

"And?"

"And I've had three men out all day. I think we have a lead on the man who managed to run off. One of my men has caught wind of someone in St. Giles making whispers about last night. My man is tracking down the source now."

"Which means that whoever is at the other end of the rumors could be the bastard who decided to sharpen his knife on my arm."

"Yes, my lord."

"Or it could be someone who likes to hear himself talk."

"There is always that chance, but in this case, I don't think so."

"Why not?"

"Because from what my man can piece together, the source is someone by the name of Mackey Crispen, a thief among other things, known for settling life's problems with a wicked-looking knife."

Brice picked up a quill and flung it back to the desk. As speculation went, it was passable, but he would not be satisfied until he knew who was paying Crispen.

"Any idea who is behind this?"

"Not yet. So far, I've found nothing that points to either

the duke or the earl. The duke is staying close to home these days."

"Most likely keeping one eye on his wife and the other on his collection of oriental vases," Brice interjected.

"As you say, and the earl has been spending most of his time at his club. He's winning at cards as much as he is losing. This Katherine Warfield makes no pretenses about wanting her son in your place, but so far, she's more complaint than anything. Which leaves your cousin, but he does not seem to have any interest outside a new kitchen wench he's taken onto staff."

Brice fingered the discarded quill. With the exception of this Crispen, they were no closer to an answer than they had been weeks ago.

"What about the other bastard? The one that died when he fell from the coach?"

Mr. Tew's one good eye seemed to glint with satisfaction. "A mean one there, my lord. Went by the name of Gord, and was known to sell his services to just about anyone who had enough blunt. He had been talking big for a few days about how he was going to come into some good money."

"How much?"

"He never said."

Reaching the end of his tolerance, Brice grated, "That brings us back to exactly where we started, Mr. Tew!" It wasn't exactly true, but he was so angry with the entire mess he wasn't willing to be patient about it. "How long will it take before you know anything more about this Crispen?"

Mr. Tew shrugged. "Could be an hour, maybe a day."

"Meaning?"

"Meaning something like this happens, and whoever is footing Crispen will want to talk. The bloke will make contact soon, one way or the other. I got my men waiting for that."

"You are awfully confident that you will get this Crispen to talk."

"He isn't known for his loyalty, my lord. He belongs to whoever has the fatter purse. Or the heavier hand."

The notion of loyalty among murderers made Brice scoff. He came to his feet in one swift motion, paying his injury little heed. "I want this brought to an end as soon as possible."

"Yes, my lord." The investigator took his leave with a series of jerking nods indicative of one who was relieved to be on his way.

"Brice?" Vianne's hushed voice came from the doorway.

He looked up to find his sister and Colin waiting to enter. He drew a steady breath, but winced at the ache in his shoulder. The stitches the doctor had taken that morning were still tender.

"Come in."

"I hope we aren't disturbing you," Colin remarked, guiding Vianne forward.

"No, I was finishing up with some business."

"I trust it's going well?"

Brice caught the knowing look in his brother-in-law's eyes and knew he was hiding no truth. Colin understood only too well what kind of "business" he had been seeing to. "As well as can be expected."

"Is there anything I can do to help?"

The query gave Brice pause. He had not been close to Colin over the years. In fact, he had treated Colin in much the same manner he had Vianne. That the man would offer his assistance was . . . touching, in an uncomfortable sort of way.

"No, thank you." Almost clumsily, he added, "It was nice of you to ask." Discomfited, and not liking the feeling, he focused on Vianne where she sat, then instantly wished he hadn't. She was watching him as though he had sprouted wings.

"Are you . . . are you well enough to be up?" Her strangled voice had the most unsettling effect on Brice's nerves. "How are you feeling?"

A pat answer balanced on the tip of his tongue, but unbidden came the memory of his asking Elora the very same question weeks ago.

In all honesty? A shrug of her hands and then . . . *I hurt.*
Looking into the eyes so like his own he said, "I hurt."

Vianne blinked. Then blinked again, pressing a hand to her forehead. "Please, Brice, sit down," she implored.

He considered the wisdom of that. He had no desire for a prolonged discussion about the attack, but there was something about the distress on his sister's face that he could not ignore the way he might wish to.

Out of the corner of his eye, he could see Vianne following his every move as he stiffly took his seat. What she saw, or expected to see, was a puzzle, but he had the distinct impression that she found something of great import. The scrutiny was unnerving, making him feel suddenly out of his element.

Stepping to the chair beside Vianne, Colin also sat. "We had most of the story from Elora last night. Do you have any idea who might have been responsible?"

Brice was quick to note that Colin delivered his query with none of the hesitancy claiming Vianne. Obviously, his sister's husband felt no restraint in asking questions that were of genuine concern.

And beyond that, it was very much in Colin's style to push for answers to which he believed Vianne was entitled.

Brice supplied one with a shake of his head. "If you are asking me if I know who is trying to kill me, the answer is no." He glanced to Vianne and his black brows lowered. Her hands were tightly clasped in her lap, her face tense and anxious. He had seen the look often, and would have turned away if he had not caught the quivering of her lips.

She was keeping the tears at bay by a shred of control. The realization drew him up short.

"There is no need for you to worry, Vianne," he told her, his voice oddly strained. "I have hired an investigator to ferret out whoever is responsible. We have our suspicions, but I can not tell you more than that."

Vianne's wide-eyed stare was one of amazement, and Brice didn't know if it was because of what he had said or how he had said it. Either way, a wobbly smile lit his sister's face. Strangely enough, it was the sight of that frail joy that decided for Brice. It dawned on him that it had been years since Vianne had heard anything other than disdain from him. She obviously was having trouble dealing with that.

"You will be careful, won't you?" she asked, struggling to get the words out.

"I will try my best."

"Are you sure there is nothing we can do to help?"

"Yes."

"If there were, you wouldn't tell us."

Even if Brice wanted to agree, he hesitated, studying Vianne more closely than he had in years. "I will . . . let you know."

She nodded, clearly not trusting herself not to burst into tears. As though afraid that she would make a complete fool of herself, she rose and offered a weak excuse.

"If you will both pardon me. I want to check on Elora. She was quite exhausted from . . . from everything." She made her way to the door, the tears she had been holding back slipping down her cheeks. But her lips were curved into a full smile; fragile, erratic, but definitely a joyous smile.

Rain swept against Brice's house, dotting the windows in a constant reminder of the gloominess to be found outside. Sitting in the front salon, Elora silently absorbed the welcoming warmth from the fire as well as the pleasure of Vianne's company.

Vianne was unusually quiet, which suited Elora well. Her mind was overrun with too many notions to offer Vianne conversation, engaging or otherwise. She sat silent, and thought about Brice.

She had not seen him at all that day. He had left the house earlier, much to everyone's amazement. She shut her eyes briefly, wondering how he could be so careless with his own well-being.

"I beg your pardon, my lady." Cobb's hushed voice jerked Elora's eyes open. She had not heard him enter or approach Vianne. "The Reverend Platt is here to see Miss Simmons."

Vianne turned an inquiring look to Elora. "Reverend Platt?"

"Yes," she returned in surprise. "A friend from home." She wasn't certain why Josiah would pay her another call, but she was pleased and asked the butler to show him in.

"I didn't know you had friends here in London," Vianne wondered aloud.

"Josiah is here on church matters."

Before Vianne could inquire further, the minister walked in, his pale face looking all the more pale above his dark, somber clothing.

"Elora, I trust you are well." The smile he gave her was as thin as his brown hair.

"Yes, I am, but I didn't expect to see you again, Josiah." There was a friendly astonishment in her voice.

He fingered a small box he held, its wrapping damp from the rain. "Yes, I know, but I received this from Mother. She asked that I give it to you." His gaze slid uneasily to Vianne.

"Oh, I am sorry," Elora apologized. Quickly she saw to the introductions before imploring Josiah to stay for a visit.

"Only if it won't put you to any trouble," he insisted.

"Please stay," Vianne returned.

"Very well." Josiah sat on the Chinese settee beside Elora, the small box in his hands suddenly cumbersome. He placed it on the seat between them. "Mother said it is for your wedding." He chuckled and scratched the back of his head. "I admit, I don't know what it is."

The sound of his laughter, his habit of scratching his head in confusion were all dearly familiar to Elora.

"Should I open it now, or should I wait?" she asked.

"Now, I would think."

She removed the plain brown wrapping from the box and set the lid aside to find a small Bible in white leather.

"Oh, Josiah, this is lovely." She inspected the fine tooling on the cover. "I shall write to your mother this very day to thank her."

Almost embarrassed, Josiah waved his hands in something close to a shrug. "She'd appreciate that. I think . . . I think she misses you like a daughter."

"I miss her." Truly touched by the gift as well as his words, Elora turned to Vianne. "Josiah's mother has always been such a sweet woman." She glanced back to the minister and the smile she gave him was as gentle as the one he bestowed on her. "Josiah, too, has been a good friend."

"I suppose there is something to be said for friendship."

Elora's heart flipped against her ribs. Brice stood in the doorway. Her gaze jumped to his.

"Brice." She rose in an unconscious welcome, drinking in the sight of him, wondering again why he was not in bed recuperating.

He came forward in a fluid, masculine stride that bore no evidence of any possible discomfort. His advance brought him to Elora's side and his right arm circled her waist.

"How are you today?"

She gave him a pointed look. "I could ask the same of you."

He refrained from commenting on the wound to his shoulder. Instead, he turned to the others. "Vianne, Reverend."

"A pleasure, my lord," Josiah said.

"And most unexpected. I didn't think your visit to London was to be lengthy."

The sharp edge to his words sent Elora's brows upward even as Josiah laughingly remarked, "Lengthy is as lengthy does." He sighed ruefully and continued. "Praise be to God, He created Heaven and earth in six days. You'd think we ministers could deal with our issues in less time, but that is the way of mortal men." He stood with another laugh. "Like all mortal men, time is an issue I need to address."

"Are you leaving?" Elora asked.

"I'm afraid so." He paused and spread his arms wide to encompass Elora and Brice. "May God bless you and keep you both according to His tender mercies and loving kindness. May He remember you for thy goodness sake."

His blessing touched Elora deeply. "Thank you, Josiah."

Vianne came to her feet. "I'll show you out, Reverend. There are several matters that require my attention elsewhere, and I am sure there are a thousand things my brother and Elora wish to discuss."

As soon as the door was shut, Elora turned within Brice's hold and looked into his shuttered face. "You don't like Josiah, do you?" It was the most delicate way she could think to inquire into his opinion. Considering the darkened jade of his eyes, she was convinced that his temper was sorely abused.

"I don't like him."

She had guessed as much, but she wasn't prepared for such a bald admission. "Why?"

Because you're mine, and I want the warmth in your voice and the joy on your face directed at me and not at that man.

It had been bad enough to see Elora's unbridled joy when Platt had visited a week ago. But to walk in today and hear her pleasure when she called the man her friend, and to see the answering delight in the reverend's gaze, had made him want to lunge across the room and wring the minister's neck.

It was jealousy, pure and simple, but realizing that didn't make it any easier to bear. Never having experienced it before, he wasn't accustomed to the feeling, not any more than he was used to any of the feelings that had assailed him since Elora had come into his life.

He looked down into her beautiful face. She had asked him why he didn't like Josiah Platt. He gave her the only answer he was capable of giving.

His arm tightened about her and he caught her lips in a fierce kiss, snatching her startled gasp and making it his own. His mouth slanted over hers, molding the soft curves, shaping them until they parted and his tongue surged into the warm recess of her mouth. In bold, hungry swipes, he explored, caressed, claimed the sweetness as he would claim all of her as his own.

His breathing turned ragged and still his arm did not relinquish its hold. "You're mine, Elora, do you understand?" he breathed against her lips.

Swept away by the forcefulness of his reaction, Elora struggled for some measure of reason. "Yes, I understand." But she didn't. She had done nothing to prompt his startling behavior. "I'm sorry Josiah's visit upset you."

"I don't like him here."

"Why? He is a friend, as close to a brother as I ever had."

"What he feels toward you is not a sisterly affection."

That startled her. "What?"

"The looks he gives you are not those shared by siblings."

"No, Brice, that isn't so." The thought was so ridiculous as to be amusing. "We have known each other for many years. What you see is nothing but the comfort that comes from a long familiarity with each other. An ease of manner, that is all. Josiah considers me as I do him, a close, but purely platonic friend."

He regarded her warily, wanting to believe her, but he was still grappling with the uniqueness of jealousy. The longer he had to deal with it, the more he decided he didn't like it one damned bit.

"All right, he is your friend. But know that I am not complacent with the idea."

His manner was so absurd, that it was all Elora could do to keep from laughing. There was absolutely no reason for his resentment. But for some reason she found it wonderfully endearing.

The glory of her love suffused her in a warm glow.

It was horribly sad that he did not love her in return.

Her insides seemed to slowly sink into her feet, but she had no girlish illusions about how Brice felt. Love simply did not exist in his life, nor did he wish it to. If she thought her telling him how she felt would change matters, she would confess all. But as disinclined as he was toward emotions of any kind, she knew he would not welcome her love, and she didn't think she could stand the pain of that kind of rejection.

A lovely image floated into her mind; that of Brice in the coach, making her a lifelong pledge. It had been a rare moment for them, touched with a poignant tenderness that even now made her heart ache. But she was not foolish enough to believe that what had passed between them had been a shared love. He had given her respect and even friendship. Nothing more.

Dejectedly she was forced to accept the truth for what it was. She had always wanted a marriage founded on love. She was going to have to be satisfied that the love was only one-sided. It was better than nothing.

It was worse than her worst nightmare. She wasn't certain how she was going to endure a lifetime loving Brice and not being loved in return.

She leaned along his chest, savoring the feel of being held against him. "Did you come in here to debate the issue of friendship?"

Her attempted smile skimmed along his nerves, dissolving his ire by slow degrees. "No, actually, I wanted to give you these."

Ignoring the pain in his arm, he reached into his jacket pocket and removed her spectacles.

"My glasses. I wondered where they had gone to."

"If you remember on the ride to Lady Barbara's last night, I tucked them into my pocket."

She took the glasses in hand and noticed at once the fine, solid gold rims. "These aren't mine."

"I had new ones made up for you. Yours were crushed."

She didn't need to be told how. Memories flooded back. The thought of how Brice had nearly been killed, again, sickened her with dread. Her eyes drifted shut and her forehead came to rest against his chest. She had almost lost him.

"Brice, I can't bear to think that someone is out there even now plotting . . ." She couldn't finish. "Why?" She looked up then, wanting an explanation. "Why is this happening? Who is doing this?"

"I don't know. I wish I did, but I don't."

"You need protection."

"I have a man looking into the matter." It was a slight stretching of the truth of Harold Tew's investigations. "I don't want you worrying over this."

"I am worried."

He could see that and it bothered him. But his own reaction to her distress bothered him even more.

Silently he cursed, as he had found himself doing repeatedly in the past weeks. All day he had been beset by the most ungovernable inclinations to feel what he bloody well did not wish to feel. First with Vianne and now with Elora. It was as if his entire universe were changing and he was being swept along by forces he could not even begin to control.

Almost resentfully, he debated whether he should continue to stand there and discuss the matter. But gazing into her eyes, he was hit full force with the undiluted concern shining out at him. How could he possibly scorn such pure, selfless emotion?

Sighing deeply, he relented. She was to be his wife, he reasoned, the very woman who had saved his life. If anyone was entitled to know the details of the affair, it was Elora.

Still, it wasn't easy following through with his decision. It had been too long since he had included anyone in what he considered his own personal matters. For several seconds, he simply stood until he finally gestured for her to take a seat.

"There are several who could be responsible," he began, sitting beside her. "My cousin Thorbon is my heir. He could want my title as well as my wealth."

"Thorbon?" Elora's eyes rounded. "This is terrible. Do you really think he wants to . . . to kill you?"

Brice shrugged. "It is only one possibility. Katherine, too, has cause to want to see me dead."

"Why?"

"Because after Thorbon, her son is next in line to inherit." Leaning back, he explained, "If Thorbon were to come into the title, it would only be for a matter of a few years. He is elderly, has no wife, no children, so the title would pass to her son very quickly."

"Do you think she would go to these lengths to see that her own son is the next marquess?"

"Perhaps." She must have heard the lack of conviction in his voice because she regarded him warily.

"There's more you're not telling me, isn't there?"

She was a sensitive little thing, Brice thought, picking up on the most remarkable subtleties. "You're right. I have reason to think that the Duke of Westford and the Earl of Stanley also might be to blame."

"Oh, my God," she whispered, her face paling.

Again, he was struck by her dismay. Giving into the instinctive impulse to calm her fears, he took hold of her hand. "I knew I shouldn't have told you."

"No, no. I'm glad you did. It's just that I never thought so many people could be responsible. I assumed one lone madman was behind all the trouble."

"There is, I just don't know which one."

"But four? There are actually four people who would wish you such harm?" She shook her head, visibly trying to come to terms with his revelations. "What do the duke or the earl have against you?"

"On Stanley's part, revenge. I told you last night that he has lost a great deal of money to me."

The composure Elora was trying so hard to contain slipped. "He thinks to collect by killing you?" she demanded hotly.

She was so outraged that Brice could not suppress a smile. "Obviously not, but my death would satisfy some warped need he has for retribution."

"What about the duke?"

"Calm yourself, little protector." He gave her hand a gentle squeeze.

"I can't. This is just too impossible to believe. Tell me about the duke."

It was as royal a command as any Brice had ever heard. Surprisingly, he didn't bristle as he normally would have. Instead he wondered how she might behave if she ever truly lost her temper. He could just imagine those gorgeous eyes of hers burning with anger, her cheeks flushed. It was an appealing picture.

"The duke's motives are not quite so simple, I'm afraid. He sees himself as the next great private curator of sorts. We both collect antiques, and I possess several that he would love to have. I believe he sees me as his only hindrance to collecting as he would."

Silence fell in wake of his words, but only for several seconds. Before Brice could even gather his next good breath, Elora came to her feet, eyes flashing and cheeks glowing just as he had imagined.

"This is outrageous!" she cried.

"Elora . . ."

"Who do these people think they are?"

"Elora, I . . ."

She plopped her hands on her hips. "We have to do something, Brice."

His hand shot out, closed about her wrist and hauled her back down beside him. *"We* are not going to do anything," he informed her in a commanding voice that far surpassed the one she had used. "You are going to remain as removed from this as possible. I am taking care of the entire matter."

"But . . ."

"No buts."

"Brice . . ."

"Elora." He would not discuss it further. The inflection in the single word said as much.

Her ire seemed to slowly dissipate. She laid a caressing hand along his cheek. "Promise me you will be careful."

The soft velvet of her eyes held a soulful yearning that ran through his veins like a liquid heat. "I promise."

And he was amazed that he meant what he said. He wanted very much to stay alive and well, not because he had a fear of dying, but because quite unexpectedly staying alive had come to have real meaning. There was a lifetime ahead of him. He just hadn't thought about it in a long while.

Chapter

13

"Tell me, Miss Simmons," Lord Thompson said, "what in London has captured your interest thus far?"

"Other than the marquess," someone added playfully.

A round of laughter forestalled Elora's reply. Blushing slightly, she gazed quickly to Brice. He was dressed formally in silver and black, a combination she thought not only suitable for the glittering gala they were attending, but also magnificently becoming on the most handsome man she had ever seen.

"I have not visited that much of the city, so I don't know how unbiased an answer I can give you. But I found the coffee shops quite intriguing."

The Earl of Stenfeld sputtered in disbelief. "Surely you cannot mean to say that you actually gained entrance into a coffee shop."

"Oh, no," Elora assured him.

"Then what do you find so intriguing?"

Smiling in genuine artlessness, she said, "The fact that I am *not* allowed to gain entrance."

There wasn't a woman present who did not entertain the exact same sentiment. In a spontaneous outburst, they laughed in a shared understanding, casting playful gibes at the men.

Elora looked about at the smiling faces, not entirely at ease with their laughter or their attention. They seemed to find her every word entertaining. She had no clue as to why. She merely spoke honestly, politely, offering her opinion and hardly more than that. But for some reason, they hung onto her every word as though they were drops of wisdom. It was quite unnerving.

She peered up at Brice again. She could not be sure if he sensed her discomfiture or if it showed. In any event, she was extremely grateful when he slipped his arm about her waist and suggested that they partake of the punch.

"Thank you for rescuing me," she whispered as they moved away.

His eyes gleamed with the beginnings of a mocking suspicion. "Are you really thirsty or would you prefer a few moments out of this crush?"

"Oh, the latter, please." No sooner had she spoken than she noted his lips curl with a small smile. "Is something amusing?"

"Yes, you." He directed their path toward one of the many doors opening out onto the terrace.

"Me?"

He paused to nod to an acquaintance. "Mmm. I find it amazing that you are intimidated by this crowd. You haven't the slightest notion as to the depths of your own courage."

"Courage?" She laughed self-consciously. "I lack courage entirely."

"Not when it counts."

It was a reminder that she could have done well without. Every time she thought of the danger Brice was in, she was swamped by the most sickening fear. A shiver skittered over her skin.

"Are you cold?" he asked, feeling the slight tremble.

"No. I think it is just the excitement of the night." It was a partial truth she hoped would suffice. She could not tell him of the anxiety she carried within her. As adamant as he was about not accepting help from anyone, she knew he would not welcome her concern, not any more than he would welcome her love.

They walked out onto the moonlit terrace, but instead of stopping at the wrought-iron rail as Elora expected, Brice guided her down the steps and into the intricately designed formal garden.

"Are you sure this is proper?" she asked, wondering how far from the view of the house Brice intended to lead her.

He arched one black brow upward, making him appear wickedly handsome. "Are you worried?"

"No, not at all." Personally she didn't care what destination he had in mind, especially when he looked at her in that hypnotic manner of his where the green of his eyes glistened with rakish, masculine intent.

Unfortunately, she knew that the majority of the people they had left behind would make it their business to interest themselves in her whereabouts. "Proprieties being what they are, I thought I should at least ask where you're taking me."

"Well, this should satisfy the gossips as well as your need for a respite." He ushered her to a raised goldfish pond, its circular wall constructed of stone. The pool stood clear of bushes and latticework screens, so it was in plain view of the house no more than thirty yards away. It was also far enough removed to offer a very public type of privacy.

"This is perfect." She sighed. Moonlight glazed the water with a silvery luster. The scent of boxwoods clung to the air, the muted strains of a waltz floated overhead. If it weren't for the distant sound of hundreds of voices, Elora could have easily imagined them in a most magical spot.

"We are as visible to scrutinizing eyes as if we were back in the ballroom," she laughed. "I can't imagine even Lady Barbara being offended by this."

"Don't imagine too hard," he remarked in mild disgust. "You would be surprised what would and would not offend her."

Seeing his disgruntled look, she smiled gently. "You are too hard on her, Brice. She really is quite sweet beneath her sharp tongue."

"You are one of the few people to think so."

"Perhaps, but I like her all the same."

That came as no surprise to Brice. Elora had the most unique ability to think and act unlike anyone he had ever met. It was as natural for her to save a person's life as it was for her to befriend one of the most cantankerous women on Earth.

He gazed down at her upturned face, the delicate features edged in the moon's soft light. Suddenly he wished he had escorted her to a spot much more private, even if it had been for only a few stolen seconds. At least then he would have been able to savor her curves pressed against him and feel her mouth soft and warm beneath his own.

A surge of desire swept through him, driving into his gut with stunning force. His blood began to pound, and mentally he damned the edicts of society, damned spying eyes and damned the three feet he kept between himself and Elora.

"Brice, are you unwell?" she asked, wondering what had given his jaw such an unyielding cast.

"I will be better once we are married."

She tipped her head to one side in confusion. "I beg your pardon?"

He swallowed a grunt of frustration. She didn't have the slightest notion of what she did to a man. "I am trying to remember my good intentions in bringing you out here."

"Why?"

"Because," he stated succinctly, pinning her with a dark gaze, "if I don't, I am likely to take you in my arms and kiss you until you can't think straight."

Elora's mouth formed a silent *O*.

"Exactly," Brice confirmed, when he saw that she finally understood.

"Do you wish to go back?" she whispered, eyes as round as the full moon above.

He reached for her hand and tucked it into the crook of his elbow. "That might be wise."

Elora shook her head in amazement. She didn't know what had caused his wanting to kiss her. Like those other times when he had swept her into his arms, it was something that just seemed to happen without warning. She admitted, however, she was entranced whenever he did kiss her.

Brice was right, this was not the place for such.

She looked about at the lovely site, and her lips took on a wistful curve. Even if complete privacy had been theirs, this was still not the place for them. This setting was for people in love, for people who could let the music and the moon hold them enchanted. Those people would stare into each other's eyes, search out each other's souls and bask in each other's love.

It was a beautiful picture. But for her that was all it would ever be.

"Elora?"

She smiled her yearnings away, but deep inside her, she wanted Brice's love more than she had ever wanted anything in her whole life.

Self-consciously she murmured, "Here I am rooted to the ground. This little pond seems to have cast a spell on me."

He caught her chin and tilted her face up, curious about what had made her voice a quivering hush. The desire he had felt just seconds ago was forgotten before the strained look on her face.

"Now it is my turn to ask if you are unwell."

"Of course I am fine. I'm just being silly." In an attempt to make light of her preference for obscurity, she forced a laugh. "You know how overwhelmed I am by hordes of people."

He knew, but he was not convinced by her explanation. The impression that she was leaving a great deal unsaid unsettled him. That restless sensation rankled as much as her evasion, and an evasion it definitely was, right down to her sudden shift in mood.

It surprised him that he was even mindful of her mood, yet he was. Since the night of his stabbing, his sense of awareness seemed to have been heightened, and he had begun to feel and see things he hadn't experienced in years. At this moment, he distinctly felt that there was something troubling her. He did not press the matter, but that didn't keep him from wondering.

It was something to which he paid a great deal of attention in the coming days. Through the rounds of balls and teas and dinners, he detected in Elora an undercurrent of tension lingering just beneath her smiles. She had never hidden the fact that she preferred a simple evening at home to a grand ball, but he could not shake the impression that her discomfiture was more than a simple case of nerves.

At first he credited his perception to nothing more than an overactive imagination. After all, it had been a long time since he had actually given any thought to how someone felt. He could very well be imagining the longing that would fill her eyes, or the wistful turn that would hinder her smile for no apparent reason. But the more time he spent in Elora's company, the more he sensed something that he could only describe as sadness.

Deciding that the social requirements would have to be neglected for one night, he sent a note up to her room, requesting that she dress for a quiet evening to be spent at home.

Moments later, a curious-looking Elora joined him in his study. "Brice? Is something amiss?"

Drawing an intricately wrought box from one of the cabinets, he swept her with an appreciative gaze. The simple lines of her sapphire dress hugged her curves, and without her spectacles, the blue of her eyes was pure and bright.

"No, there is nothing wrong. I simply thought you could use a night away from the frenzy of it all."

"Oh?" Surprise mingled freely with gratitude in her voice. "Are you sure? I don't want to disrupt any plans that you made. And Lady Barbara had agreed to accompany us to the opera."

He rested one hand on her shoulder. "I am so sure that I have already sent word to Lady Barbara." His brows lowered fractionally. "That is of course if you have no objections."

"No." She was quick to assure him before her expression turned sheepish. "I confess, I would much rather spend the hours here with you."

"Then it is settled."

With a mastery that never failed to amaze Elora, Brice had his sister and Colin informed that they would not be going out. Cobb was instructed to have the fire in the grate stoked to a crackling blaze, and everyone was told that he and Elora did not wish to be disturbed.

"Have I ever mentioned to you just how commanding you are?" she teased, sitting beside Brice on the rug before the fireplace.

"Not until this moment." He placed the rectangular box of foreign origin between them.

"What is this?"

"A game the Egyptians called senet."

"Egyptian?" Elora stared at the richly carved piece. The ebony sides were detailed with raised images of animals, while the top was laid out in three rows of ivory squares. The artistry of the box was beautifully simple and meticulously crafted.

Elora was fascinated. Given Brice's extraordinary collection of rare artifacts, she had no doubt that the box was an original and not just a copy. Which meant that it had to be thousands of years old.

"It's exquisite. But what are we doing with it?"

"I thought we would play." Not favoring his shoulder at all, he removed his dark gray jacket and laid it aside.

"You know how to play ancient games?"

From a drawer built into the short end of the box, he removed the numerous playing pieces. "I know how to play senet."

As though it were an everyday occurrence to be playing a game that most people had never even heard of, he handed seven wooden cubes to Elora and kept seven little pyramids for himself. As he explained, the rules of the game involved a player moving all seven of his or her pieces across the thirty squares on the board. Throwing a knucklebone determined how many squares a player could advance one of the pieces.

"I think I will enjoy this game," Elora said. Lining her cubes up in a neat row on the rug, she was captured by a good-humored, albeit competitive spirit. "I shall trounce you soundly."

Brice liked the sparkle in her eyes. He hadn't seen it as often as he would have preferred lately. "Don't be so sure of that. There is more to this game than you think. The Egyptians equated a great deal of symbolism to the game."

"Oh?"

"Supposedly one plays against Fate, and the squares on the board symbolize the pitfalls of the netherworld."

Elora stared at her cubes. The seemingly innocuous game suddenly took on a different slant entirely. "Then what meaning is attached to victory?"

Brice made himself more comfortable, bending one leg and resting his forearm across his knee. "The prize for winning is eternal life and all its glories."

One of those glories, Elora knew, was love. Her spirits dropped and try as she may, she could not get a rein on her wayward heart. It ached for what she would never have.

The slightest flicker of emotion crossed her face, and she dipped her head in an effort to hide her feelings. It would do her little good to bemoan her circumstances. Life did not come with a set of promises, where the love you felt for someone was reciprocated.

"Elora?"

Brice's deep voice brought her head up. Belatedly she remembered to smile. "Shall I throw first or will you?"

Brice studied her intently. There it was again, the almost forced curve of her lips and the slight unease about her eyes. What had put that look on her face? Two months ago he wouldn't have even noticed. But now he did and he damn well wanted to know the cause.

"Are you feeling ill?"

She shook her head. "No."

"Then what is bothering you?"

His close scrutiny sent her delicate brows upward over eyes that rounded just a little too quickly. "Nothing is bothering me."

For a moment he considered allowing her the excuse, but only for a moment. In a careful, even voice he asked, "Do you remember the night you tried to walk out of the house? You managed to come down the stairs, but you could barely stand up without the support of the wall. Still, you tried to tell me you were strong enough to leave."

Elora recalled the night vividly. He had cursed her for ever coming into his life. "I remember."

"I believe I told you never to play faro because you don't have the face for it. You could not lie then about your hurt and pain because despite your best efforts they showed all over your face." His voice drifted to a husky murmur and he reached out to trace the satin of her cheek. "You cannot lie now. Something is wrong and I want to know what it is."

A trembling began in her stomach, intensifying until she had to swallow. She couldn't tell him, she just could not. To proclaim her love and have it rejected would wound her more deeply than the pistol's shot ever had.

"I suppose I am nervous about all that has happened. My life has changed drastically in a very short amount of time." It was the truth, but not the one he sought. She plucked up one of her cubes and turned it slowly in her hands. "And I can not help but fear for your life."

He did not doubt that for a second. "What would make you feel better?"

Having your love. She turned her gaze to the ceiling. "A small wedding would help."

"As you wish."

She looked at him skeptically. "Truly?"

"If the truth be known, I have no great fondness for the type of pageantry that accompanies the ceremony."

She sighed in heartfelt relief. "I can not tell you how glad I am to hear that. I have been on pins and needles at the thought of hundreds and hundreds of people crowding about, making a fuss. I really would prefer a small gathering of your family—Vianne and Colin, Lady Barbara." She tilted her head at a thought. "You have never mentioned your parents. I assume you would wish them to witness our marriage."

The hand that had stroked her cheek clenched into a mighty fist, straining the tendons into prominence. His voice when he spoke was as taut.

"My parents are dead."

She sensed him freeze up instantly, a barely contained shimmering of energy entwining with his muscles. "I'm sorry, Brice. I did not know."

"It happened years ago. It is not something I speak of." He returned his attention to the game, his hand unclenching. "Are you ready to play?"

Elora regretted her words that had so readily bared his anguish. Obviously his parents' death was a very raw subject.

She recalled Vianne telling her that Brice had endured bitter grief in his life. Was the death of his parents the source of his sorrow? It was impossible for her to know, but whatever the cause, she longed to comfort him. If he would allow, she would put her arms about him and help ease whatever suffering he held. But by his own words, he would not discuss this with her.

Wishing to alleviate the strain that lay between them, she focused on the game, determined to recapture the amiable mood that had existed earlier. If Brice would not let her help, then she could at least make the evening as pleasant as she could.

An hour . . . and three rounds . . . later, she was ruefully questioning her resolve. She had wanted to lighten the mood, but not necessarily at her own expense. Through the course of their game, a good-natured competition had sprung up, but she had lost all three rounds and Brice was doing nothing to hide his enjoyment of his wins.

"Are you sure we're throwing the same knucklebone?" she asked in cheerful suspicion.

Brice collected his pyramids and cocked a black brow at her light indignation. "Are you accusing me of cheating?"

"Not at all. I simply do not understand how I can throw the same piece as you and achieve such horrid results." Not wearing her spectacles, she squinted for a better view of the obnoxious little die.

"It's all in the wrist," he told her, a grin pulling at the firm line of his mouth.

She sent him a shaming look, and could not contain her mirth. Sweet ripples of her laughter floated about them, drawing Brice's appreciative look to her lips.

The fire's glow danced on the gold strands of her hair and gilded the contours of her body. Her generous curves were sumptuously defined and he followed the shape and outline of her with a bold, masculine gaze.

Raising a hand, he traced the clean line of her cheek, his eyes following his hand's descent to her neck. Unexpectedly, he caught sight of a small mark on the edge of her jaw and he leaned closer for a better look.

"What is this? A scar?" He had never noticed it before and he ran a finger over the faint, jagged line.

Elora's amusement died abruptly. Eyes filling with the remnants of a long-ago fright, she lifted a hand to her neck, her fingers brushing Brice's.

"Yes, it's a scar."

Her sudden anxiety startled him. Gone was her easy gaiety. In its place was a tension that glazed her eyes and stiffened her voice.

"How did you manage a cut like that?" From the look of it, Brice knew it was years old, and the cut that had produced it had to have been quite deep for it to have left such a permanent imprint.

"It happened when I was young." One of her shoulders rose in a jerking shrug. "I don't really remember how."

But she did remember. He could see that in her expression as clearly as he could see the scar itself. He sensed that there was much more to the story than what she was telling him, and while he normally wouldn't have pushed at all, he now wanted to hear every detail of what had occurred.

He caught her chin between his thumb and forefinger. Instantly, she flinched as though she had been burned.

"Elora?" He raised her face toward his, concerned and not a little stung by her involuntary reaction. Annoyingly, he realized that it wasn't the first time she had behaved in just such a manner. On more than one occasion in the past weeks, she had recoiled from him.

"How did it happen?" The repeated question and the implacable frown that accompanied it left no room for argument.

"I fell against a table when I was eleven or twelve," she said succinctly.

"And?" Despite her obvious reluctance to continue, he persisted, not really certain why he did. But he could not shake the sensation that the more he inquired, the more he would discover about himself.

"And I cut myself."

"What caused you to fall?"

Elora tried to look away. Brice's hand held her firmly in place. "I really don't want to talk about it. It happened a long time ago."

"But I want to know."

She did not want to tell him. The recollections associated with the scar dragged to mind the worst of her stepfather's brutality. Even now, eight years after the fact, the horrible episode had the ability to make her insides go cold.

By Mr. Gillet's order, she had been tidying his workroom. Plates of half-eaten food had been scattered about his desk. Empty wine bottles had been strewn haphazardly over ledgers and piles of bills. Muddied boots and rumpled clothing lay neglected on the floor, while piles of various wares had been stacked about in a random fashion. For a thirteen-year-old, the chore of putting the room to rights had been monumental.

She had wanted to be finished with her task before her stepfather returned home, but hours of work had seen her well behind her goal. He arrived before she could be out of his drunken sight and as she had feared, he had taken out his displeasure on her.

"Please, Brice."

"How did this happen?"

It was useless. He was going to persist. "My stepfather," she whispered.

Coming to his knees in one powerful surge, Brice grasped her by the shoulders and pulled her up until she was kneeling close before him. His face rigid, his expression grim, he stared deeply into her eyes.

"He hit you?"

Her hand fluttered to the wall of his chest in a feeble attempt to diffuse his anger. "Brice, I told you once before that he is a cruel man."

"Yes, but you never said that he was a bastard who went about striking children, and no doubt women, too."

"Yes . . . well, he did."

Raw fury ripped into Brice. In a bid for some kind of control, he shut his eyes and tipped his head back. *Damn it all to bloody hell and back!* The thought of someone, *anyone,* striking Elora, hurting her, made him want to tear that person apart.

His eyes snapped open. Once again, he could see her that day in this very same study, looking up at him as he urged her to marry him. *Promise me you'll never hurt me,* she had pleaded. At the time, he had merely been insulted by the request.

Now, he realized that her entreaty had been based on a fear she had of her stepfather, a fear of being abused.

In a move that surprised them both, he swept her up against him. "Are you all right?"

She released a shaking breath. "Yes."

"Are you sure?"

"As I said, it happened a long time ago."

"But the memory of what he did still bothers you. I can tell, I can see it in your eyes."

His reaction amazed her. She had not expected him to express such concern for her well-being. In their association, he had been generous and honorable and protective, but he had not expended himself emotionally on her behalf. The fact that he did now warmed her heart, and alleviated her distress.

"I try not to dwell on what my stepfather did. No good can come of that. I am thankful that he is gone from here and that I will never see him again."

He looked back to the faint line on her jaw and tried to cool the anger racing through his veins. He pictured the young child she had been, suffering at her stepfather's brutal hand, and he gathered her more tightly against him, impelled to protect the woman she was now. The impulse to shield her from a long-ago hurt engulfed and startled him, for he realized that deep inside him, he ached for her suffering.

He felt his body warm as she flowed along his length, her soft curves finding a natural fit to his hard planes. Relying on barely remembered instincts, he offered her his comfort.

Pressing his face into the golden mass of hair, he breathed in the sweet scent of her and in his mind pictured laughter and sunshine. It was a purely aesthetic imagining, but he relished that impression as much as he did her warmth and softness.

Elora closed her eyes at the exquisite feel of him. It had been so long since she had been held with such precious care. The pleasure and easing of spirit that flooded her only made her love Brice all the more.

She leaned back ever so slightly and pressed her palm to his cheek. Spurred by all the love in her heart, she brought her mouth to his and kissed him with a tender passion.

Brice went utterly still for the space of one thunderous heartbeat. He knew her to be a passionate woman, but always at his prompting. To have her initiate the kiss was a pleasure unlike any he had ever known.

He returned the kiss, deepening it with a hungry slant of his mouth on hers. With no coaxing, her lips parted and their tongues entwined in an ardent play that quickened pulses and brought a low moan to Elora's throat.

The sound traveled Brice's nerves to a place deep in his gut. A surge of desire shot through him and his body reacted as it did to her alone; hardening instantly, fiercely. Her softness was an enticement of the senses, and in one raging second, he was desperate to join his body with hers.

His movements strong and sure, he lowered Elora to the thick rug, following her down, bending one leg so that his knee rode between her legs and his hips covered hers. His hands roamed at will, molding her rounded hips and cupping her thrusting breasts.

Everywhere his fingers touched, Elora felt shocking jolts of pleasure ignite. Each tremor was a sweet torture that collected as a heated coil in the pit of her belly, urging her to hold him close, and closer still. Her hands clung to his shoulders and she arched into him until her breasts and thighs were pressed full-length to him. And all she could think was that she loved him. Body and soul, heart and mind, she wanted to belong to him.

"Are you going to want to take my clothes off again?" she asked in a breathless whisper, as his mouth trailed a line of kisses to her neck.

"Yes," he groaned, his fingers already releasing the row of tiny buttons that ran down the front of her bodice.

"I'm glad."

Her throaty words tugged mercilessly at Brice's control. Even as he pulled aside the fabric of her dress and chemise, he could feel waves of heat curl deep into his loins.

Another low moan caught in Elora's throat as he drew her nipple into his mouth and caressed the sweet flesh with his tongue. She threaded her fingers into his hair and held him tightly, drifting on a heated excitement, floating higher and higher on each and every new sensation he was making her feel. The fiery coil within her belly had lowered and her hips rose of their own accord.

Brice absorbed her gentle thrust and felt his restraint slip another notch. His mind warned that this was madness. Unless he wanted to take her right there, he was going to have to stop. Soon.

But the feel of her was too good, too right, and he was loath to give her up. He couldn't. Not yet, not when her body was responding so perfectly to his, not when her breathless sighs were like a siren's song.

He wanted to have all of her, and his hand followed his mind's urging. His fingers trailed over the flat of her belly to her thighs. Even through the fabric of her clothes, he could feel the warm curve that extended from hip to knee, and he skimmed the outer contour with a searching hand that made Elora draw in a shaking breath.

His mouth came back to hers, and his fingers retraced their path. Pulling her dress aside, he stroked higher along the inside of her leg until he found what he sought.

"Brice," Elora gasped, stunned by the feel of his fingers against her flesh. Her eyes flew open and she grasped his wrist.

But he did not remove his hand. If his sanity depended on it, he wasn't certain if he could. The feel of her was delicate and feminine and perfect.

Eyes smoldering with desire, he whispered, "Are you frightened?"

She swallowed, straining for a breath that seemed locked in her chest. "I . . . I don't know."

"I won't hurt you." He brushed his lips over hers. "Do you want me to take my hand away?"

How could she answer? To even think that his hand was there between her legs was utterly foreign. But the pressure of his palm was creating the most wondrous sensations she had ever felt.

The green of his eyes beckoned, asking her to trust him. In her breast, her heart squeezed painfully. Knowing that he did not love her, would never love her, she also knew that what he was asking of her was as right as it was shockingly blissful. Her hands lifted to circle his neck and urge him back to her. Her lips sought his and she gave him his answer.

It was the answer he wanted above all others. Groaning, he captured her mouth, kissing her in a tender assault. His blood raced through him in wild torrent, sweeping him toward the absolute limit of his restraint. All the while his fingers stroked over the soft heat of her, he knew he was consumed by a torment of his own making.

His touch fractured Elora's world. Shivers raced out in every direction from the center of her, and she fought for breath. Blindly seeking to assuage the urgent need he was creating, she arched upward, her movement increasing the intimacy of his touch.

In the next instant, she felt him move away. Stunned, she watched him roll to his side and then up to his knees. He sat back on his heels and braced his hands on his thighs, his head lowered between broad, tightened shoulders.

His departure was too sudden and she plummeted down to reality in a jolting crash. Staring at his back as he faced the glowing flames in the grate, she wondered a little frantically what had happened.

She sat up and pulled her bodice into place, never once taking her eyes from Brice.

"Did I do something wrong?"

He turned his head and looked at her over his shoulder. The sight of her uncertainty made him curse his lack of control. Pivoting about, he faced her, but at a distance meant to cool his blood.

"You didn't do anything wrong," he assured her, dragging in a deep breath and then another. "In fact, had you done anything more right, we would have had our wedding night now instead of after the fact."

"You're talking about making love again, aren't you?" She still did not know precisely what that entailed, but she was getting a clearer picture of it all the time.

"Yes, I am talking about making love. And had I not stopped when I did, I would have made love to you right there where you sit."

Her brows arched in guileless wonder. "In all honesty, Brice, I think I would have liked that."

He bit his lower lip and it was only by the most supreme act of self-control that he did not reach out and give her what she wanted, what they both wanted.

"It is time, Miss Simmons, that we married."

Chapter

14

"THREE DAYS," ELORA SAID TO HERSELF. "IN JUST THREE DAYS, Brice and I will be married."

She could hardly contain her amazement as she wandered into the east wing of Warrington Hall. Three days ago, Brice had declared that it was time that they marry. Now, she was here at his country seat, preparing for that very event.

True to his word, Brice had arranged for a small wedding to take place in three days' time. Only a handful of guests would be present, among them, Lady Barbara. Vianne and Colin were already moved in, and the remaining guests would be arriving here tomorrow.

She defined "here" with an encompassing look about her, and not for the first time, shook her head in awe. She had thought Brice's town house to be wondrously grand with its rich appointments and exotic, oriental furnishings. But *this* . . . This sprawling mansion, with its history dating back to the eleventh century, was beyond her wildest dreams.

Her first sight of the house had taken her breath away. It had been built in several stages, the structure boasting styles that included Elizabethan as well as English Baroque. Still, the eclectic manner did not detract from the building's appearance. In Elora's opinion it only added a certain charm.

She made her way through the quiet gallery, her footsteps echoing off the floor-to-ceiling wainscoted walls. According to Mrs. Cobb, this wing was maintained, but not used. Elora had to wonder why, because there was a lovely splendor to be found in this part of the house that she much preferred to any other portion of the mansion. Even the fine layer of dust on the floor, the furniture draped in holland covers and the smell of disuse in the air could not hide the warm grandeur.

Despite that, Elora confessed on a laugh that she was most likely going to get horribly lost. Room led to room, and halls opened into salons in a seemingly endless design that she had yet to understand. Still, she derived a much needed serenity from exploring the deserted rooms.

The past days had been a whirl of activity as the entire London household had been packed up and moved. Somewhat dazed, she felt like her mind was playing catch-up with her body. Completing the hasty arrangements for the wedding had only added to that disjointed feeling.

Entering a wide hall off the gallery, she moved slowly down its paneled length. Doors lined the walls that were bare save for three paintings. She stopped at the first two portraits which hung side by side.

The image of the man bore a striking resemblance to Brice. He had the same black hair, lean jaw and firmly chiseled lips. He carried about him an air of authority, his bearing that of a man ready to challenge the world, and win.

The woman seemed joyfully serene, as though she were supremely content with life. Her light brown hair and generous smile proclaimed her to be in the prime of life. And the deep, glittering green eyes announced her relationship to Brice.

It was immediately obvious to Elora that the couple portrayed on the canvases were Brice's parents.

A gentle smile pulled at her lips. It was strangely touching to look upon these two who had given life to Brice. He had only mentioned his parents once, and that had been to tell her that they had died. Somehow, just seeing their faces was oddly satisfying. For some reason, she felt closer to the man she was going to marry.

"I love your son," she whispered up to the still faces. The blue of her eyes clouded. "I hope to make him happy."

She moved farther down the hall, and stopped at the third painting. For an instant, Elora thought it a portrait of Brice. On closer inspection she realized her mistake. The man in the painting had gray eyes, not green.

She frowned slightly, wondering who this could be. There was no denying the extraordinary resemblance to Brice, and to the painted images of Brice's parents.

A brother? It was a logical conclusion, but Brice had never made any mention of a brother. Then again, Brice never talked about his personal life at all, so there was no reason to think he would have mentioned a brother. Still, the similarities between the portrait and Brice were too marked for there to be any other explanation.

Looking back down the hall, she tilted her head to one side, a puzzled look on her face. Why would Brice hang these paintings where no one would see them? It was rather disturbing to think that he had purposely relegated their images to this isolated spot. There was something depressing about that.

Rubbing a shiver from her arms, she retraced her steps to the end of the hall. But even after she had gained the main portion of the house, she could not dismiss the matter from her mind.

It followed her as she let herself outside and strolled the plush grounds that surrounded the house. She hated to think that Brice had put the paintings where they were because he disliked his family to the point that he could not bear the sight of them.

She wanted to believe that he had shared a loving relationship with his parents. For his sake, she hoped that he had experienced the tender love and care that only a parent can bestow upon a child. But that could very well be nothing but wishful thinking on her part. She knew only too well that wishes did not always come true. If they did, Brice would love her as she did him.

Her steps brought her to the front of the house, and she spotted Brice. He stood tall and straight, an imposing figure who made her pulse trip. His dark head was bent toward a short, almost lumpy-looking man.

She closed the distance between them, but before she could offer a greeting, the man climbed into his waiting carriage and Brice turned to face her.

"I did not mean to interrupt your conversation," she offered, gazing into the green eyes so similar to those she had seen in the paintings.

"You didn't interrupt. We were done."

"Was he someone I should know?" Thinking the man was one of the hundreds of people in Brice's employ, she added, "I have yet to learn all the names and faces of your staff. I am afraid it's going to take me a few more weeks."

The corner of Brice's mouth quirked upward, yet despite that encouraging sign, Elora couldn't help but notice the slight narrowing of his eyes. For several seconds he said nothing, and she had the distinct impression he was grappling with the idea of replying.

Finally, he glanced quickly to the departing carriage and heaved the sigh of a man arriving at some inner decision. In a gesture that seemed characteristic of both wariness and surrender, he reached out and toyed with a blond curl that grazed her neck.

"His name is Harold Tew. He's the investigator I hired to find out who is trying to kill me."

Elora didn't know what she had expected to hear, but it certainly was not that. Shocked, she looked from Brice to the retreating vehicle and then back to Brice.

"Why was he here?" Apprehension put a fine edge to her voice. "Is something wrong?"

"No, nothing is wrong. He simply came to discuss the progress he has made to date."

The fear she felt for Brice darkened her eyes. "Has he found out who it is?"

"No." He snorted in supreme disgust. "He had been following a lead, someone by the name of Mackey Crispen, but the man mysteriously disappeared, knife and all."

"Knife?" Her voice rose an octave. "You mean the man who stabbed you?"

"The very same."

"What is Mr. Tew going to do about this?"

"There is nothing that can be done, Elora."

"There has to be." She could not bear the idea of Brice being in danger. If anything should happen to him, she would likely shrivel up and die herself. "Brice, this is terrible."

"Not any more terrible than anything else that has happened in this entire mess."

"That . . . that Mackey Crispen man is still out there. What's to stop him from trying to . . . trying to . . ." She could *not* get the horrible words out.

"Mr. Tew and I agree that if the bastard was going to make another attempt, he would have done so by now."

Elora bit her lower lip, drawing a little comfort from what he told her. "I suppose you're right."

"I believe I am, but I didn't tell you this to upset you." Shoving his hands deep into his pants pockets, he grimly added, "You asked and so I told you."

Which for him, she realized, had not been easy. Part of her dearly wanted to push the matter, but Brice rarely confided in her and his doing so now pleased her greatly. She would not disparage that by asking questions he was not ready to answer.

She let her eyelids drift shut briefly before she gazed lovingly up to his lean face. "Brice, my mind will be at peace only when I know you are safe."

It would have been impossible for Brice to have missed the emotions shining in Elora's eyes. They were profound and undeniable, and they had prompted him to confide in her. Weeks ago he would have shied from doing so, and from

Elora herself. But during the course of those weeks, his life had changed in ways he could not even begin to comprehend.

Without delving too deeply into the why of it, he accepted what she offered. "Come, walk with me." He took her elbow in his warm hand. "I want to inspect the grounds."

Neither said anything more for several seconds. Elora relinquished her fears for the time being, preferring instead to bask in the pleasure she found in just being with Brice. The simple act of strolling with him brought her a contentment she had never known. It warmed her deeply to know that over the weeks, an easy companionship had grown between them.

"Thank you for telling me about Mr. Tew."

Her gentle voice drew his gaze to the elegant contour of her profile. "You're welcome."

"You might think this odd, but I feel relieved knowing the man is near."

"I will not have you worrying about this, Elora. I would prefer that you concentrate on our wedding."

She exhaled on a sigh that was in part a laugh. "As far as I can tell, all the arrangements have been made. Vianne has been dashing about in one direction, Mrs. Cobb in another." She pressed her fingers to her forehead. "I shudder to think what a large wedding might have entailed. I finally had to take myself off for a few moments."

Brice scanned the acres of sweeping lawn surrounded by dense forest. "Well, there are certainly enough places here in which to find quiet. Where did you end up?"

"The east wing of the house."

Brice came to a stop, his hand jerking Elora to a halt beside him. "The east wing is closed."

She regarded him carefully. With her one statement, he had lost every bit of his calm and now was poised on the brink of a brittle tension.

"I know the wing is closed."

"You should not have gone in there."

"I was not aware that I was not allowed to."

His mouth became a bitter slash. "It is not a matter of your not being allowed, Elora. I would simply prefer that you not do so."

"Why? Is there some danger?"

"No."

The finality in the single word as well as the fierce scowl on his face gave Elora pause. For reasons that he would not explain to her, he did not want her entering a part of the very house in which she was going to live. It did not make sense. Not any more than having his family's portraits hidden away.

"Brice, why is the east wing not used?"

The answers roiled through Brice, demanding release. He spun about on his heel and searched the sky for control. But that will of iron that had seen him through the past three years had been gradually eroded by this one small woman who had burst into his life and forced him to feel once more.

A part of his mind commanded that he turn and walk away from her and all she inspired. A louder voice insisted that he could no longer deny the truth of his past. As though by some unseen force, he felt driven to give voice to words that for too long he had not even allowed himself to think.

"Those rooms were for my parents' private use," he choked out, engulfed by all the love he had felt for his family.

Elora stared at his back, shaken by the agony she heard in his voice. "Brice, I found their pictures."

He didn't say anything for a long moment. At length he whispered, "And Robbie's, too."

"Yes. Is he your brother?"

"Was."

Elora bowed her head. His parents were dead, his brother as well. "I am sorry, Brice."

He spun back to her, the green of his eyes as dark as the bordering forest. "For what?"

"For your loss. I know how it feels to lose your parents. It is a hurt unlike any other."

"You can not know my hurt."

She shook her head slowly, feeling his anguish. "No, not any more than you can truly know mine when my mother and father died. But I do understand how it feels to lose their love, and not be able to love them in return." She gazed deeply into his eyes, wanting to cry at the pain she saw there. "You did love them, didn't you, Brice."

Of course I loved them. More than anyone could possibly know.

His face hardened with unspeakable emotions, and his body stiffened until for one terrible second Elora was not sure what he would do. Then, on a groan that emanated from the depths of him, he stalked away.

She watched him make his way toward the trees. In a quiet stricken voice, she asked, "Is it so terrible to love?"

Her words chased him through the day and into the night, pursuing him as he prowled his darkened rooms seeking relief from his torment.

Is it so terrible to love?

He could still hear her tearful voice, making his stomach clench until his muscles strained with the effort to keep the answer at bay.

Pacing to his bed, he flung himself onto its surface, staring at the shadows overhead. But for all the solidity of the massive piece beneath him, he felt as though he were poised on a precipice, tilting precariously in two different directions. The safe, manageable life that had been his lay in one direction, beckoning him back to cool, guarded, aloofness. In the other direction lay a huge void, its only known quantity, Elora.

He tried to elude the issue, but it remained crystal-clear in his mind. Elora would be his wife in little more than a day; he would be spending the rest of his life with her. And unless he chose to live separately from her, she was going to continue to eat away at his defenses until he was as vulnerable as he had been when his parents had died.

The admission cost him dearly. He came to his feet, trying

to retreat from the past. But Elora's words came back once more to haunt his mind.

Is it so terrible to love?

He forced himself to reply, *yes, because it leads to pain.* Damnably, part of him mocked that rationalization with a steadfast serenity, a peace of mind that was grounded in the memories of his childhood. That childhood had been filled with love.

Is it so terrible to love?

He didn't know. He was not certain he wanted to.

"You arc all thumbs today, Elora." Vianne looked to the spoon Elora had dropped.

Elora set her cup on the side table, grimacing slightly as the saucer rattled in her hand. "Prewedding jitters, I suppose." She retrieved the spoon and set it beside the cup.

"Well, you are entitled. All brides feel nervous the day before their wedding."

"Some more than others." Restively, Elora rose and walked to one of the long windows of the blue and white salon. There she wrapped her arms about her waist and stared unseeing at the beautiful park behind the house.

The day before my wedding. Her stomach lurched. Tomorrow she was going to marry a man who by his own choice refused to love her. Oh, sometime during the endless night just past, she had finally realized the bitter truth of the matter. Well into the wee hours of the morning, her mind had recalled again and again the moment yesterday when Brice had told her about his parents.

It had never been a case of his not believing in love, or not understanding it. It was that he would not *let* himself love. Most especially her, and she, like the ridiculous idiot that she was, could do nothing except love him with all her heart.

She was a fool. She had been from the very start to have ever believed that she could enter into a marriage that held no love. She was an even bigger fool to have thought that she could live content, loving Brice and not have his love in return. Her only excuse was that she had assumed that he had had no basic understanding of the emotion. If it had been lacking in his life, then he could not possibly know how to go about loving someone.

That had been a reasoning with which she had been able to live. Brice could not be at fault for something over which he had had no control. But that had never been the truth. She knew that now, and the knowledge was cruel. He knew how to love. Or at one time he had. She could not discount the fact that something had happened to turn him into the man he was now. Still, the foundations of love were within him and if he so chose, he could love again. But he chose not to love her.

Her glistening eyes swept the green lawn as a relentless query repeated itself again and again in her thoughts. Was she lacking? Was there something about her that prevented him from wanting to love her? She knew the answer in her heart, and the tears that threatened filled her eyes.

"Elora." Vianne's sympathetic voice sounded from behind her. "There is no need for such nerves."

Elora scoffed lightly. "No, you are right. If there is a need for anything it would be pity."

"What are you talking about?" Vianne set aside her cup and joined Elora at the window. Seeing the tears, she asked, "What is the matter?"

Elora took a series of shallow breaths, her emotions too close to the surface to contain. She did not wish to burden Vianne with her sorrow, but the words seemed to tumble out unchecked.

"I never wanted much in life. A husband, children, a home. Just look what I will have." She lifted a hand to indicate the splendid room. "All this." All that was meaningless.

Vianne laid a soothing hand on Elora's arm, concern and alarm draining the color from her cheeks. "Elora . . ."

"Did you know that I am horribly naive?" Elora continued, unable to keep the cynicism from her voice. "Well, I am, right down to my toes. I believe in all the good things in life, like love and friendship and hopes and dreams coming true."

Her eyes reflecting her misery, she whispered, "I love him, Vianne. I love Brice until it hurts inside. I really thought I would be able to live my life without his love." A travesty of a smile pulled at her lips. "Silly, naive me."

Strangling on her hurt, she fled, desperately needing the sanctuary of her room. Behind her, Vianne stood motionless, blinking back tears too painful to bear.

Seconds ticked by in complete silence and still Vianne remained unmoving until at last she swiped angrily at her wet eyes. As though that simple act nourished her strength, she marched from the salon into the huge foyer. A quick glance at the footman standing attendance at the closed library doors told her that Brice was within.

Not waiting to be announced, she pushed open the double doors and swept into the room, her every step gilded with a trembling, consuming rage. Not caring if the footman was watching curiously, not paying the slightest heed to Colin's welcoming smile, she marched up to Brice where he stood by the fireplace and slapped him across his face with all the strength she possessed.

"I hate you!" The tears she had controlled only seconds earlier rushed forward once more. "I will not stand for any more!"

Colin rushed to her side, grasping her by the shoulders, but beyond that he did not interfere.

One arched black brow was Brice's only indication that he was affected by her outburst. "I trust you have an explanation."

"Don't you dare say anything to me! For three years I have stood by while you have relegated me to the position of nonentity. I have done everything humanly possible to try and ease your suffering, and to what end? You step all over people's feelings, caring as little about them as you do about yourself. Well, I am through. For all I care, you can go to the devil!"

Three years of anguish tinged her every word and they

211

spilled forth in an angry torrent. "You aren't the only one to have suffered, Brice. I loved them, too. When Mother died, a part of me died along with her. The love I have for Father and Robbie is still a sad yearning within me.

"I know how much you loved them, I know how hard you tried to save them. But do you think that I did not suffer at their loss? Do you think that you alone felt the hurt?"

Shaking with her ire, she spat, "You have let this consuming sorrow of yours turn you into something cruel and selfish. And you are going to destroy Elora just as you have destroyed yourself." Her shaking hands blindly reached for Colin's. "For her sake alone, we will remain for the wedding. But after that, if I never see you again it will be too soon. I can only pray for Elora's happiness."

She wrenched out of Colin's hold. He caught up with her in two long strides to usher her out of the room.

Much as Vianne had done only moments ago, Brice stood rooted to the floor. The red imprint of Vianne's hand was emblazoned across his cheek, but he did not feel the sting. He did not feel or hear or see anything other than his sister's face as she hurled her truths at him.

You are going to destroy Elora just as you have destroyed yourself.

Elora adjusted her spectacles on her nose and took a good long look at herself in her mirror. Having spent the past hour crying into her pillows, she had regained her composure, if not her pride. She shook her head in disgust.

"You have made a fool of yourself this time," she told her reflection. "You have never wallowed in self-pity, so there is no need to begin now. Brice will not love you. There is no more to be said."

Her reflected image stirred as Elora turned away for the door. She needed to find Vianne and apologize for her outburst. Vianne did not deserve to be on the receiving end of such an emotional blunder.

She left her room but went no farther than the stairway when she met Cobb.

"I beg your pardon, miss, there is a gentleman below by the name of Harmen Gillet. He wishes a word with you."

In one sinking swoop, Elora felt her insides drop. "Mr. Gillet is here?" Every horrible memory of him filled her with dread.

"Yes, miss," Cobb replied carefully. "I told him I would inquire if you were receiving, but he was most insistent that you would wish to speak to him."

She laid a hand to where her stomach should have been and swallowed with difficulty. Her stepfather could not be here, he just could not. She truly thought she had seen the last of him, and she hated to think what had brought him here. It could not be anything good.

Panic seized her. She could make up any excuse in the world not to go below, but what would that really accomplish in the end? Harmen Gillet had found her, and if he had been so bold as to seek her out now, there was nothing preventing him from returning again and again. That was a horrifying prospect she wasn't certain she could bear. Better to have the meeting over and done with.

"Very well, Mr. Cobb." She followed the butler to a small receiving room on the first floor. Just outside the door, she stopped and adjusted her spectacles that were already firmly in place.

She did not want to go in there, did not want to speak to, much less look upon, her stepfather. But what choice did she have? She better than anyone knew just how ruthlessly single-minded he could be. He had always forced her to his will. This instance would be no different.

A small voice within her urged her to go to Brice for help. He would protect her, he would keep her safe from Harmen Gillet. But even as she considered the thought, she denied it. Starting here and now, she was going to have to learn to protect her person from her stepfather. And her heart from Brice.

It was the only way she could envision a future for herself. If she allowed herself to rely on Brice for protection, she would let herself rely on him emotionally. That was something she could not continue to do.

Realizing that Cobb was waiting, watching her while she gripped the folds of her silk dress, she settled herself as though to do battle.

"Do you wish me to leave the door open, miss?" he asked quietly.

Heaven only knew what her stepfather would have to say. She would prefer that it not be overheard by anyone other than herself.

"No, Mr. Cobb, thank you." She started forward, then added, "Would you wait out here?"

Cobb nodded solemnly. "Yes, miss."

Grateful for that small amount of reassurance, she entered the room with her chin held high. Her gaze sought the bald, hulking shape of her stepfather at once and she advanced no farther than the middle of the room.

"Mr. Gillet," she commented in a level voice.

Harmen Gillet heaved himself out of his chair with an ease that never failed to surprise Elora. For a man of his size, he was frighteningly agile as he took a menacing stance. His thick legs braced apart, he stood as solid and unmovable as any ox. Only Elora knew that an ox was a gentle beast, and not given to the kind of brutality that typified her stepfather.

Entwining her fingers to hide their shaking, she silently watched his piercing black eyes take in the expensive cut of her dress. The permanently slack line of his mouth twisted into a smile.

"You've done all right by yourself."

Elora wasted no time with niceties. She wanted the man out of the house as of two minutes ago. "What are you doing here?"

He spread his beefy hands wide. "I come to see my stepdaughter wed. Read all about it in the papers, I did."

"I am sorry, we are having very few guests at the wedding."

"Now, Elora, I don't think a father should be counted as a guest."

"You were the man my mother married, but you were never my father."

He dismissed the notion with an ugly grimace that bared two blackened teeth. "You're going on about trivialities, girl. I'm your kin as sure as I'm standing here. I come all this way to do right by you."

"Do right by me?"

"Of course. You think I'm going to just hand you over to a man I never even laid eyes on?"

She saw the reason for his presence in that instant, and his presumption was so great that she lost much of her trepidation. "You have no claim to me. You have no say in what I do. If you think I am going to allow you to extract money from anyone for any purpose, you are sadly mistaken."

His black eyes narrowed to malicious slits. "Don't take none of that tone with me, girl. I won't stand for it, you hear?" Yanking his waistcoat into place, he reasoned, "Now, I come here peaceably, wanting nothing more than my due."

"Your due?" She was incredulous, and had her nerves not already been flayed, she would have remembered that the man was not to be goaded. As it was, she had little patience to claim as her own. Eyes flashing, she cried, "I assumed responsibility for your debts. As far as I am concerned, you are owed nothing."

"I supported you for years. Put out good money even after your mother died."

"Even after your neglect and brutality killed her, you mean. And if that wasn't enough, you tried to cheat your creditors out of what they were owed. I was left to face them. In my eyes, you are entitled to nothing but my contempt."

Her words ignited his nonexistent fuse and any restraint he might have had was snuffed out. "You think I'm going to let you have all this without getting some of it for myself?" he bellowed. He closed the distance between them in long angry strides. "You little slut, you owe me."

Elora's skin prickled with fear, but before she could utter the first sound, brilliant lights and roaring thunder erupted everywhere as Gillet's fist crashed against the side of her head.

She tried to check her fall, but the force of the blow sent her to the floor. Dimly she felt herself crumble, the room seeming to explode in violence.

Brice came through the door at the same second that Gillet had raised his hand. But even as he lunged to reach Elora and yank her out of the way, she reeled under the impact of Gillet's brutal hand.

Blinded by a blazing fury, Brice swung his fist into Gillet's face, toppling the man with that one savage blow. Gillet collapsed in a fleshy heap, but still Brice was not satisfied. He grabbed the half-conscious man and shook him viciously.

"You bloody maggot, if you ever come near her again, I will kill you." He shoved Gillet away with every ounce of his strength, cracking the bald head against the wood floor.

Disgusted, he surged to his feet, leaving the way clear for two stalwart footmen to drag the limp form away. In three strides, he reached Elora and went to his knees, gathering her into his arms.

"Elora." Frantically, he searched her bloodless face, praying for the first time in three years, praying for her well-being, praying that she would forgive him. "Oh, God, Elora."

"Brice." Her voice was nothing more than a muted vibration. It was the sweetest sound he had ever heard.

Standing, he held his precious burden as though his very life depended on it. And it did. Rushing from the room, he knew that if anything were to happen to her, he would not be able to live. He would not *want* to live.

"Send Mrs. Cobb up." He threw his order to a waiting Cobb as he hastened up the stairs. In only a matter of seconds, he laid Elora on her bed and sat beside her.

"Elora, look at me. Please tell me you are all right."

She blinked groggily, seeing two images of Brice instead of one. A lopsided grin trembled on her lips. "Hello."

Unbidden, tears came to his eyes. He let them fall. Unable

to help himself, he gently pulled her into his arms again, burying his face in the wild tumble of her silken hair. "Forgive me, forgive me. I never meant to hurt you."

But he had done that very thing. She had been afraid of her stepfather, yet she had gone off to face him on her own. Instead of coming to him for help, she had turned to a servant for support. The support he should have given her, the support she wouldn't ask for because he had been too wrapped up in an anguish he should have abandoned long ago.

"Oh, God, what have I done? *What have I done?*" If Cobb hadn't come to him when he had, there was no telling what might have happened. He ground his eyes shut, but all he could see was Gillet's hand striking her head. Once again, he felt himself wither.

"Elora, tell me you forgive me." He pressed his lips to her forehead. "Tell me you love me."

Elora swallowed against the dizziness swirling about her head, but she heard his words clearly. "Brice?" She lifted trembling fingers to his face. Had he actually mentioned love?

He turned his head to kiss her palm. "Are you in pain? Do you hurt?" Before she could reply, he ordered, "Lie still. You must take care." He pressed his cheek to hers, savoring its softness. "I've been a fool, a selfish idiot . . ."

"Brice, no."

". . . blinded to your goodness, heedless of all you have been trying to give me. From the very start, I couldn't see past my own warped convictions." Savage regret strangled his throat. "I let myself be torn apart by my grief. Instead of confronting the truth that Mother and Father and Robbie had been killed, I rejected life. I rejected you."

Elora felt his torment clear to her soul, and her heart reached out to him. "Brice, you must not torture yourself this way."

"I am so sorry."

"For what?"

"For hurting you the way I have. For taking out my

bitterness on you. You never deserved that." His mouth hovered above hers. "From the first moment I looked into your eyes, you made me feel again, made me live again. I didn't want to and I was angry with you for that." His lips brushed hers. "Tell me you forgive me."

"There is no need."

"Yes, there is. For so much, especially for failing you when you needed me most."

"You did not fail me."

"I did. I should have been the one to confront that bastard downstairs. Instead, you were left alone because you felt you could not come to me." He kissed her with a fierce passion, wanting to erase her suffering. "I've been so thoughtless, cruel in the worst possible way." He scanned her features desperately. "Tell me I can hope. Tell me there is still a chance that I haven't lost you forever."

It could have been a dream, but the warmth of his lips was all too real, the emotion in his eyes all too poignant. Both were brimming with the promise of love. "You haven't lost me, Brice."

Fresh tears glistened his gaze again. "I love you."

She had hoped, dared to dream, but until that moment had never thought it possible. "You do?"

"With all of my heart," he vowed, staring into the cobalt depths of her eyes.

A smile as glorious as a new dawn spread over her face. "Oh, Brice, I love you, too, but I feared . . . I feared you would never love me in return."

He called himself ten kinds of a fool. "I tried not to. I fought it from the first moment I saw you, but I can't fight it anymore. I don't want to fight it." Tenderly, he covered her mouth with his and when he spoke again, his voice was low and rough. "God, but I do love you."

Chapter

15

"YOU LOOK BEAUTIFUL, ELORA."

Smiling, Elora turned to Vianne. "Do you think so?"

"How can you doubt it? Just look at yourself."

Elora checked her reflection in her mirror. Her hair was swept up to the crown of her head, the intricate twists arranged about the coronet of her veil. Her wedding dress was unlike any she had ever seen, for it lacked adornment of any kind. Without a single frill, the pure white satin fell from the elevated waist in soft folds. The effect was simple and elegant, and the perfect backdrop for a floor-length veil spun of the most gossamer lace.

"This is too beautiful for words." Vianne sighed, lifting the veil for another look at the pattern of entwined hearts surrounded by roses. Her gaze lingered on the delicately wrought linked hearts, and a good portion of her smile faded. "I hope you will be happy, Elora."

Elora saw the disquietude in Vianne's green eyes, and reached for her friend's hand. "Have you spoken to Brice at all today?"

"No." The lace slipped from Vianne's fingers. "This morning was so hectic, and there was no time this afternoon. But even if there were, it is very . . . awkward."

The details of Vianne's break with Brice had been re-counted to Elora last night. Colin had thought it best to explain the circumstances to Elora so she would not be left wondering about the tension that was sure to exist between the brother and sister.

"I wish you and Colin would not leave until you have had a chance to talk to Brice."

Lifting one shoulder into a small shrug, Vianne summoned a weak laugh. "Brice is not one for discussions with me."

"Brice was not one to speak of love, but he has."

Vianne slowly shook her head. "Which I must confess baffles me. But if you say he has actually told you he loves you, then I can only believe what you say."

"He has told me he loves me. When he carried me in here yesterday, it was nearly all he *could* say. I thought I was imagining it at first."

"But you weren't."

"No. He was overflowing with emotions he had held within him for too long. Not just love, but remorse and regret. Which is why I think the two of you should talk."

Vianne lifted the veil once more. "I don't know, Elora."

"I will not ask you to make me any promises. But if you feel as though you could stay for a while then please do."

Vianne regarded Elora cautiously. "You have that much faith in him?"

"Yes." There was a great deal she and Brice needed to talk about, so much that Brice would have to share with her. She didn't expect that to happen immediately, but when he had confessed his love, he had made the first step toward being whole again. "I have complete faith in Brice."

"I truly want to believe there is a chance for a reconciliation, but . . ."

There was no need for her to continue. Elora knew Vianne was afraid to hope. "Please think about it, at least."

"I will." As though she could not stand the thought of dwelling on the painful subject on what should be a most joyous day, Vianne brightened. "This is most unusual to have an evening wedding. I like the idea immensely. Are you sure you are feeling all right?"

Elora had lost count of the number of times Vianne had asked that of her. "Yes, I am fine," she assured her.

"Does your head still hurt?"

"Only a little, just above my ear. But I am too happy to fret over a slight headache."

Mary Cobb bustled into the room, her mobcap fluttering with her hasty passage. "It is time, it is time." She handed Elora the single white rose she was to carry then paused in wonder. "Oh, miss, you are a rare sight."

Elora turned her radiant smile on the woman. "Thank you, Mrs. Cobb."

The housekeeper's eyes misted over. "I am so happy for you, miss." She sniffed, reaching into her pocket for her hanky. "I am so happy for his lordship. I never thought to see this day." Quickly, she dabbed at her eyes and collected herself. "Everyone is waiting at the chapel."

Vianne drew Elora into her arms for a hug. "Then I had best go. Colin will be waiting to escort you."

Moments later, Elora stepped down from the carriage in front of the stone chapel that had seen the blessings of generations of Warfields. The setting sun cast a golden glow to the wide steps covered with a white carpet, and to the rails decorated with garlands of flowers. Out from between the double doors, strains of organ music floated on the gentle breeze.

"Nervous?" Colin asked, placing her hand on his forearm and leading her into the small vestibule.

"No," she said. "Only happy."

That happiness glowed in her heart like an unwavering light, and when Colin escorted her down the aisle to Brice's side, it shown like an iridescent radiance in her eyes.

Brice stared into the shining blue orbs and felt his heart turn over in his chest. He had seen that look often, the blue boring straight into him, searching out his every nerve until he was fused with her. Time and time again, he had wondered at the cause, but now he recognized it for what it was. A rare and priceless love. From that very first moment she had opened her eyes and looked up at him, she had been giving him that love.

Elora placed her hand in Brice's, the strength and warmth evidence of the power of the man himself. She gazed lovingly into his burnished green eyes and knew that there had never been a more handsome, compelling, loving man. The last trait had been nearly forgotten, but she had all the years ahead of her to help him remember.

She turned to the vicar and listened to the words that bound her to Brice for a lifetime. Beside her, Brice stood solemnly waiting to pledge himself to this woman for whom he had waited a lifetime.

"I, Brice Christopher Stephen Warfield . . ." *will love you, Elora, from this moment until the end of time, with each beat of my heart, with my body and soul, until my dying breath escapes me and I am nothing but ashes on this poor earth. And even then I will give you my love.*

"I, Elora Miriah Simmons . . ." *give you my love, my life, my happiness, all that I am or will ever be, forever more.*

In words too mundane for the heart, the vicar pronounced them man and wife.

Brice turned to Elora and, before the small assembled group, cupped her face between his palms and kissed her with an abiding and everlasting love. When he lifted his head, the blue in Elora's eyes returned that love tenfold.

They walked up the aisle amidst offers of congratulations and the laughter of good tidings. Brice made only one prolonged stop and that was to listen to several pointed and risqué comments that Lady Barbara insisted on whispering in his ear. Waiting good-naturedly, Elora turned to adjust her veil, and noticed Josiah Platt standing behind the last pew.

Her smile widened. She hadn't known that Josiah had been invited to the wedding. Knowing how Brice felt about her friend, she had not asked that his name be included on the guest list. Apparently, Brice had set aside his own feelings and had invited Josiah to please her.

She lifted her gaze to her husband, the blue of her eyes softening. If possible, she loved Brice more than she did just moments ago.

Brice straightened at Lady Barbara's wicked laugh and took Elora's elbow again. Elora turned to give Josiah another smile, but he was gone.

Minutes later Brice was lowering Elora from his coach to lead her into the foyer to receive the congratulations from the servants. Mary and Ambrose Cobb stood proudly, their faces wreathed in smiles.

"Are you happy?" Brice asked, when they finally walked into the blue and white salon.

In answer she stepped into his arms and curled her fingers about his neck. "Happier than I have a right to be."

He touched his lips to hers, but even as he deepened the kiss the guests began to arrive.

"Ha!" Lady Barbara exclaimed. "I knew you would waste little time, Warrington."

Brice muttered something about interfering old ladies, earning Elora's shameful glance. Nonetheless, she could not contain her guilty giggles for she, too, had wanted the kiss to continue.

The guests numbered fewer than a dozen. Despite the intimacy of the gathering, Brice's chef produced a wedding feast fit for royalty itself. The sumptuous courses pleased and teased the palate, but Elora discovered rather quickly that she tasted very little of what she ate. Her mind was too consumed with overwhelming joy to fully appreciate the food set before her.

"I am going to have to apologize to your chef," she confessed to Brice when the men at last joined the ladies in the drawing room.

"Why is that?"

"Because," she admitted, not the least bit contrite, "throughout the entire meal, I could concentrate on nothing but you."

The green of his eyes glistened and he could not resist the temptation to steal a kiss. As appetites went, his was raging, and it had nothing to do with food. A little irritably he resigned himself to the fact that it would be at least another two hours until he could, in all respect to their guests, sweep her up the stairs and claim her as his own.

A wry grin tugged at his lips, drawing Elora's questioning gaze. Bending his head close to her ear, he explained, "I have spent a good portion of the last few years not giving a damn about conventions. Now, when I have a hunger that cannot be ignored, I find I am bound as tightly to those customs of etiquette as if I were wrapped in chains." He regarded everyone with an ill-concealed look of annoyance. "I wish they would just disappear."

As Elora's most fervent wish that Brice love her had come true, she glanced about half expecting to see their guests vanish before her eyes. But as the next hour progressed and everyone remained in clear sight, she could only mollify Brice with her sympathetic smiles.

"You are looking radiant, my dear," Lady Barbara declared, giving Elora a thorough head-to-toe examination. "Happiness looks good on you."

"Thank you, my lady."

Casting a look to Brice where he stood conversing with several guests, Lady Barbara proclaimed, "It looks even better on Warrington. I would say that you have definitely had an excellent effect on the man."

"I hope so."

"Aack." Her gnarled hand sliced the air. "No more of this modesty of yours. It is enough to drive me to the brink. I have known the man since he was in leading strings . . . although I daresay he would not wish for me to admit to such . . . and I can tell you that too many years have gone by since I have seen that smile on his face." She gentled her words with a quick pat to Elora's hand. "He deserves some joy in life, especially since the incident with his parents. It nearly ruined him."

"I think he is beginning to recover."

From the smile curling Lady Barbara's lips, it was obvious she agreed. "I think you're right."

Elora felt her heart swell with emotion. If she did nothing else in her life, she would be a gratified woman knowing Brice had been given the love and happiness he deserved.

As though he felt the touch of her gaze, Brice turned his head abruptly, his smile expanding.

I love you, his eyes vowed.

I love you, hers answered.

Content . . . for the moment, Brice turned back to the amiable conversation from which he had temporarily withdrawn, waiting for the interminable hour to pass.

It did, finally, and not a second too soon to please him. Having satisfied every propriety he intended to for one night, he crossed to Elora's side.

"The hour is getting late, sweet," he hinted in a low voice for her ears alone. He took her hand in his own and drew her from their guests toward the doors. Just short of exiting, he slowed, and then stood still.

"Brice?" Elora questioned.

His mouth turned down at one corner and his black brows slowly descended. "I will be just a minute."

Wondering what had put the unsettled look on Brice's face, she watched him make his way to Vianne and Colin. Brother and sister stared at each other, and even from where Elora stood, she could feel their anxiety. She understood that years of hurt and anguish lay cold and all too painfully real between them. Silently she hoped for both their sakes that they could reconcile.

Her wish seemed to come true in the very next heartbeat. She could not hear what Brice said to his sister, but whatever it was, brought Vianne's arms about his shoulders for a hug.

Elora's smile was radiant as Brice escorted her from the room. She didn't say anything until they reached the great stairway. There she laid her hand on his chest, her expression one of adoration.

"You, my lord husband, are wonderful." She rose to her toes and pressed her lips to his. "You made Vianne very, very happy."

Not completely at ease with the scope of the feelings he had been experiencing for the past twenty-four hours, he pulled her near, her softness as steadying as it was arousing. "You make me very, very happy."

In one fluid move, he swept her into his arms and carried her up the stairs. The urge to capture her lips was overpowering and as he kicked his bedroom door shut behind them, he joyfully gave into the craving.

He molded her lips to his own and, still holding her against his chest, slowly advanced toward the fireplace. But even there, he was reluctant to release her and so he simply stood near the crackling fire and did what he had ached to do for so long.

Elora gave herself up to the tempestuous kiss, parting her lips for his tongue, curling her fingers about the strong column of his neck. Beneath her thighs and along her back she could feel the hard muscles of his arms flex.

"Brice," she gasped when he at last lifted his mouth from hers.

"Yes, love." He pressed his lips to the wildly pulsing vein in her neck, making exquisite tingles race down her body.

The sensation made it almost impossible to think, and if she hadn't had certain confusions, she would not have bothered with a conscious thought at all. She could not imagine anything more heavenly than for Brice to continue kissing her.

But all along, he had made no secret about wanting her without her clothes. He had told her that on their wedding night, removing her clothes would lead to their making love.

"Is this when you . . ." Her breath caught as he flicked his tongue at her earlobe. "Is this when you take off my clothes?"

His head came up, his smoldering green eyes reflecting his wonder and passion. There was no trembling in her voice, no shyness in her gaze. The look on her face proclaimed only a budding desire and an ingenuous eagerness.

He nearly groaned, wanting nothing more than to remove her clothes until every splendid inch of her was revealed to him. Instead, he loosened his grip about her and let her slide down the length of him.

"It is easy for me to forget how innocent you are, love." He wanted this night to be perfect for her. Unfortunately, her unconscious and all too stimulating responses to him, and his own burning desires, were making it difficult for him to remember that she was a virgin.

"Come." He took her hand and led her through his dressing room and into hers. "Your things have been moved in here." He nodded to the room just beyond. "That is your new bedroom."

Elora stepped into the spacious room, the blue and silver decorations a pleasing complement to the gold and blue found in Brice's room. Nonetheless, she could not contain the lines of bewilderment that puckered her brow.

She had known that she would be given rooms connecting to Brice's when they were man and wife, but she hadn't expected a bedroom specifically for her own use. Nor did she want one. Her parents had always slept in the same room, in the same bed, and that was what she had envisioned for her and Brice.

"Is this where I am to sleep?" she asked, disappointment evident in her voice.

He studied her face carefully. "Don't you like it?"

"It's beautiful."

"But . . ."

"But it isn't . . ." She cast him a quick glance and held her tongue. She had no wish to offend him. "Is it customary among husbands and wives of your station to sleep apart?"

Having no idea where this conversation was going, Brice narrowed his eyes. "Only if they desire."

"Is that what you desire?"

Is that what he desired? "No! Not at all."

Her worry fell away like a visible sigh. Seeing her relief, Brice circled her waist and pulled her against his chest. "Is that what you thought? That I would want you to sleep apart from me?" He did not need a reply as it was written all over her face. In a tender voice he avowed, "I have waited forever for you. I am not about to abandon you to your solitary bed, not when I have only just discovered our love."

She leaned her forehead against his throat and hugged his words to her heart. "Brice, I love you so."

He held her tightly. "Say it again."

She did, again and again and again until he had to still her words with his mouth.

He stepped away only when the kiss threatened to blossom out of control. Determinedly, he rang for Elora's maid and then entered his own rooms. Studiously, he avoided looking back at the tempting picture Elora made, knowing that if he did, the maid would enter and be extremely embarrassed.

A half hour later, Elora looked down the length of her nightgown, suffering an embarrassment of her own. Somewhat ruefully, she decided that there wasn't an awful lot for Brice to remove. A fragile white lace comprised what little there was of the gown's deep-cut bodice and long billowing sleeves. And the length of the nearly transparent silk skirt was saved from immodesty only by the folds that created concealing shadows.

In all her life, she had never worn anything so beautiful. Nor so revealing. She could only hope that Brice liked it.

The door connecting their rooms opened and he walked in, his eyes coursing slowly over her curves. Nervously she clasped her hands, excruciatingly aware that every detail of her body was visible through the lace and silk.

He came to stand within arm's length still dressed in his formal black pants and white ruffled shirt. The shirt's cuffs had been rolled back over tanned forearms and the buttons had been loosened to the waist exposing the wide planes of his chest.

Almost reverently, he lifted a hand to the cascade of blond curls tumbling over her shoulders and down her back. Unnameable emotions filled him, feelings he had never experienced in his entire life, feelings irrevocably entwined with the love he felt for this woman.

Bending slightly, he scooped her into his arms and carried

her into his bedroom. The sight of her, the feel of her, sent his blood pounding, his body reacting as it always did to her, instantly, hungrily, demandingly.

The fire had burned down to smoldering coals, and by the light provided by that heated golden glow, he brought her to his bed and set her down on her feet.

"Do you know how beautiful you are?" he asked, skimming his hands over her shoulders and down her arms. The movement pulled her gown away and it floated to the floor like a soft cloud.

Before Elora could fully realize that she was standing naked in front of a man for the first time in her life, Brice settled her under the sheets in the center of his bed. Then with quick, efficient hands, he divested himself of his clothing.

Elora watched him remove his shirt and then his pants, his form cast into enveloping shadows by the fire's meager light. Memories of the night when she had gone to his room to warn him of an intruder came back to her now. He had climbed naked from his bed, and she had glimpsed long hard thighs and a sleek back that tapered downward to taut buttocks. That night she had looked away hastily for the sake of modesty. Now she gave in to the desire to openly, gladly behold the splendor of his body.

Brice slid beneath the covers beside her and she held out a hand, unconsciously wanting to touch the sculpted perfection of bone and sinew. At his look of astonishment, she hastily withdrew her hand.

"I'm sorry." Horribly uncertain, she stared down at the sheet pulled to her chest. "I told you . . . I do not know what . . . what to do . . . what I am allowed to do."

He caught up her hand and brought it to his chest, trapping it there with his own. "Oh, God, Elora, do not apologize. I want you to touch me. I just did not expect that you would want to."

She blinked in genuine surprise. "Why would you think that?"

He choked on an incredulous laugh. "I don't know. Not

once have I ever known you to think like any other woman. I don't know why I should expect you to do so now."

"What would other women be thinking now?"

Running his hand over her waist, he whispered, "It doesn't matter." All that mattered was that despite her innocence, she wanted him as much as he wanted her. "Touch me to your heart's content."

Elora rolled to her side to face Brice, her hand slipping up through the hair on his chest. The rough texture brought a curious smile to her lips, and her other hand joined the ardent play.

"I like the way you feel." She smiled, running both hands over his chest, lingering on the flat male nipples.

"I'm glad," he got out on a strained breath.

Hearing his near groan, she jerked her gaze to his. "Does this bother you?"

In answer, he stroked her breasts with his hand, and watched her melt. "Does this bother you?"

"No." She sighed as a languorous pleasure stole down her body.

"It feels the same to me."

She looked at him. "Does it?"

Distracted by the silken feel of her nipple hardening to his finger's touch, he nodded.

The revelation that he was experiencing the same glorious sensations as she brought Elora to her elbow. "I did not realize that we were so very alike."

"In most ways."

"You mean that when I kiss you, your stomach seems to want to knot of its own accord?"

Delighted by her eagerness, he admitted, "My stomach . . . among other things."

"What other things?"

In his wildest dreams, Brice had never *ever* imagined himself having a conversation such as this on his wedding night. But he could not, would not deny Elora her exploration, even though it was making a shambles of his self-restraint.

Reining in on the discipline that had seen him through the past three years, he took her hand and lowered it beneath the concealing sheets to that part of him that was making urgent demands.

Her eyes widened and he smiled.

"In one or two very elemental ways, dear wife, we are not alike."

Beneath her palm, she could feel the hard length of him, but she could not garner a clear image of what it was she held. Still, she trailed her fingers over him, marveling at the incredible combination of satin and steel.

Brice's breath came in on a sudden intake and got caught. A shudder wracked his body and his eyes drifted shut.

"Oh, my," she sighed, moving her fingers into the thatch of hair and the heaviness of him below. "We are definitely not alike."

Her untutored hands were the sweetest fire he had ever known, and they were taking him to the brink faster than he would have believed possible.

He clamped his hand over hers, pulled it away, and in one lithe move, pushed her onto her back. Catching her lips in a searing kiss, he slanted his mouth over hers. Tongues entwined, breaths mingled and he lost himself to the passion she evoked.

Elora kissed him back with a passion born of love. She met the thrust of his tongue with hers, unconsciously turning her head to increase the friction of their lips. The shift sent a wondrous heat straight to the pit of her belly, making her tremble and arch. Her breasts pressed to the hardness of his chest and she relished the feel of him.

"I love you," she whispered into his mouth, her hands clinging to his back, learning the contours, memorizing the form and feel of his muscles rippling under her hands.

Those three words speared deep into his heart, the same heart that, until recently, had been frozen. That she had saved that heart and made him whole again was a humbling pleasure just short of pain.

His gaze burning into hers, he vowed, "I love you, Elora."

He kissed her again, but it was not enough. It would never be enough. He had been starved of love for three long years, and he reacted as any starving man who had been given his sustenance would. He wanted her to the depths of his being, he wanted to be one with her, and a kiss, simple or otherwise, would never satisfy the all-consuming need he felt for her.

He skimmed her neck with the tip of his tongue, slowly making his way to her breasts. He kissed and caressed her softness, wanting to draw her pleasure out, wanting to give her as much pleasure as she gave him.

She moaned low in her throat and her insides clenched when his mouth closed firmly on the coral tip of her breast. Of their own accord, her hands slipped into the thick black hair, holding his head to her, reveling in the shivers that spiraled out from his mouth. The tugging pressure teased and lured and increased until she thought she would be consumed by a scorching, molten urgency.

"Brice." His name escaped her lips on a frantic little cry.

He replied by bringing his mouth to her other breast. "I love you," he told her as his lips brushed the full lower curve of her breast. "I love you," he vowed, kissing the small red scar marring her skin. "I love you," he groaned, tasting the satin of her flat stomach.

She had no defense against his hands and mouth. Every nerve in her entire body trembled and her senses were as tightly coiled as the ache centered in the core of her. She reached for his shoulders, wanting to hold him, needing the feel of his mouth on hers, but he angled himself farther down her body and parted her thighs with a firm but gentle hand.

Carefully, he caressed the silken heat of her, gentling her, teasing her, drawing a moan from the depths of her. Then he lowered his head and worshipped the sweet flesh as he had the rest of her.

This time when she cried his name, there was no mistaking the panic in her voice. Her eyes flew open and she arched upward, straining away from the devastating caress at the same time her body sought more.

"Brice, stop," she cried, gasping for breath. The tender assault was more than she could bear. "Oh, please . . ."

He raised himself over her, his burning gaze delving into hers. Cupping her chin in one hand he asked, "Did you mind so terribly?"

Nearly overwhelmed with a raging desire, she was also shocked to the core of her. "No, it was . . . you shouldn't have . . ."

He understood. It was too much too soon for her maidenly sensibilities. "I did not mean to frighten you."

"You didn't . . . not really." Color flooded her face. "It was too wonderful."

Her throaty confession was Brice's undoing. He claimed her mouth, tilting his lips over hers and experienced a jolt of such pure desire that he felt the last of his control slip.

His hand returned possessively to the heat between her legs, stroking the sensitive flesh. Elora moaned low in her throat, trembling, feeling as though her body were turning to liquid fire. Helplessly, her hips arched upward and his fingers slipped into her clinging warmth.

Brice settled himself between her thighs. With one hand he raised her hips to receive him and he thrust forward unerringly, taking her low cry of pain into his mouth, making it his as he made her body his.

Elora stilled beneath him, the surprise of the slight pain intruding into her bliss. But it was not enough to block out the incredible reality of what had just occurred.

In wonder, she searched Brice's taut face. "You're . . ." She could not get the words out.

He said them for her. "I'm inside you, love. That's where I belong."

But even as he spoke, he knew he could not possibly explain exactly what it was that he felt. Countless times, her gaze had captured him, held him, joining her spirit to his. And during those times, reality had vanished, reasoning had been destroyed until all he had ever wanted was to be one with her.

That consuming need, the raw hunger burned in him now and he gloried in it.

He thrust into her tight warmth, only to withdraw and then return in deep, penetrating strokes that made Elora cling to his back. The coiling sensation within her slipped lower, collecting where she and Brice were so intimately joined.

Her breath came in ragged little gasps as she twisted beneath him. The ache inside her increased with each surge of his body into hers, gripping her muscles as she sought an end to something she could not even begin to define. Against Brice's lips, she whispered his name, and he increased his driving tempo, fighting his own storming desires, holding himself in check until she exploded in ecstasy.

She did in the very next instant. Pulsing waves burst through her, spreading out in every direction, wringing a low cry from her throat. The sound tore through the last of Brice's restraint and he thrust into her, giving her all of him, filling her with his need and his life and his love.

The fire's glow bathed their bodies as their breathing slowed. They lay entwined, neither moving, neither willing to relinquish the other.

Her eyes slumberous with passion, Elora gazed up at Brice. "I never knew."

He kissed the corner of her mouth. "Neither did I. Until this moment, 'love' in the phrase 'making love' never held any significance for me."

"Is it always like this?"

His lips found the other corner of her mouth. "For us it will be." She was as tempting in the aftermath of passion as she was in its throes. Astoundingly, that was beginning to have a decided effect on him. Carefully, he began to ease out of her, but she looped her arms about his shoulders.

"Don't go," she whispered. "I like the feel of you."

Passion and lust and love all collided in his gut. He wanted to be gallant and courteous for her sake and let her body gradually become accustomed to his. But when she tempted him with such honest and seductive pleas, it was difficult for him to remember anything other than he was still sheathed within her incredible softness and that he was hard again in one swift, flashing second.

"Oh, my," she breathed, feeling the effect her words had on him.

"That is what you do to me." Unable to help himself, he thrust gently. In answer, she lifted her hips.

It was the last coherent thought either had. Passion erupted in a torrid whirlwind that belied the ecstasy of moments past. Their bodies met in perfect harmony, giving, taking, and always loving. Their mutual need rocketed them to dizzying heights, before it broke upon them in endless swells of pleasure that left them sated and nurtured and endlessly, ardently in love with each other.

And even then, it didn't end. In his mind, Brice relived all those times when the deep blue of her eyes had claimed his body . . . and a soul he hadn't known he had. Now he felt consumed by an overpowering force to claim her in the same way.

He loved her until their breaths were torn from their bodies and their skin was flushed and slick. He loved her until every pulsing ripple of her body became his, and he could no longer define her as being separate from himself. He loved her until all his yesterdays were laid asunder and the only thing left for him was all his tomorrows with this one precious woman.

Chapter
16

WEARING NOTHING BUT A SMILE, AND BRICE'S WHITE FRILLY shirt, Elora snuggled into her husband's lap. They were seated at the table in their private dining room just off Brice's bedroom. Spread out on the linen tablecloth was a breakfast of strawberries and cream, an assortment of pastries, hot chocolate, coffee and champagne.

"This is wicked," she declared in a whisper. Still, she did nothing to remove herself from Brice's lap. She liked feeling the warmth of his bare chest against her side, the support of his arm at her back and the strength of his legs beneath her thighs.

Brice, too, greatly favored the present seating arrangements. Her curves were cuddled most distractingly against him. Every time she reached for something to eat, he was taken to new heights of blissful torture.

Easing himself beneath the snug fit of his black pants, he reached around Elora for a strawberry and dragged it through the bowl of sweetened cream. "Are you afraid that I will corrupt you?"

"That would not be possible."

"Why not?" He brought the berry to her mouth.

"Because corruption is vile and base and you are capable of being neither." She parted her lips, anticipating the sweet juice and smooth cream. But instead of placing the fruit in her mouth, Brice dabbed the cream onto her lower lip.

"You missed." She laughed, and began to lick the white fluff, but Brice quickly lowered his head and took care of the matter himself. His tongue stroked over her lip before it slipped into her mouth.

Elora leaned into his chest, and gave herself up to the kiss despite how outrageous she found it. She gladly followed his lead, just as she had done throughout the night.

He had shocked her repeatedly, yet he had always been tender and loving, teaching her that there was no need for embarrassment between them. But just thinking about the things she had discovered sent a crimson stain up her chest and into her face.

"What is this?" he queried, noting her increased color. "Don't tell me you're embarrassed?"

"Brice, I normally do not eat cream, or anything else for that matter, in this way."

Not the least bit repentant, he fed her the strawberry and drawled, "Tastes better, don't you think?"

He was so blasé that Elora yielded to another laugh. "You are incorrigible. Imagine what our guests would think if they knew what we were doing."

"They would most likely think me the most fortunate man alive. But you needn't worry yourself about it. Our guests are probably long gone by now."

"They are?"

He gave her a pointed look. "Elora, this is our honeymoon. Even Lady Barbara wouldn't dream of imposing on us."

He did have a point. She and Brice were the center of each other's attentions to the distraction of all else. She had to admit she preferred it that way.

Despite her happiness, she couldn't help thinking of Vianne. "Did your sister and Colin leave also?"

He heard the question behind the question. "If you are asking me if we have parted for good, the answer is no. I told her I would call on her soon." Sighing, he brushed a long strand of hair over her shoulder as he contemplated his brief discussion with Vianne the day before.

"Is this terribly difficult for you?"

His brows flicked upward in question. "Is what difficult?"

"Mending the estrangement that has existed between you and Vianne."

"It's awkward."

"Vianne said the same thing."

"Did she?"

"Yes, before the ceremony yesterday."

"She had it right. It's been years . . ." His hand tangled in the length of her hair. "We have not been close since my parents and my brother died."

"How did it happen, Brice?"

His brows flicked upward as though in silent denial. From the slight gesture, Elora could tell he found it difficult to answer. "If you would rather not discuss it, I understand."

His mouth twisted down at one corner. "I've never spoken to anyone of their deaths. It was always too painful."

"Is it now?"

Pausing, he considered the question, sorting through a tangle of emotions. He still felt an emptiness within him, but surprisingly, the anguish which had hounded him for years had lessened.

"No, it's all right. I don't mind telling you." He exhaled in wonder. "I think Mother would be pleased."

"What makes you say that?"

"It was very much in her nature to worry about her children's well-being, whether that be physical or emotional."

"She sounds wonderful."

"She was. So was Father. There was never a pair like them, laughing, teasing, hopelessly in love with each other. As children, Robbie and I would try and guess how many times during the day our parents would stop just to kiss each other."

Elora smiled at the mental image of the people in the paintings loving their way through the day. "Who won?"

Brice grinned slightly. "I would say my father."

"If you are anything like him, then your mother was a lucky woman in her own right. I think I would have liked her."

"Really?"

She nodded. "And your father and brother, too. Were you close to Robbie?"

"Very."

"He was older than you?"

"By three years. He was supposed to have inherited." All traces of his smile vanished.

Against her back, Elora felt Brice's arm tense. "What happened?"

He tilted his head back against the chair. "The war with France was finally over, the Treaty of Paris had been signed. As far as everyone was concerned, Paris was open to the world again. My parents and brother, like so many others, flocked to the city. No one had any idea that Napoleon would return from exile."

Elora remembered reading the accounts of those frightening months in 1815. It had seemed as though all of England had groaned in despair when Napoleon had resumed power. France had suddenly become the enemy once more, King Louis had been forced to flee while thousands of Europeans had literally been caught in the backlash of a political nightmare.

"When Vianne and I received word that my parents and brother had been arrested, I tried everything I could to secure their release; money, political pressure . . . all of it. Nothing worked. They were executed." Shadows of his grief flickered across his face.

Unconsciously Elora smoothed her fingertips over the lines of his strain. She could not even begin to imagine the frustration and anger he must have suffered. He had had a chance to prevent the deaths of those whom he dearly loved. Sadly, his efforts had been in vain.

"I'm so sorry, Brice."

"So am I."

"It's no wonder you became so bitter toward life."

Scoffing, he smoothed a lock of hair over her shoulder. "I was weak."

"Why do you say that?"

"I should have been stronger, I should have been able to handle the loss. Vianne did. She went on with her life while I . . . I cut myself off from everyone."

"You judge yourself too harshly, Brice. We are not always capable of controlling our feelings, especially when it comes to those we love."

"I couldn't get past the hurt."

"That is not a failing on your part. The sorrow you felt, and still feel, is a testimony to your love for your family. They were so fortunate to have been the recipient of such a love." Her fingers trailed down his jaw to the base of his neck. "I consider myself blessed that you love me as you do."

He shook his head slowly, his gaze never wavering from hers. "No, it is I who am truly blessed. I seriously doubt that I deserve you."

"You should not feel that way. You can't continue to condemn yourself for what was. What is important is that you are willing to come to terms with the past, and that you want to make amends. Vianne knows that."

Silently Brice agreed. Vianne did know. He was profoundly grateful for that. He dragged a deep, almost satisfying breath into his lungs. For the first time in three years, he felt free of an awful weight.

Running his knuckles over her cheek, he asked, "How did you become so wise?"

"I'm not, really. I just know a wonderful man when I see one."

A chiding laugh worked its way from his throat. "Before I know it, you're going to say that I have a heart of gold."

"No," she teased, tilting her head from side to side as though to weigh the notion. "Most likely silver."

"Silver?" he repeated, a little stung.

"Oh, yes, your heart is pure and fine. But unfortunately it

is horribly tarnished from lack of use." A gentle smile graced her lips and she cupped his face between her hands. When she spoke, her voice was quiet, compassionate. "But you shouldn't be offended. Gold hearts are quite common. Yours is much more precious for its very scarcity. Love from a silver heart is priceless."

Brice knew a *priceless* treasure when he saw one. He had surrounded himself with the finest the world had to offer. But he knew that *nothing* he had collected or was ever likely to, could compare to the treasure of Elora herself.

He crushed her to him. "God, I love you." His mouth came down on hers with a fierce tenderness, sealing his avowal in a manner that spoke more eloquently than words.

The kiss swept Elora into that world of passion that she had come to share with Brice, a world where only the two of them existed. Her arms circled his shoulders and she returned the kiss, parting her lips eagerly for the entrance of his tongue into her mouth.

He tasted of champagne, she of strawberries. The combination was heady stuff that added to the rapidly increasing urgency of the moment. His mouth sought her neck as his fingers made easy work of the buttons running down the shirt she wore. In mere seconds, he parted the fabric and one hand closed over the fullness of her breast.

"Oh, Brice." A shudder rippled through her. He felt it against his palm, all along his chest, and he gloried in her unbridled passion.

Their lips met again, taking, giving. She trailed her hand over the hard plane of his chest, searching out the flat male nipples, wringing a low moan from him before caressing the tightened muscles of his abdomen.

And all the while, his hands stroked over her breasts, drawing her nipples into hardened buds. In an enticing pattern, his fingers created a burning path, skimming over the satin of her stomach to the juncture of her thighs.

Elora needed no encouragement, and parted her legs, welcoming Brice's touch. When his fingers slipped into her sweet, moist secrets, she could not contain the low moan of pleasure that broke over her lips. Against his thighs, her hips undulated helplessly, gracefully, caressing the rigid proof of his desire.

Brice's blood pounded through him in a wild dash that amazed him. They had spent the better part of the night entwined in each other's arms, taking each other to the heights of passion. He should be sated, replete, incapable of the fierce kind of hunger he was feeling now. But it was as though with every touch of her hand, with every kiss she gave him, his hunger only grew, doubling and redoubling in intensity.

Quickly, he shifted her so that she sat astride him, her breasts teasing his chest, her mouth a hair's breadth from his own. Even more quickly, he saw to the fastenings of his pants. It was not until that moment that Elora realized exactly what he intended to do.

Shocked, once more, she looked down at their positions and blurted out the first thing that came to mind. "I thought we were going to have breakfast."

Green eyes glimmering with a raging fire, he reached behind her and scooped a dollop of cream onto his finger. Smiling wickedly, he plopped it onto her nipple.

Lowering his head to her breast, he breathed, "Breakfast is served, my lady."

Vianne was anxious to be home. Yesterday's wedding festivities had been beautiful, but emotionally draining.

Sitting in the private dining room of the Painted Horse Inn, she thought back on the moment when Brice had sought her out. Even now, she could not believe that he had apologized to her.

Forgive me. Two simple words, quietly spoken. He had said little more than that, but it had been enough to assuage the years of hurt and lay the groundwork for a healing between them.

Once again, her heart swelled with emotion, just as it had yesterday. Brice was whole for the first time in three years, and all because of Elora. Her delicate blond beauty and loving nature had made Brice want to live life as it should be lived.

That was a rare accomplishment, one to which Vianne gave great credence. It was one of the reasons she and Colin had chosen not to spend the night under Brice's roof, and had traveled the few short miles to this inn. More than most couples, Brice and Elora needed privacy in order to begin their marriage on the right foot.

Vianne wished them all the happiness they deserved.

The door behind her opened to admit Colin, surprisingly enough, accompanied by Thorbon. Vianne smiled in wonder.

"Thorbon? This is a delightful chance meeting."

Colin cupped his hand over her shoulder. "I told him the same thing. The world is certainly shrinking when we should all end up in the exact same inn at precisely the same time."

"Mere coincidence," Thorbon remarked, pulling on the points of his waistcoat. "I'm bound for Essex."

"We should hope for more such flukes, then," Vianne commented lightly. "We don't see nearly enough of you, Thorbon."

"Is that supposed to mean something?" His harsh voice gave Vianne a small start.

Her brows rose in question. There was no reason for Thorbon to sound defensive, but there was no mistaking his tone of resentment. A little helplessly, she glanced up to Colin. "I didn't mean anything untoward, Thorbon. I simply meant that it's been a long time between visits."

Thorbon settled himself in one of the chairs at the table. Apparently all too willing to drop the matter, he asked, "What brings you out to Hampshire?"

"Brice's wedding," Colin replied.

To Vianne's amazement, Thorbon's face assumed a deep reddish tint.

"I should have known," he snapped, looking from Vianne to Colin. "I'm his heir, damn it, but I wasn't even invited to the wedding."

Dismayed by her cousin's outburst, Vianne didn't know what to do. She had thought it a little odd that Brice had not included Thorbon in the wedding party, but she had assumed that Brice had had his reasons.

"I think Brice and Elora wanted to keep the wedding as small as possible."

Once again, the door opened to admit the innkeeper. Pale, hollow, he sped forward, the frayed ties of his once white apron fluttering behind him.

"I beg's your pardon, m'lord, m'lady. I don't mean to be disturbin' you none, but it's a mighty favor you could be doin' me this mornin'. If you've a mind." The lined, pockmarked face took on a desperate look. "Please."

"Of course," Colin said.

The innkeeper heaved a sigh that Vianne thought should have come from a man three times his size. "'Tis a good man, you are, sir. Knew it the first time I set me eyes on you. But the truth of the matter is that I'm in a bit of a spot."

Taking pity on the nervous innkeeper, Vianne asked, "What sort of spot?"

"A parson he is, the gent that just arrived. A touch on the timid side. He be requestin' a private room, he does." A sickly smile pasted itself to the thin face. "I got me only this one private room, and since you'll be leavin' shortly, I be wonderin' . . . hopin' is more to the point, if you wouldn't be mindin' to share it. If you could. If you would."

"By all means," Colin assured him.

"Ah, thank you, sir, thank you." The man's head bobbed repeatedly. "Knew you was a good man, knew it I did from the start."

As hastily as the innkeeper had entered, he exited, only to return moments later and hold open the door for Josiah Platt.

"Reverend, this certainly is a day for surprises," Vianne declared, then laughed at the near comical expressions on all three men's faces. "I suppose I should explain that Reverend Platt and I met in London recently. He is a friend of Elora's." Quickly she saw to the introductions.

"Old friend of the new marchioness, eh?" Thorbon asked as Josiah lowered himself into one of the chairs.

"Yes, you could say that." Josiah spread his hands in a small shrug. "Elora and I have known each other for close to ten years. Lovely girl, just lovely."

"You'll get no argument from us," Vianne chuckled.

"She made a beautiful bride."

"What?" Thorbon's shout brought Vianne half out of her chair. "You were at the wedding? You, a *friend* of the bride?"

It was all Vianne could do not to wring her hands. The poor Reverend Platt was looking truly aghast while Thorbon appeared as though he were going to go into apoplexy at any second.

"Please, Thorbon," she began, "you must understand that Brice—"

"Oh, I understand the boy only too well." His jowls flapped with his indignation. "Treats me like some old fool. How do you think that makes a body feel, I ask you? Like some feebleminded stallion that's been put out to pasture, is how."

"I'm certain that isn't the case," Colin interjected in an attempt to calm him.

"No? Well, I say differently. He's been like a cold fish for years now."

It was the truth, but Vianne bristled anyway. "Thorbon, you are talking about my brother. I will not stand for your criticism." She set her shoulders firmly. "I grant you that Brice has not been himself for some time, but he has had his reasons. I would beg you to exercise a little understanding in this matter."

Her cousin drew himself up to his full height. "I've understood all that I intend to. But not this time." He gestured wildly to Josiah. "Not when I'm overlooked in favor of some *friend.*" On that, he stormed from the room, leaving Vianne shaken, and embarrassed.

Feeling as uncomfortable as Josiah looked, she explained, "I do apologize, Reverend. My cousin has been . . . upset lately."

"I fear I have caused a slight commotion," Josiah replied.

"No, no," Colin reassured him. "You simply had the misfortune of getting caught in the middle of a family squabble."

Vianne thought squabble was a mild word to describe Thorbon's hostility. His feelings ran closer to bitterness. As Colin handed her up into their coach moments later, she reflected on that animosity, and the entire encounter that had just taken place.

Thank goodness the reverend was a forgiving man. He had readily accepted their apologies. She wished that Thorbon could behave as agreeably, in this instance, forgive and forget. But the acerbity she had seen etched into his face told her that wasn't likely to happen.

Bliss. That was the only word Elora could think of to describe the three days she and Brice had been married. A happiness she had never known filled her life from the first moment she woke in Brice's arms until the last minute at night when she drifted to sleep beside him. Each second of the day was a celebration of their love, whether Brice was showing her his collection of oriental artifacts or whether they were pursuing more amorous delights.

The days were also a source of never ending surprise. Elora had glimpses of Brice that she had never seen before they were married. Every time she looked into his eyes, she marveled at the emotions she saw there. The smile that had rarely come to his face now lingered more often than not. A little rusty, at times crooked about the edges, the smile was her gauge of just how far Brice had come since he had spoken those magical words, I love you.

For reasons she could only sense deep inside her, she felt that she was seeing Brice as he had once been. Intense, loving, an ardent, passionate man. If he was occasionally too intense, too ardent, she gladly welcomed the depth and power of emotion from a man who had for too long been frozen.

She discovered very quickly that behind the handsome

face was an extremely intelligent man, capable of the most shrewd business reasoning. But also behind his virile exterior was a depth of compassion that touched her deeply. Surprisingly, she realized that the fears instilled within her by her stepfather had all been laid to rest because Brice was wonderfully tender and protective. He was also amazingly bawdy.

The latter caused her to blush with startling frequency, something that delighted Brice to no end. But while her shock and embarrassment were inevitable, they usually resulted in Brice sweeping her into his arms. With that she had no complaint.

Which was why she could only laugh when Brice suggested in a too casual tone that they play a "private and very interesting" game of senet.

"What do you mean by 'private and interesting'?" she asked, giving him a wary look as they sat before the fire in her bedroom.

"I mean just that." He set out the game pieces. "I think if we put our minds to it, we can come up with some way of making this game more fascinating."

She gave him a shaming look. "Brice Warfield, I know you well enough to know that you have already given this a great deal of thought."

Grinning unabashedly, he confessed, "You have found me out, wife."

Elora took in his humor and her heart flipped over. The smile did incredible things to his face. The curve of his lips, the creases beside his mouth, the sparkle in his eyes made his handsome face that much more handsome.

"You need to smile more often," she told him, her voice slightly husky.

"If we play this game by my new rules," he teased, a wolfish gleam in his green eyes, "I will most likely smile for the rest of the day."

She had seen that look before and knew precisely what it meant. She may have been incredibly naive three days ago, but she had learned some things very quickly.

"All right, what are these new rules?"

Stretching out on the thick Persian carpet, he propped himself up on a forearm. "They aren't rules so much as stakes. Whoever loses a round, loses an article of clothing."

Shocked, again, Elora's mouth fell open. But in the end, she agreed to the game because she knew exactly how the contest would end.

More than an hour later, clad in her chemise and stockings, Elora looked at her husband and thought that he was far too smug. His smile was lazy and seductive, his gaze boldly masculine as it tried to strip away what little clothing she still wore.

"You have not been the least bit fair," she said, throwing the knucklebone.

"Why is that?" He trailed his gaze up the curve of her leg, past the frilly garter to the exposed skin of her thigh.

"Because you started out with more clothes than I. You have lost three rounds and you still have on your shirt and pants. I have lost three rounds and I am sitting here like this." She leaned forward to move one of her pieces, and the front of her chemise gaped open, affording Brice a tantalizing view.

"You don't need to remind me," he got out in a throaty murmur. "But if you are complaining, I will see what I can do to divest you of the rest of your clothing."

"That is not what I meant." But she had to fight down a curious tide of anticipation that caused her hands to shake. Having Brice lounge there, looking so cool and unperturbed, watching her remove piece after piece of clothing was doing strange things to her pulse. The fact that he was still practically fully clothed only seemed to make her all the more conscious of the differences in their states of undress. "It is very possible, Brice, that you could lose this round," she insisted, striving to sound as cool as he appeared.

"I could," he agreed, throwing the knucklebone, but the heat in his eyes proclaimed that he had every intention of getting her out of her chemise first.

He did that in an amazingly short amount of time, much to Elora's embarrassment . . . and delight.

Cheeks stained pink, she sat as demurely as she could, and regarded the stockings she had lost in the last two games. "I should have known better than to have played this game with you," she protested breathlessly. This game of slow, deliberate disrobing had subtly, but irrevocably seduced her senses. She knew that Brice was very aware of that, and she knew that *that* was what he had intended all along.

"I believe you lost that round," he reminded her in a deep voice full of potent, male promise.

She grasped the hem of her chemise, and felt every inch of her skin heat up. Quickly, not wanting to lose her nerve, she pulled the garment over her head.

Even before she looked up, she felt the weight of Brice's stare stroking over her breasts, sliding down her stomach to her legs, touching everything along the way. Hot, purposeful, it made her insides tremble.

"I believe the game is over," Brice muttered. He came to his knees, cupping her head between his hands and raised her face to his. In the next instant his mouth came down on hers in a tempestuous kiss that belied the casual, unperturbed appearance he had given.

His tongue thrust past her parted lips, delving deeply in a plundering kiss. He captured one full breast and stroked the generous swell, circling the tightened crest with his thumb as his other hand coursed down to her hips. He urged her firmly to his thighs and any thought that he might have been cooly unaffected was instantly put to rest. The hard length of him pressed intimately against the softness of her belly.

Her hands clung to his shoulders, her fingers biting into the rippling muscles through the fabric of his shirt. The garment was a barrier of the worst kind and she sought to rid him of it. But when she would have slipped the first button through its hole, he lifted his head and sat back.

Dazed, bereft of the feel and scent and heat of him, she watched him reach into the pocket of his discarded jacket and remove a small velvet box. From its interior, he lifted a delicately wrought silver chain, and fastened it about her neck.

"Brice?" Curiously, she ran her fingers along the fine links until she encountered the single pendant lying in the shadow between her breasts. Lifting the piece, she discovered a perfect, shining silver heart, a sparkling diamond in its very center.

Kneeling before her, Brice circled his arms about her waist again. In a voice brimming with emotion, he said, "You are the keeper of my heart."

He caught her to him, their mouths meeting with a near desperate urgency. He had given her his heart to hold and cherish, and with an abiding love, she accepted it and made it hers.

Hands worked feverishly to rid him of his clothes, and in moments he was laying her back against her bed, his mouth coming down fiercely on hers. It was not a time for teasing pleasures. The flagrant nature of their game had seen to that. They were caught by a wild hunger born of their love and their boundless need for each other.

In a headlong assault toward rapturous paradise, Elora entwined her arms about his neck, and felt his body as though for the first time. The heat and strength of him permeated her skin, melted her bones and filled her senses with joy and passion. She raised her hips, silently telling him that she needed him now, that instant, deep inside her where her blood dashed wildly through her veins.

A groan, low and deeply male, vibrated from Brice's chest. Lying above her, his weight braced on his forearms, he slanted his mouth feverishly over hers and answered her need with his own.

He surged into her body, and she felt herself fracture into a million pieces, each as radiant as the diamond on her silver heart. Glorious pleasure of the mind as well as the body shivered over every nerve, rolling and swelling through her, taking her to the edge of bliss.

She arched up to meet Brice, fueling their desire, hastening their ascent toward ecstasy. He thrust into her again and again, strong and unerring, wanting her as he had never wanted another, wanting her with every fiber of his body, wanting her past the bounds of reason. He pulled her more tightly to him, his hands beneath her hips, and she convulsed around him, sweeping him to his own shattering release.

Breathless, they held each other close for a long moment before Brice eased from her body. Rolling onto his back, he cradled Elora's head on his shoulder, her legs entwined with his.

"Thank you for the necklace," she breathed, fingering the silver heart that still retained the heat from his body. "I will cherish it forever. Just as I cherish you."

He looked down into her eyes. "That makes us perfectly matched, love, because I cherish you more than my life."

A soft smile stretched across her lips. "Have I told you today that I love you?"

He pretended to think about the question. "I can't remember. Tell me again."

"I love you."

"I like the way that sounds. Tell me again."

She did. Again, and again and again.

Chapter
17

"I'M NOT CERTAIN I AM EVER GOING TO FEEL COMFORTABLE UP here," Elora confessed. Adjusting her knee about the horn of her sidesaddle, she gathered her reins into one hand so she could push her spectacles more firmly into place on her nose.

The look Brice gave her from atop his mount was both encouraging and loving. "You're doing fine, Elora. No one feels comfortable the first time they ride."

"I haven't exactly ridden. All I've managed is a walk."

"You are on a horse, the horse is moving. That qualifies as riding."

She had to laugh at that. "You're playing with words. But I love you for trying to make me feel better."

That was exactly what Brice had been trying to do, only he hadn't realized it until she made mention of the fact. He was so in love with Elora that caring and worrying and comforting were second nature. Again. Just as they had been years ago.

His gaze drifted off toward the tall steeple of the chapel nearly hidden by a wall of trees. In the shadow of that steeple rested the three markers erected in honor of Robbie and his parents.

He waited for the torment to engulf him, but all he felt

was a vague impression of that anguish. Bittersweet memories clouded his mind, but the pain of the heart was gone. He did not need to be told why.

Elora was the embodiment of all that was good in life, love and laughter, compassion and caring, hope, faith and trust. If he lived forever, he would never understand what he had done to deserve her. Certainly none of his actions of the last three years had warranted his being gifted with her love.

He watched her adjust her spectacles once more, and gave up trying to figure it all out. Whatever the case, he was going to spend the rest of his life making her as happy as she made him.

"Just relax, Elora. Your horse is the most gentle mare in my stable."

"I know." But she did not sound convinced.

"It might help if you took your mind off the horse itself and concentrated on something else."

"What do you suggest I think about?" She was too occupied with the mechanics of simply staying in the saddle to notice a very wolfish grin spread across his mouth.

"Picture me between your legs. You rode quite well last night, if I remember correctly."

Her mortified gasp was accompanied by an embarrassed squeal. *"Brice Warfield!"* But the indignant tone of her voice was ruined completely by her laughter. "How can you just blurt such things out that way?" She laughed again, and without realizing it relaxed into the fine leather of her saddle. "You are going to corrupt me."

"But you still love me."

Her smile softened. "I will always love you."

"Good, because I want to show you a favorite spot of mine deep inside that copse of trees, and as long as you're willing to be embarrassed, again . . ." His words trailed off as he noticed one of the grounds keepers rushing across the lawn toward them.

"My lord, my lord!" The lanky man held his flopping hat in place on his head to keep it from flying off. Panting, he reached Brice and Elora and skidded to a halt. "My lord, you've got to come quick. It's the chapel, my lord. Someone's taken to smashin' the windows and breakin' the benches."

"What?" Brice demanded.

"There be glass everywhere, my lord, and the altar, God help me, looks like someone took an ax to it."

Brice swore viciously, his eyes taking on a feral gleam that made the frantic man take a step back.

"See that her ladyship returns to the house."

"Aye, my lord."

Elora shook her head, wanting to accompany Brice and face whatever it was he would find together. "Brice . . ."

His darkened gaze swung back to her. "Do as I say, Elora," he bit out. Digging his heels into the sides of his horse, he raced toward the chapel.

Dismayed, Elora watched him leave, and did as she was told. But it wasn't easy remaining at the house, waiting patiently for him to return. As she paced from one room to the next, she was besieged by thoughts that she had been too happy to consider for nearly a week.

It had been easy to forget that someone had repeatedly tried to kill Brice. Days spent in laughter, nights given up to passion had made the real world seem far away and not the least bit threatening.

Now that threat came rushing back and she moaned, sinking down into a chair in Brice's study. Whoever wanted Brice dead was responsible for vandalizing the chapel. She knew it as surely as she sat there.

Her stomach twisted with fear. Someone was still out there, watching, waiting. This act of violence was a brutal reminder of that.

The sound of Brice's footsteps sent her racing into his arms.

"It's him again, isn't it?" she whispered.

Grimly, Brice nodded, enfolding Elora against his chest. "There can't be any other explanation."

She tipped her head back and saw a dangerous, carefully controlled anger. "Will you send for Mr. Tew?"

"I already have."

She could not bear to think that his life was in grave peril. "How much longer can this go on?"

He tightened his arms about Elora. The moment he had walked into the chapel, he had decided that he would no longer sit and wait for someone else to make the next move. He had decided that his time of waiting was over.

He met with Harold Tew within the hour. Behind the closed doors of his study, Brice stood at his desk, a thin roll of tobacco clenched tightly between his teeth.

"I am returning to London tomorrow."

"Do you think that is wise, my lord?" Mr. Tew asked. As if he were in some way uneasy with Brice's intentions, he shifted from one foot to the other, his one good eye darting about.

The narrowing of Brice's eyes had nothing to do with the silver smoke curling about his head. "It is not only wise, it is necessary. I intend to flush this bastard out once and for all."

"That would be easier done here than in the city."

Brice jabbed his cigar into a silver dish. "Perhaps, but I will not have her ladyship endangered again. She will remain here. I want extra men hired to protect her while I'm gone."

"If that is what you wish, my lord, but I must tell you that we will not have to wait very long for our man to make his next move."

"Meaning what?"

"Meaning this damage done to the church is out of character for our killer. He wants you, but will settle for something that belongs to you instead. The bloke is getting tired, frustrated. He'll get careless before too long."

"Fine, but I will not have him getting careless within a hundred miles of my wife."

Harold Tew shifted his weight back to the other foot. "I am afraid that he may be closer than that right now."

Brice straightened, seeking and finding the investigator's

unspoken disclosure in that one bulbous eye. When he spoke, his voice was cold, lethal. "Who?"

"Your cousin Thorbon, my lord."

"Thorbon?"

"Yes, my lord. He was in the area the day after your wedding. Stayed at one of the local inns. We've had our eye on him the entire time."

Brice exhaled sharply and shoved away from his desk. Disbelief and relief, anger and confusion impelled him to pace to the far end of the room and back. *Thorbon.* Of all the people he had suspected, his cousin had been the last person he had truly believed responsible.

It was difficult to accept. But damn, Thorbon was his rightful heir, and would stand to gain considerably by becoming the next marquess. It was rather improbable that the man would choose to seek the title now when he was nearing the end of his life. If he had been covetous all along, it stood to reason that he would have attempted to obtain the title years ago.

"Are you certain?"

"I'm not positive at this time, my lord, but your church has been ransacked, and the man was here. I believe he hired someone to do his dirty work." Mr. Tew spread his hands wide in a gesture that told Brice to draw his own conclusions.

He swore and swung away toward one of the windows.

"I'll know better for certain in a day or so, my lord, after we question the locals."

"Where is my cousin now?"

"Left yesterday. According to the innkeeper, your cousin was headed from London to his home in Essex. I have one man there now, watching him."

Brice stared at the garden outside, but saw none of its beauty. He had not wanted to think that it could have actually been Thorbon. Or Katherine for that matter. Knowing that someone actually wanted to kill him was bad enough, but for that person to be related made the situation all the more deplorable.

He tipped his head back and considered the irony of it all. He, who had treated people, Thorbon and Katherine included, like cast-off shoes, was now beset by feelings of regret. God only knew what they must have felt for years.

"All right, Mr. Tew." He turned to face the investigator. "See that you have your men here by first light tomorrow. I will return to London then."

Elora sat in the blue and white salon as patiently as she could, but after ten minutes the strain of waiting for Brice and Mr. Tew to emerge from the study took its toll. If she had had her way, she would have been included in that meeting, but Brice had been most insistent on the matter.

Her anxiety was like a living thing vibrating through her. Driven by restlessness, she left the house and made her way to the bower of rosebushes at the far edge of the formal garden.

Repeatedly her gaze sought the house, fear clouding the sapphire hue of her eyes. Brice's reasons for meeting privately did not sit well with her. It hadn't been a matter of trust or lack of faith. He simply had not wanted her to worry, and as he had explained, hearing the details of the investigation would definitely make her worry.

"Stubborn man," she declared, pulling a leaf from one of the bushes. "Doesn't he know that I will worry more if I am kept in the dark?"

"Hello, Elora."

She jumped and turned at the unexpected sound of Josiah's voice. "Josiah," she breathed, laying a hand over her chest. "You gave me a start."

He grimaced slightly. "I am sorry, I didn't mean to frighten you."

"That's quite all right." A tardy smile came to her lips. "You just took me by surprise, but I confess that you do have the most uncanny ability to show up when I least expect you to."

He lifted a hand in apology. "I should have had one of

your servants announce me, but I didn't think it was necessary."

"Of course it isn't necessary. We're old friends."

His expression turned wistful. "Always that, friends."

Tipping her head to one side, she regarded him curiously. "What brings you here, Josiah?"

"My business in London is complete and I am returning home. I hope you don't mind."

"Of course not, I could never mind."

Glancing down over his stomach to the tips of his shoes, he hunched his shoulders. "I can not help but detect a certain resentment toward me on your husband's part. I don't want my presence to be the cause of any strife between you."

"You are worrying for nothing," she assured him gently. "Brice understands that you are my friend."

For a long moment, Josiah merely stood there as though considering that. "Well," he declared at last, his smile wide, his brown eyes glowing. "Then I shan't give it another thought. I would have offered my congratulations to you on your wedding day, but I wasn't certain how the marquess felt."

"You should have stayed."

"I know that now." He scanned her face. "You look happy, at peace with yourself."

"I have never known such happiness." Just as quickly as she spoke, she silently amended her words. The joy that had been hers until that morning had been shattered by some madman's hand.

"Elora, what is it?" he asked, seeing her distress.

Sighing heavily, her fingers rose to clasp the silver heart lying against her chest. "I'm frightened, Josiah."

"Of the marquess?" His eyes widened.

"No, no. He is . . ." She paused, trying to capture the right words. "No," she murmured, her eyes radiant with love. "He is the most wonderful, caring man. I have never met anyone who is as compassionate. He is the love of my life."

"Then what has you frightened?"

"Just this morning, someone ravaged the chapel."

"Oh, dear Lord." His voice lowered to a whisper. "Blessed Lord, have mercy on the souls of the wretched."

"We think it is the same person who has been trying to kill Brice."

"What makes you think that?"

"There is no reason not to think so. This act of vengeance on the church was directed at Brice." She wrapped her arms about her waist.

"How can you be so sure?"

"I don't know what else to think. There is no room for coincidence when someone is trying to kill you."

Josiah placed a comforting hand on her shoulder. "Perhaps you are overreacting, Elora. Perhaps someone holds a grudge against God. Or it could be that someone possessed of a sinful nature is crying out to the Lord for help."

She looked heavenward. "I would like to think so. But I have a bad feeling about this."

"Does your husband suspect anyone?"

"In particular? No."

"But he does have suspicions . . . as to who is responsible."

"Yes." She didn't elaborate. Even though Brice had not cautioned her to silence, she knew that what he had told her was to be held in the strictest of confidences. "I just wish for it to end, Josiah. I wish that whoever is responsible will be caught, or will cease in this madness."

"You must have faith, Elora. The Bible tells us, 'Behold, he travaileth with iniquity, and hath conceived mischief, and brought forth falsehoods. He made a pit, and digged it, and is fallen into the ditch which he made. His mischief shall return upon his own head, and his violent dealings shall come down upon his own pate.' "

"I try to believe in justice, but it is difficult when the person you love best in life could die."

Josiah shrugged slowly. " 'The wicked shall be turned into hell.' "

Elora looked back to the house. "Is it wicked to pray for that, Josiah? Is it wrong for me to hope that whoever is to blame for the attacks on Brice be punished?"

A shallow smile came to Josiah's thin mouth. "The Lord will show you the right path in all things. He will lead you and teach you, for He is your salvation." Taking her hand, he bowed his head.

Prayer seemed to be Elora's only hope, and if there was ever a time to appeal to God, now was that time. She gave Josiah's hand a quick squeeze before stepping away. "I will do my best not to become discouraged," she promised.

"That is all you can do."

Still, she could not shake her dread, and was anxious to return to the house. "Will you be able to stay for a while?"

"No, no, I should have been on my way before now, but I wanted to pay my respects." He scratched the back of his head.

"Are you sure?"

"Positive."

"If you must, then." Each time they parted, she had thought never to see Josiah again. Somehow she got the unmistakable impression that this would indeed be the last time she saw her friend. "Take care of yourself, Josiah."

"I will." He gazed at her, brown eyes filled with emotions Elora could not fathom. Reaching out to the nearest rose-bush, he plucked a dried, faded bloom and tucked it into the lace that edged the modest neckline of her dress. "The Lord be with you, Elora." Then he turned and walked away.

Elora hastily made her way back through the garden, intent on seeing Brice at once, regardless of what he thought. He was too stubborn for his own good, especially in this matter.

She squared her shoulders as she neared the wide terrace behind the house. He had made great strides in the past week. His manner had been as loving as she could have possibly wanted. But in this instance, he had reverted back to his old habits.

He had spent too many years pushing people away and he had done that very thing once again by not allowing her to be present for his meeting with Mr. Tew. Well, she was not about to let him force her out of any portion of his life. Loving someone meant taking the good with the bad and Brice needed to learn that right now.

Her chin came up as she marched down the hall to the closed study doors. Fueled by her love, she stepped into the book-lined room, her snapping gaze finding Brice immediately.

"I need to talk to you this instant," she told him in no uncertain terms, making her way toward the window where he stood. "You cannot shove me aside like some mindless idiot. I am your wife and I love you." She was only mildly aware that Mr. Tew was no longer in the room, but even if he had been, it wouldn't have made any difference to her.

Stepping up to Brice, she ignored his mild look of shock and declared, "I love you. Do you understand what that means? It means that my days are not complete unless I can look upon your face. It means that any happiness I have in life will be made all the more sweet if it is shared with you. It means that I will go through the years with you by my side, holding you to me at night, taking you into my body." She paused for breath, and her voice lost its edge. Lovingly, she vowed, "I will bear your children, and ease the frown from your brow. And it means that I will share all that life brings to us, both the good and the bad."

The green of Brice's eyes glimmered with a fire of the love that burned in his heart. His hands shot out and he pulled her into his embrace, burying his face in the silk of her hair.

"What is this all about?"

"I am so frightened, Brice. I love you and I want you safe. I cannot stand you shutting me out. Not with this." She leaned back slightly until she could look directly into his eyes. "Not with anything. I know you thought to spare me, but all you truly did was close yourself off just as you have done for so long."

He lowered his forehead to hers. He had not realized what he had done. But she was right, he had excluded her.

"I'm sorry."

"I know it is difficult after all these years, Brice."

"I haven't shared my life with anyone in so long. I meant only to protect you."

"I do not need to be protected from the truth."

His lips covered hers. The kiss was honest and giving. "Forgive me."

"There is nothing to forgive. I love you, but you needed to know how I felt."

His chest filled with a deep breath. "You want to know what was discussed in the meeting."

"Yes."

He sighed again, and stepped back. "Tew believes Thorbon is responsible for all the attacks."

Elora tilted her head to one side in astonishment. "Why Thorbon?"

"Because he was in the area the day of our wedding."

Like Brice's earlier reaction, Elora could hardly credit that the affable old gentleman was responsible. The thought was sobering and horribly sad.

"Is he certain that it is Thorbon?"

Crossing his arms over his chest, Brice shook his head. "No, nothing is definite. That is why I have to return to London." He pinned her with his gaze. "Alone."

She stilled. "Alone?"

"Yes, I need to see this thing ended. Now. I will not spend another day with this hanging over our heads."

"But why alone? Why can't I go with you?"

His hand curled over her shoulder. "This is not a matter of my shutting you out. This has only to do with your safety. I will not put you in harm's way."

The blue of her eyes darkened, and her lips trembled. "Then you are going to be in danger. Again."

"Possibly. Hopefully not."

"But you have no guarantees of that."

He shoved an impatient hand back through his hair and walked away. "There are no guarantees in life, Elora." If he had learned anything three years ago, it had been that.

His growing frustration struck her hard and her objections caught in her throat. She had asked that he confide completely in her, but she was making it all the more difficult for him by refusing to accept the truth of what he said. It *would* be easier for him if she were here and he was free to do what needed to be done.

Going to him, she slipped her arms around his waist. "It pains me to think of you going off like this, but you are right. If you think it would be best for you to go alone, then you must. Promise me you will be careful."

"I promise."

"I will worry about you the entire time you are gone."

"I will feel better knowing that you are here and safe." He brushed his lips over hers, then sought to ease her fears. Forcing a lightness into his tone, he teased, "I expect to be welcomed home with open arms. I will bring you roses suitable to wear, and not like this poor thing." He flicked a finger at the dull, dried blossom tucked into the lace of her bodice.

"Oh, this," she remembered, pulling the flower from her dress. "Josiah picked it from one of the bushes and gave it to me earlier."

Brice cursed soundly, not even trying to keep his displeasure from showing. "What the devil was he doing here?"

"He was returning home and wished to pay his respects."

With all that had occurred, hearing about Josiah Platt was just one more thing to tempt Brice's ire. "You know how I feel about him. I do not like him sniffing about you the way he does."

"Yes, I know how you feel. But he was very sweet, very concerned for my happiness." She lifted her mouth to his. "I never did thank you for inviting him to the wedding. It meant a great deal to me to have him there."

She kissed him with an ardent passion that spoke of hopes

and dreams and undying love, vanquishing thoughts of murder and reverends and Brice's endearing jealousy. "I love you, Brice. Hurry home to me."

He held her securely against him, but it was a moment before he could say anything. "I will." Over Elora's head, he stared straight ahead, his gaze steady, unflinching, resolved.

Chapter

18

IF SHE LISTENED HARD ENOUGH, ELORA COULD STILL HEAR THE sound of horses and coach coursing down the lane, fading into the early morning fog that refused to surrender to a feeble sun. Standing near the house, she adjusted her spectacles, hoping to catch one last view of the team and vehicle that bore Brice to London, but the ashen mist proved as obscuring as any stone wall.

A sense of time remembered came over her, and she could not shake the impression that she had somehow come full circle. The first time she had seen Brice, he had been enshrouded by a damp fog. That same concealing mist now hovered over the ground swallowing him from what might be her last sight of him. Of their own accord, her fingers closed about the silver heart nestled against her chest.

She turned away with a shiver that raced over her entire body. The frisson was just one of too many she had experienced since Brice had told her of his plans. Through the night, such shivers had threatened to make her tremble, but Brice had held them at bay. With his arms holding her close, his words of devotion bathing her mind and her senses, she had fought down her fears for his safety. She had taken the love he offered and given hers in return.

Her hands rubbed over her arms in the only defense she had now. The woolen shawl did what it could to alleviate the bite of the morning dampness, but there was no helping the chill that settled inside of her.

She lifted her gaze to the house, but made no move to enter. Without Brice, it looked cold and empty, nothing more than a barren collection of rooms, architectural components without meaning. Much like her life would be if Brice did not return to her.

She closed her eyes in prayer. "Come back to me, Brice. Come back so I can spend the rest of my life loving you."

She couldn't go in. She would end up pacing from one room to the other, picturing Brice at his desk, at the dining room table, in his bed or hers. Those memories were too fresh, and it would ravage her soul to think that if Brice were to die, those memories would be all she had left.

Pulling the shawl more closely about her, she made her way over the lawn. Even at this hour, a shadowy figure moved among the nearby trees, watching her steps closely, guarding her in Brice's absence.

She knew the man was there at Brice's order, and she tried to accept that. Still, it was rather unnerving to be followed so scrupulously, even if it was for her own good. But in this as in most things, Brice was resolute. The guard and two others as well were to keep her safe.

Her wandering path took her into the thick copse of trees behind the house, although she gave no thought to a destination. She knew only that she needed to keep her mind occupied and off horrible images of Brice lying dead. Not for the first time, she sent up a silent prayer for his safety.

As though directed by her prayers, she found herself at the stone chapel. Wrapped in layers of white mist, it stood forlornly, its beautiful stained glass windows reduced to ragged, gaping holes.

Helplessly, tears rose to her eyes. Five days ago, she and Brice had been married in this chapel. Only then flowers had decorated the structure, and music had floated in the air. Today, a stillness hung oppressively in the clearing like a horrible foreboding.

She pushed open the double doors and walked up the aisle. The shards of glass had been cleaned away along with broken pieces of wood from the pews and altar. Still, small remnants of the assault remained scattered about and with each step Elora took, a crunching noise echoed off the walls. The sound was mournful, eerily so. As she sat in one of the pews, it encompassed her as surely as the morning chill.

Why would anyone do this? she asked herself. The violence that had prompted the act was frightening, utterly foreign to her way of thinking. Despite all the animosity she had encountered in the past months, she still could not reconcile fury and hatred of any kind.

The sound of a boot stepping on broken glass came from behind her and she turned about sharply. Stunned, she found Josiah standing at the back of the church watching her.

"Josiah?"

When he remained silent, she came to her feet. "Josiah, what are you doing here?"

He shifted from one foot to the other, not saying anything.

Through her glasses, Elora squinted slightly, thinking he appeared not at all like himself. "Are you all right?"

Finally, he responded with a smooth nod. "Yes, I am well."

But he did not look well. His face was flushed and his eyes seemed to glow with an odd sheen. "Josiah, I thought you had returned home."

"This wasn't supposed to happen," he explained quietly.

She tilted her head to one side, barely able to catch his words. "I beg your pardon?"

His shoulders rose into an exaggerated shrug, his arms spread wide at his sides. "No, it wasn't supposed to be this way."

"I don't understand. What are you talking about?"

"You."

"Me?"

" 'This is the Lord's doing; it is marvellous in our eyes.' "
He slowly moved from his place in the doorway in an
ambling, casual stride. "It was supposed to have been taken
care of in London." His thin mouth twisted from side to
side. "Now, I will have to see to the matter myself."

A tiny tremor skipped up Elora's spine. There was something terribly wrong with Josiah that set her nerves on edge.
"Why are you here?" she repeated.

" 'This is the day which the Lord hath made; we will
rejoice and be glad in it.' "

"Rejoice in what?" His peculiar manner made her nervous. She looked through one of the broken windows,
unconsciously searching for the guard she knew had been
following her.

"He's not there," Josiah said.

Her gaze shot back to his. "What?"

"The man you're looking for. The man your husband
hired to protect you." He smiled broadly, taking another
step closer. "He's not there."

"Where is he?"

"Under one of the trees. Perhaps dead, perhaps not." He
cast an unconcerned glance about. "I'm just not certain how
hard I hit him."

Fear seized Elora. It combined with a horrible sense of
absurdity. She had always known Josiah to be kind and
gentle, yet he was calmly telling her that he had possibly
killed someone.

"Josiah, what have you done?"

"You weren't supposed to leave me," he whined, shaking
his head. "I wanted you to remain, to become my wife."

"Your wife?" They were friends. She had never thought of
him as more.

"You should have been mine, but all you could think of
was paying off your stepfather's debts." He stood at arm's
length and looked calmly into her eyes. "I had to punish you
for that."

"But you helped me find the post with Lord Ashton."

"Yes, yes I did. I shouldn't have, but you were so pitiful. It was wicked of me to have given in. I should have made you stay with me and Mother."

Elora's heart and stomach collided.

Josiah's head rolled back on his thick neck, his eyes closing as he raised his voice. " 'Discretion shall preserve thee, understanding shall keep thee: To deliver thee from the way of the evil man, from the man that speaketh forward things; Who leave the paths of uprightness to walk in the ways of darkness.' "

He straightened, his glazed eyes staring straight into her. "You chose to stray from the righteous path, the path God put forth for you at my side. As my wife."

Too numb to utter a sound, Elora stared horrified. He was rambling on about wickedness.

"But I don't—"

"I will hear none of your blasphemy!" he roared. His indifference exploded and rage rose up in its place. "You had to be punished!"

Elora jumped back, but cruel hands shot out and clamped viciously about her arms.

"You can't go away," he explained calmly, reasonably. "You must be chastened for your sins. I tried, I really did, but the clumsy fool couldn't even shoot straight."

Reality struck her in a single cold, abhorrent blow. That night in London, she had nearly collided with Brice. In the blanketing fog she had seen the pistol raised and thought to save him, but all along the pistol had been aimed at her. *Her.*

Frantically, she pulled at the fingers biting into her flesh. "It was you who shot the pistol," she breathed in horror.

"Oh, no, not me. Someone I hired to kill you."

"Why?"

"God gave you to me. But you never loved me as I loved you. You had to die. You were supposed to that night—you didn't, so I had to come to his house. I could have fulfilled the Lord's wishes then, but the marquess found me out before I could even open the door."

"You hired those men to attack our coach." She strained back from his punishing hold.

269

A huge sigh escaped him and his voice took on a pleading note that was all the more frightening for its lack of anger. "Don't you see that you left me no choice? You could not be allowed to go on disobeying the Lord's command." He lifted a hand to stroke her shining, golden hair, his sight directed into some far-off realm located in his twisted mind. "I used to dream about this hair. I would picture it spread about your shoulders, drifting down your back." His fingers loosened the curls from their combs, pulling strands free until her hair hung in cascading waves. "Is this how you wear it at night? Is this how you go to your husband's wicked bed, with your hair tumbling about your breasts?"

He caught the mass in his fist and viciously dragged her face up to his, his eyes darkening with a virulent rage. "Does he suckle you and spread your legs for his evil lust? *Do you whore for him?*"

Fear and pain engulfed Elora in huge waves. "Josiah, please don't do this."

"Down on your knees, harlot!" He forced her to the floor at his feet. His hand still clenched in her hair, he bent over her, forcing her back into a brutal arch. "Pray for forgiveness, pray to your maker to deliver you from your wickedness."

"I haven't done anything wrong," she choked out in pain, his body looming over hers, filling her vision. Hands trembling uncontrollably, she grabbed at his wrists, but her efforts were futile.

"Silence!" With his free hand, he fumbled in his jacket pocket and withdrew a knife. Its blade shone dully in the chapel's muted light.

Elora's heart lodged in her throat, her eyes riveted to the curved steel blade clutched in Josiah's sweating hand. This could not be happening. Josiah had been her friend, but he was going to kill her.

Brice! her mind screamed, her fingers clenching the perfect silver heart on its fragile chain. But Brice had gone to London to put an end to the madness. He had no way of knowing that the killer was here and she was going to die.

Fear such as she had never known raked through her. Twisting frantically, she tried to break from his hold. He held her fast, his eyes rolling until only white showed in his ruddy face.

"'The Lord hath utterly destroyed them, he hath delivered them to the slaughter. For my sword shall be bathed in heaven; behold, it shall come down upon Idumea, and upon the people of my curse, to judgment.'"

"No, Josiah, you can not do this," she cried, arching away from the knife he raised above his head, swallowing against the taste of terror that clogged her throat.

"'The sword of the Lord is filled with blood, it is made fat with fatness, and with the blood of lambs and goats.'"

Into his abrupt silence that followed his ramblings came a small but distinctive click. Lost in his own world, Josiah had no idea that the sound belonged to a flintlock's hammer locking into its tumbler. Nor did he feel the pistol pressed to the base of his skull until a deep voice dragged him from his private world.

"Let her go."

Caught in her terror, her vision infused with nothing but Josiah, Elora could hardly believe that Brice was there. But she had heard his voice and just behind Josiah, she could see his solid, powerful form. Unable to contain her frightened sobs, she would have sagged in relief, but Josiah's fist still retained its hold.

"Let her go," Brice warned, "or I will take great pleasure in splattering your brains from here to kingdom come."

Some of Brice's command penetrated a part of the thick euphoria clouding Josiah's brain. He jerked up, but the pressure boring into the back of his head stayed his movement. Somehow his mind made sense of the meaning of the cold metal, defined it as a pistol, and finally recognized that it was Brice Warfield holding that pistol.

He released Elora from his grasp. She swayed momentarily, then scrambled out from his reach. On her knees, she struggled across the floor to one of the fallen pews, and only then became aware of four men standing within the chapel, pistols raised and trained on Josiah. One of those men was Harold Tew.

He motioned his men forward and they rushed up the aisle. Strong hands grabbed hold of Josiah and wrenched the knife away. Only then did Brice cock his pistol and lower it to his side.

Josiah stared about wildly, gawking at Brice and then the two burly men who held him immobile. "You are interfering with the Lord's work," he babbled. "She must be punished." His gaze swung crazily to Elora crouched on the floor. "You are a sinner!" he insisted, trying to convince her he was telling the truth. "You must love me. You must!"

Elora choked back a wounded cry, shrinking from the insane stare stabbing at her.

A low growl sounded from deep in Brice's chest. "Get him out of here."

Before Elora's stricken gaze, Tew and his men hustled Josiah away. In the next instant, Brice was at her side, pulling her into his arms, holding her protectively.

"Are you all right?" He held her as though he would never again let her go.

She nodded, her hands gripping tightly to his jacket.

Brice dragged in one labored breath after another, battling the rage and fear that permeated his entire being. "Did he hurt you in any way?"

"No," she whispered. That was all she could say. A fierce trembling seized her body and tears welled into her eyes. Sobs wracked her slender frame, and she cried out her fear and relief as Brice carried her back to the house.

It wasn't until she was clothed in a nightgown and settled beneath the covers of Brice's bed that she regained most of her composure. Brice sat on the edge facing her, holding her hand, and not for the first time, she drew a measure of strength from his presence.

"I'm all right now," she assured him quietly.

"Are you certain?" He searched her face, looking for remnants of the horror that had quaked through her.

"Yes." The sigh she gave was quivering. "I don't know why I fell apart that way."

He brought her hand to his lips. "You had every right to cry. The bastard tried to kill you." The green of his eyes registered a savage gleam when he even thought about Platt wanting her dead. His hand tightened about her delicate fingers.

His fury was carefully contained, but Elora sensed it immediately. "Brice, I am fine. I promise."

Once again, he kissed the back of her hand. "I know." For that he would be thanking God for the rest of his life. "When I saw him standing over you with that knife, I could have easily killed him."

Elora's brows curved in bewilderment. "How did you know to come back?"

He took a deep breath and met her gaze steadily. "I never left."

"But I saw the coach . . . where did you go?"

"Only as far as the end of the drive."

Confusion danced over her face. "I don't understand. I thought you had gone to London to seek out Thorbon."

Not relinquishing his hold on her fingers, he lifted his hand to stroke his chin. "I had every intention of doing that very thing. Until you told me who was really behind all the trouble."

"Me?" She blinked in astonishment.

He nodded slowly. "I know you did not realize it at the time."

"What did I say?" She tried to think back over everything she had ever said to Brice concerning Josiah.

"You thanked me for inviting Platt to the wedding."

She waited, expecting some great revelation. "And?"

"Elora, love, I never invited him. I didn't even know he was there until you told me yesterday."

"Because of that you suspected him to be the killer?"

"That and something Tew mentioned. He said that whoever was responsible for the destruction done to the chapel was acting out of character, getting desperate. I combined that with the fact that Platt witnessed our marriage, and it made sense. Especially since I detected his possessiveness toward you right from the start."

She remembered all those times she had thought Brice jealous of Josiah for no reason. "I never knew how he felt. I considered him my friend."

"He wanted more."

"When he realized he couldn't have me, he wouldn't let anyone else have me either. Not even as a governess."

"So he tried to kill you." Brice gripped her hand more firmly. "All this time, we thought it was I who was in danger, and it wasn't. The bastard had been trying to kill *you.*" He bit back a curse. "I should have known that I wasn't the target."

"How could you have possibly known? Everyone from Thorbon to the Duke of Westford gave you just cause to suspect them."

"Yes, but in looking back, I see that what I thought could be a possible motive for murder was nothing more than farfetched speculation. It makes sense now why I could never pinpoint exactly who I thought was responsible. None of them was."

"But they all made no secret of how they felt."

"Exactly. Their threats and hostility were far too blatant. None of them is subtle enough to attempt something as covert as murder for hire. Platt, on the other hand, was devious to the point of being obsessive."

Josiah's ranting words tumbled through her mind. She shoved them away, unable to withstand the dread that came from the deranged tirade.

"I am so glad this is finally over." She peered up at Brice, a soft ache underlying the blue of her eyes. "Why didn't you tell me what you had planned to do?"

He looked down to their entwined fingers. "I couldn't, love. I know how you feel about my shutting you out, but this had nothing to do with my old habits. You would never have been able to face Platt if you had known the truth. You would never have been able to hide your fear and accusation. I couldn't take the chance that he would react to that and kill you before I could stop him."

"You knew he was going to try to kill me again."

"As much as I hated the idea of it, yes, I was convinced that he would not give up until he had either killed you, or he was killed himself. That was why I gave every indication that I was going to London, to draw him out. His behavior was becoming more and more reckless, first with the chapel and then by coming here to see you. I suspected he would waste little time in another attempt as soon as he thought I was gone."

He opened his hand and studied her palm. When he spoke, his voice was a dark whisper. "I am sorry that you had to endure what you did."

His regret touched her deeply. She curled her fingers back through his. "I would endure it again to have this madness put behind us."

"You were never in any danger, love. I was never more than a few seconds away. And Tew's men were watching you closely."

His words brought her upright, her face whitening with alarm. "Josiah said he killed one of the guards."

A quick shake of his head allayed Elora's anxiety. "Knocked the man unconscious, but he's all right."

She sighed in heartfelt relief and relaxed against the pillows again. Still, she found the entire situation horribly sad. Josiah had been harboring his twisted love for her for so many years, and she had never known how he had felt about her. "What will happen to Josiah?"

Brice could see her remorse, and for an instant considered not telling her. She had been through enough that day and he had no wish to increase her distress. But she needed to know, he reasoned. She deserved to hear the truth. "He's not sane, Elora. They've taken him to Bedlam."

The horrors of that institution were too well known for Elora not to understand the fate that awaited Josiah. "I know you will think me ridiculous, but I am sorry for him.

And his mother. I know she has her sister to rely on, but she will be horribly hurt by this."

It was nothing less than Brice would have expected from her tender heart. Leaning forward, he kissed her gently. "I think you are wonderful and perfect just the way you are."

The feel of his lips on hers was to be savored. She let the warm, firm pressure lighten her sorrow. "I love you," she vowed against his mouth.

His hand trailed about her neck, his fingers slipping into the wispy curls at her nape. "I love you, and I intend to spend the rest of my life proving that to you."

"You do not need to prove anything to me, Brice."

"Consider that pledge my eternal gift to you."

Her arms circled his shoulders. "You have already given me the only gift I will ever want from you."

"What is that?"

"Your love."

Epilogue

Hampshire, England, 1819

IN THE SHADOWS OF HIS FAMILY'S ANCIENT STONE CHAPEL, BRICE stood and stared about him, noting with a purely aesthetic eye how the brilliant sun glinted off the familiar tall spire. His face softened with a smile that was grounded in peace.

His contentment was of the heart as well as the mind and body. Elation, serenity, absolute satisfaction combined to make his life perfect.

"Brice?"

He turned to gaze at the source of his joy. Elora. His smile grew as did his happiness, doubling in dimension and intensity.

"Brice, I think I might need your steady hand."

He had no doubt of that. Kneeling before his parents' stone marker, fussing with the flowers she had lain there, Elora was very rounded with his babe. She was as beautiful as he had ever seen her.

His heart swelled in his chest as he helped her to her feet. "You're not tiring yourself out, are you?"

"Not at all. I feel wonderful, although I am anxious to have this baby born. I want to hold him in my arms."

It was something Brice, too, had dreamt of often; holding Elora as she held their child. "Soon, love."

She rested her head against his chest. "I know. In just a matter of weeks we'll have to make arrangements with the vicar for a christening."

Brice shut his eyes, hearing words from years ago echo through his mind. He had come a long way since he had stood right here and damned the vicar to hell. Elora had ushered him on his healing path every step of the way.

"We'll call on the vicar, love."

"And we must talk to Vianne and Colin about being godparents."

"All right."

"And . . ."

He lowered his mouth to hers, sealing off her words for a more ardent distraction. When he lifted his head, the green of his eyes was filled with a love whose radiance rivaled the sun shining overhead.

"Have I told you today that I love you?" she asked against his lips.

"Yes, but say it again."

She did, again and again and again.

Author's Note

While the ancient Egyptian builder and decorator of tombs, Sennedjem, actually lived during the reign of Ramses II, the *Sennedjem Papyrus* mentioned in this book is a product of the author's imagination. The papyrus, and all things Eastern, were considered to be extremely fashionable in early nineteenth-century England. Among the aristocracy, collecting artifacts was as prestigious as it was popular.